ACTS OF
ATONEMENT
MEN OF WRATH *Series*

ACTS OF ATONEMENT

MEN OF WRATH *Series*

The forbidden never tasted so sweet...

ELEANOR ALDRICK

ACTS OF
ATONEMENT
MEN OF WRATH *series*

Copyright © 2020 by Eleanor Aldrick

www.EleanorAldrick.com

Cover Photo by Volodymyr Tverdokhlib

Cover Design by Pretty Riot Graphics

Copy Edit by Ellie | My Brother's Editor

ISBN: 978-1-7345272-0-9

Library of Congress Control Number: 2020905208

First Edition: June 2020

To all the women who think they can't. This book is for you.
It's proof that you can.

"To burn with desire and keep quiet about it is the greatest punishment we can bring on ourselves."

Frederico Lorca, Blood Wedding and Yerma

Playlist

"Conversations in the Dark"—John Legend

"Girl Gang"—Gin Wigmore

"Break My Heart"—Dua Lipa

"Believe It"—PARTYNEXTDOOR & Rhianna

"Blinding Lights"—The Weeknd

"Home"—Phillip Phillips

Prologue

THREE YEARS AGO...

"You have to come clean, Mom." I swipe at my eyes, trying to keep my vision clear, but the tears just keep coming.

My chest feels heavy—as if an imaginary elephant were sitting on top of me, robbing me of my very breath. Only the proverbial elephant isn't imaginary, it's real. It's a real secret that shouldn't be mine to bear.

My mind runs through so many emotions—emotions I've never felt before. *Betrayal. Devastation. Hatred.*

Sure, my mother isn't perfect. Whose mother is? But to betray our family like this? It's unforgivable.

My mother's shrill voice cuts into my thoughts. "You have no idea what you're asking of me, Bella. You are too young to understand." Her hands practically strangle the steering wheel as she drives us home from the art exhibit—the art exhibit where I had my very first showing. "Besides, you will be off to college before you know it. This isn't something you need to concern yourself with."

Rolling my eyes, I turn to look at her. "Bullshit! Tonight was supposed to be my night. But, no. Instead, I have to walk in on—"

Mom's right arm shoots out to brace me, cutting me off mid-sentence. Her face goes pale and her eyes widen before I hear the screeching of tires and see the flash of headlights illuminating the interior cabin.

The loud noise of metal crashing against metal reverberates through my body as I slam into the center console. Before I can fully comprehend what just happened, the car begins to fishtail off the road, toward the tree-lined river. Inside the car, my body is being slammed back and forth like a rag doll. I try to reach for Mom's hand, but with all the movement, it's impossible to hold on.

Random memories flash before me... Mom flipping Saturday morning pancakes, Dad teaching me how to drive, Matt and Max jumping on my bed...

The sound of crunching metal and shattering glass has me closing my eyes, trying to avoid the glittering shards flying straight toward me. My body lurches forward as my head hits the airbag. Fine white powder floats through the air, burning my skin on contact and causing me to cough repeatedly. My nose stings and my throat burns. Realization begins to dawn as the dust starts to settle.

We've been hit by another car.

"Mom..." I call out, needing her to make this all okay, but she doesn't answer.

Despite my mother's flaws, she is still the one I turn to when I'm scared. And at this moment, I'm *very* scared.

A silent scream escapes me as soon as my eyes land on her. They focus in and out, trying to make sense of the sight before me. *Blood. So much blood.* A branch is sticking straight through her torso—puncturing God knows what—and her throat is generating gurgling noises as she tries to speak.

"Shhhh, Mom. Don't say anything. Help is coming," I softly whisper, trying to comfort her with my words because I'm too afraid to touch her. "Someone must've seen us."

I reach to undo my seatbelt in an attempt to locate my cell phone, only to find that the latch is jammed. We're running out of time. *Think, Bella. Think.* I need to get help before Mom bleeds out, but every movement causes insurmountable pain and drains me of what little energy I have left.

Wiggling my left foot, I feel what could be my phone. With great effort, I manage to scoot the object backward, despite having limited space between the dashboard and my seat. If I push it back far enough, I might be able to shimmy it within arm's reach.

I tilt my head upward in an attempt to shift my body closer to the floorboard, managing to reach out and touch the object with my fingertips. "Almost got it..." I grunt out as I push my left arm farther down, successfully grabbing the phone but unsuccessfully retrieving it. *Great. I'm stuck.* The top of my arm is now pinned between the dash and my seat, making it impossible to pull myself free.

Using muscle memory, I unlock the phone and attempt to blindly dial for help. The call will go to whoever was the last person on my call log. *I think it was Dad. God, I hope it was Dad.*

As I sit there waiting for the call to connect, the post-adrenaline crash kicks in and my mind begins to wander in and out of consciousness.

Peering out the window, I see the full moon in all its glory and am reminded of simpler times. Times in my early childhood where imagination was reality and anything was possible.

I would lie in the bed of my dad's truck and stare up at the moon, trying to memorize every nook and cranny of its surface. Sometimes I could even make out a face and pretend it was a fairy godmother, sent to grant me my every wish. *If only that were true.*

"If you're out there, fairy godmother, please send help," I cry out before my vision starts to falter and everything fades to black.

Chapter One

WILLIAM

I GRIP THE RECEIVER tightly against my ear, hearing my knuckles crack from the exertion. "What do you mean Harper hasn't been picked up?"

"Mr. Hawthorne, as I already stated, your wife has yet to pick up Harper from our mother's day out program. We've attempted calling both numbers in the system, but this is the first time I've been able to get ahold of anyone." The snarky tone of the woman's voice grates on my nerves as I try to make sense of what's going on.

"Someone must pick Harper up immediately or we will be

forced to call Child Protective Services. We will be left with no choice but to report this sort of negligence."

"I'm on my way now..." I pick up my keys and begin to head out the door. "And ma'am, if you *ever* threaten me again, I'll personally ensure you never see the inside of a childcare facility for the rest of your damned life." A huff of outrage escapes the woman, but I continue. "Seeing as how this is the first time we've received a call like this, threatening with CPS involvement for what may be tantamount to mere miscommunication is absolutely ridiculous." Seething with anger, I end the call before she has an opportunity to respond. Nobody comes between me and my child. *Nobody.*

I get into my blacked-out Range Rover, slamming the door behind me. How dare this woman even insinuate that CPS needs to get involved. Over the past six months, Harper has been timely picked up and not one complaint has been issued.

Sure, it probably wasn't smart to threaten the person who currently holds my child in her care, but she *definitely* knows who I am and knows I have the power to make that threat a reality.

I dial Heather's number again as I speed my way down the road. No answer. *Where in the hell is she?* I try and recall if she told me to pick up Harper, but nothing comes to mind. Heather had been acting distant lately—

more than usual—but I honestly couldn't be bothered to ask what the hell was wrong.

It's no big secret I hadn't married out of love. Heather was one of many women I kept on constant rotation. *I know, I know... what a manwhore.* But if you grew up like me, seeing the example my parents set, a relationship would be the last thing on your radar too. For fuck's sake, they made Peg and Al Bundy look like Mr. and Mrs. Cleaver.

After a couple of months of 'dating' Heather, we found out she was pregnant. Not wanting my child to grow up in a broken home, I did what I thought was right and asked Heather to marry me. She initially jumped at the idea of marriage and a family, so I was extremely surprised when I found a pamphlet on abortion laying on her nightstand. When I confronted her, she said she was ready for marriage but wasn't sure she was ready to be a mother, reasoning that she had to keep her 'trophy wife' figure.

I roll my eyes at the memory of it all. The only reason I was marrying her was for our child and she was going to get rid of it?

I was upfront and honest with Heather, telling her that I would only marry her if she was keeping the baby; otherwise, there would be no point in staying with her. Now before you get all up in arms about it being her body, her choice—the decision of whether or not I married her was never intended as extortion or bribery, it was just the mere truth of the situation. She was a hot fuck turned baby momma, not the love of my life, and marriage would only come into the equation if my child were involved.

I may be many things, but a deadbeat father would never be one of them.

Heather quickly changed her tune and developed a sudden case of baby fever. Not seeing it for what it was— *the first red flag*—I foolishly believed her change of heart, refusing to acknowledge what truly lay beneath it all.

Fifteen minutes later, I'm at St. Albert's ready to see my little girl and get her the fuck out of there. Approaching the main office, I see that Harper is being held by an older woman with salt and pepper hair pulled back into a tight knot.

"Mr. Hawthorne, so good of you to make it." Ignoring the sarcasm, I take Harper from the woman's arms. "I'm Mrs. Morgan, we spoke on the phone." She pats Harper on the head and continues with her mock concern. "We were unable to locate Mrs. Hawthorne. We do hope everything is okay."

"Can't kill the Devil," I mumble under my breath.

"What was that?"

"Nothing. I was just saying I'm sure she's fine. It was probably a mix up in Harper's schedule." I move to pick up Harper's bag and notice an envelope sitting on top of the baby gear. "Was this envelope here before drop off this morning?"

The shrew turns back around, a fake smile plastered across her face. "Why, yes. I do believe so. Your wife must have left it in there by accident." The woman nervously fidgets with her wire-rimmed glasses before continuing. "We didn't open it of course. It is addressed to you, after all."

Didn't open it, *my ass.* I'm sure she's already read it and it's made its way around the facility. Shaking my head, I turn around without a second glance and head back to the SUV, ready for this day to be over.

Back at the house, I put Harper down for her nap and make my way to the study, dreading whatever lies inside of the mysterious envelope. Multiple possibilities assault my mind as to what it could be, but in the back of my mind I already know.

She's left us.... Well good riddance, she could go to Hell for all I care.

A pang of guilt hits me full force as I have these thoughts. No matter how shitty of a mother she is, Harper still deserves to have her in her life, even if it is in the smallest capacity.

I pour myself a tumbler of Macallan and sit at the large mahogany desk anchoring the room. With a deep sigh, I pick up the large manila envelope and unfold the flap, dumping out its contents.

The first thing I see is a letter in Heather's handwriting, attached to it is a petition for divorce and relinquishment of custody. From the looks of the documents, she must have been planning this for a while. Enough time to hire an attorney and get our assets all divvied up and outlined.

I start with Heather's letter, in it she shares how she'd come to the conclusion that being a wife and mother wasn't what she'd really wanted out of life but that she wished me and our one-year-old the best of luck.

Really, Heather? I'm sure a one-year-old child prefers half-hearted well wishes to the actual presence of her own mother.

Finally getting to the divorce papers, I see she has overstepped the boundaries of our prenup. I already see what a huge clusterfuck of a battle this is going to be. I hope she doesn't think she's getting a dime. After all, she's the one who is walking out on our family.

Shaking my head free of the fog it's in, I start to make plans for Harper. For her sake, someone needs to have their act together in this relationship. I pick up my phone and dial my sister's number.

Ashley picks up on the third ring. "Hey big bro. To what do I owe this honor? You never call me during the week."

"Well." I run my fingers through my hair, tugging at the ends. "My life has taken an unexpected turn..."

I fill her in on the details of today's events, ending with a plea for help. Ashley agrees to come and stay with us for a month until I'm able to set up a permanent nanny situation because there is no way in hell I'm taking Harper back to St. Albert's after today.

"I'll get the jet out to you tomorrow morning. My assistant will email you the specifics once everything is confirmed."

I let out a big sigh of relief, taking a grateful sip of amber liquid. Maybe, just maybe, Harper and I can come out of this unscathed.

One month later

I find myself sitting at the conference room table with Ren, Aiden, Titus, and Hudson, my childhood friends and co-founders of WRATH, our private security company. We all met in prep school, with the exception of Aiden— Ren's older brother—who ended up joining our band of merry men after his tour in Afghanistan.

A little over three years ago, we were all off doing our own thing—Ren was a tech genius by day and notorious womanizer by night; Titus a private investigator up in the Hamptons, getting the lowdown on cheating husbands for their wives; Hudson, an accountant with his own private firm here in Dallas; and last but not least, Aiden, fresh out of the NAVY trying to figure out where he was going next.

As for me, I'd just finished my Master's in Business and was ready to make a name for myself, independent of my family drama. I was full of ideas on what to do, but the one that stuck out the most was the one that included my honorary brothers. I'd pitched the idea of partnering up and forming a private security firm, utilizing all of our different skill sets. The men agreed, and here we are, three years later and a nationally recognized name, serving the who's who of our fine country.

The clock strikes five and we've just wrapped up our weekly case management meeting.

"It's officially happy hour," Titus announces while making his way to the bar.

Feeling the need to vent, I catch the guys up on the disaster that is my life. "Ashley flies back home on Sunday, and I have yet to find a full-time nanny for Harper," I huff out while kicking my feet up on the table and throwing my head back on the chair.

"Can't your sister move here permanently?" Ren asks.

"No. I asked her, and she shot me down immediately. Can't say that I blame her. I would rather live in sunny Palm Beach than here in Dallas too. So many horrible memories for her here. I'm surprised she's even stayed this long."

"She's your sister. Of course she'd come help you when you needed her. But if you need a nanny, I'm sure Isabella would help through the summer. She's going off to college in the fall, but it would give you enough time to secure a permanent live-in nanny for Harper until then," Aiden offers as he pats me on the shoulder in sympathy.

These guys. I'm once again reminded of how true and loyal our brotherhood runs.

"Wait, doesn't Bella watch the twins after school? Matt and Max are more than a full-time job. I know this from personal experience." Ren laughs out loud as I remember the last prank they pulled at Harper's baptism brunch. Those boys managed to get into the kitchen and pour an entire container of salt into the chocolate fondue.

"To Bella's defense, she wasn't on watch duty, I was," Aiden sheepishly admits. "Plus, it's temporary. It's just until William finds a more permanent solution and seeing how it's Friday, I don't think he'll be able to find a better substitute nanny."

"Thanks, Aiden. I really appreciate the help. If it's okay with you, have Bella stop by the house tomorrow morning so she gets a chance to meet with Ashley and go over Harper's schedule." Breathing a sigh of relief, I start to relax a little.

"Of course. Any word on the baby momma front?" Aiden asks.

"*Yeeeesss.* Do share!" Titus bellows from the bar across the room. "Last we all heard she was in New York trying to bag herself a younger boy toy!"

"God. I hadn't heard that one yet, but I wouldn't put it past her." I roll my eyes and sigh. "Honestly, marrying her was a mistake. I just didn't want Harper growing up in a broken home. *So much for that.*"

Titus slams his whiskey glass onto the table. "Forget her ass. There are plenty of hot fish in the sea. That broad has no clue how good she had it. Just mark my words, she'll come crawling back to you the moment her dumbass realizes it."

"If that's the case, I'll gladly remind her where she can shove it. I wouldn't keep her out of Harper's life, but she can't just come in and out of our lives whenever she pleases. That isn't healthy for Harper." I try to stay calm but this conversation needs a change of subject, *pronto.*

If I keep dwelling on that woman I'm liable to lose it and show up to the house piss drunk. I'm too old for that mess. Honestly, having to take care of a screaming baby while having a major hangover is not appealing. Been there, done that, not doing it again.

Chapter Two

ISABELLA

COFFEE. SWEET NECTAR OF THE GODS.

Holding my favorite mug in one hand, I take a giant sip of the rich black liquid. *Mmmmm. So good.* Closing my eyes, I allow the caffeine to enter my system, one delicious gulp at a time and savor the quiet before the storm.

The twins aren't up yet, and this is the only time I have to myself before chaos descends upon me.

Ever since summer hit, the boys have been on a mission to decimate the house. It's a miracle I've been able to keep them in check thus far since they have the attention span of a gnat, quickly getting bored of whatever activity I've set up for them.

It's times like these that make me really miss Mom. I'm really not a bitter Betty, it just feels like a real mom would be able to do so much better than a big sister.

Taking one more sip of coffee, I pick up my phone and lazily peruse social media before remembering Dad sent me a message last night. Something about William and his daughter, Harper. Gosh, that really is a shitty situation he's in. To have his wife leave them like that is beyond insane. Who in their right mind would leave *William*? The man is *gorgeous.*

I may or may not have fantasized about his piercing blue eyes and strong jawline warming my bed on more than one occasion. I mean, can you blame me? The man is a Greek god, any hormonal teenager would be lusting after his full lips and chiseled body. Not to mention, he's also an amazing father and extremely smart businessman.

William was the one who came up with the idea to make WRATH a national firm as opposed to the small local deal it originally was. Thanks to him, they now have contracts throughout the states with some extremely high-profile clients.

The man truly is the whole enchilada, and that woman is seriously delusional if she thinks she can do better than him. To each their own, I guess.

DAD: Hey Bella, William needs a nanny for Harper, and I told him you'd be okay with stepping in for the summer until he finds a permanent live-in.

He's in a bind and this would really help him out. If you're okay with taking on one more kiddo, then meet him and his sister over at his place tomorrow morning. You'll be going over Harper's schedule.

Gaaaawd, Dad is lucky Harper is an easy baby. What was he thinking, offering without asking me first?!

"Bella, Bo Bella!" Matthew sing-songs as he runs into the kitchen, signaling the end of my quiet time.

"G'morning, booger butt. Where's your brother and what do y'all want for breakfast today?" I ask while running my hand through his platinum blond hair.

The twins look so much like Dad, with bleach-blond hair, green eyes, and an olive complexion. I, on the other hand, am the spitting image of our mother with dark ebony hair and pale gray eyes—the only exception being my ability to tan, giving me the same golden complexion as the boys. I sometimes catch Dad staring at me with the saddest eyes, knowing I must be a constant reminder of the woman he lost.

If only he knew...

"Max is brushing his teeth," Matt says, snapping me back into the here and now. "It's Saturday, we want chocolate chip pancakes, *duh!*" He giggles as he rubs his belly.

"Chocolate chip pancakes it is." I quickly spin around and head toward the pantry, pulling out the necessary ingredients and laying them out on the counter.

Max saunters into the room and sits at the butcher block island with Matt. They start chatting about the latest Marvel movie and I decide there's no time like the present to break the news about the newest addition to *Bella's Summer Camp*.

I pour the ingredients into a mixing bowl and stir. "Guess what, chicken butts?"

"What?!" they both shout in unison.

"Miss Harper will be joining us on all of our summer adventures, starting with a trip to the zoo on Monday, if her dad clears it, of course. Does that sound like fun?"

I had to sweeten the pot with an excursion, in case they weren't keen on having a one-year-old cutting in on their summer vacation—it seems to be working. Their eyes are as wide as saucers and their tiny faces are aglow with excitement.

"Heck, yeah!" The boys high five and quickly start talking about all the animals they want to see. "We have to make a stop at the snake exhibit. They are *so* cool."

I shudder remembering the last time I took Matt and Max to see the reptiles. It was feeding time and I couldn't get the vision out of my mind for days, but the boys seemed to love it. I roll my eyes and shake my head as I mutter under my breath, "*Boys.*" It'll be nice to have a little girl in the mix, switching things up.

After breakfast, Dad agreed to watch the boys so I could go meet up with William, Harper, and Ashley. To be honest, I'm sort of nervous.

Full-on confessional—remember that whole bit about how I may or may not have fantasized about William? Yeah, well, I totally downplayed that. Every time I'm around him—which isn't often, thank goodness—I get all weird and turn into a loon. I seriously pray I don't make a fool of myself.

Giving myself a mental pep talk, I finally force myself to get out of the Tahoe. Once outside, I come face to face with my dream home. It's a beautiful Cape Cod style house nestled smack dab in the middle of University Park. It's absolutely gorgeous, with gray shingle siding, white shutters, ornate molding, and white trim around the front double doors.

Just as I'm about to step onto the porch, the front doors open and William steps out.

"Bella, thanks for helping us on such short notice." He moves to hug me, and I freeze. He's never hugged me before and the sudden display of affection catches me off guard. When he notices my reaction, he quickly steps back. "*Soooo*, that's your ride? Very mom-mobile for an eighteen-year-old, no?"

"I guess. It's a necessity while carting around two six-year-olds from soccer, to hockey, to karate. It was that or a minivan, and no offense to moms everywhere, but *no thanks*. It's social suicide for someone my age. Not that I have much of a social life, but still. It would be nice to forgo the mom bus in case I ever went out with friends." Noticing the smirk on his face and the fact that I'm rambling, I quit while I'm ahead and shut up.

"Well, whatever the reasoning, it suits you. You took on a huge role and stepped up for the boys after your mother..." He trails off, not really wanting to finish that sentence. Losing our mother three years ago was a blow to everyone who knew her, and still a major source of sorrow whenever she's brought up in conversation. "Look, if caring for Harper is too much on top of what you already have going on, I totally understand."

"No, it's fine." My voice comes out thick and forced. "I already talked to the boys about it and they're excited. Plus, it's only temporary through the summer, right?"

"Yes, maybe even sooner if I'm able to find a live-in nanny before then." He motions toward the house with his left hand and continues. "Please come in." William presses his palm to my back, his pinky connecting with the exposed skin of my midriff and shooting tiny jolts of electricity up my spine as he ushers me into his home.

I only see the Hawthorne family on holidays or special occasions and I've only been inside their home once, at Harper's baptism brunch. Stepping into the foyer, the home is just as stunning as I remember. It's decorated in a coastal farmhouse theme with calming shades of gray and ivory throughout the entire main floor.

"Hey Bella, I can't believe how big you are! I haven't seen you in ages. Since you were fifteen, right?" Ashley walks up to me while holding Harper and reaches over for a side hug. "You're such a beautiful young lady now, your mother would be so proud."

I hug her back, bopping Harper's nose as I pull away. "Hey. Yes, the last time I saw you was at my mother's funeral." I give her a sad smile and try to change the subject. "So, you've been helping William with Harper?"

"Yes, I have. Come, let's go into the kitchen and grab some coffee while we chat."

"You said the magic word, coffee." I raise my hands skyward in praise. "Show me the way and I will follow." I chuckle while keeping pace.

We step into the all-white kitchen. It's finished with nickel hardware, a massive marble island, and a gorgeous fireplace in front of the breakfast nook. Totally Instagram worthy.

Ashley hands Harper to William and points me toward a barstool. "Sit. I'll make your coffee. How do you take yours?"

"Black. No fuss. Makes it really easy on the mornings the boys and I are running late. Which is more often than not." I laugh self-deprecatingly.

"Girl, I understand. Trust me. I honestly don't know how you do it with two boys. I've been helping my brother for a month, and don't get me wrong, I love my niece, but I'm in no hurry to have a baby permanently." She shoots me a smile while simultaneously pushing a cup of coffee toward me. "Your father is truly lucky to have you, Bella."

"There was no other choice. My family needed me, and I couldn't just check out on them. That would have been all kinds of wrong," I say, shrugging my shoulders.

"Not everyone thinks the same way you do, Bella," William growls out, pinning me with his brooding gaze.

Crap. I'm guessing I hit a sore spot. "I'm sorry. I didn't mean to say anything offensive," I quickly apologize, not realizing I might've rubbed the shortcomings of his crappy ex in his face.

"Don't pay Mr. Grumpy Pants any mind, Bella." Ashley waves her hand toward William. "Now, let's talk about the schedule. Harper is up by seven a.m., naps at noon, dinner at five-thirty and in bed by seven. William heads out to the office at eight forty-five a.m. and returns at five-thirty p.m. That is, unless he's out of town for business. How will that work with the schedule you have going on with the boys?"

"Matt and Max are both up at six a.m. sharp. *Yay me.*
Which means I'm usually up by five or five-thirty a.m. if I
want to get ahead of the curve. If it's okay with everyone,
we could be out the door by six forty-five and here in time
for Harper's wakeup call." I take a sip of coffee and
continue with my train of thought. "We could all have
breakfast here, then set out for our daily activity, whether
it's out of the house or something here in the back yard.
We'll all be back inside for nap time, followed by learning
activities and dinner." Ashley and William both nod, so I
continue. "I could prepare dinner, but the boys and I don't
have to eat here, if it's too much of a strain. Plus, I'm sure
Dad will start to miss my cooking."

"Anything in this kitchen is at your disposal,
including the food, so don't be shy about it. Chef will be
out on maternity leave until the fall, so I know William
will appreciate all of the help you can give when it comes
to cooking. That man can burn water." Ashley snorts as
she slaps her knee. "Anyway, feel free to take any
leftovers home to Aiden, that way you'll kill two birds
with one stone."

"You really are the modern day Mary Poppins,"
William blurts out, half in awe and half in sarcastic
disbelief.

"I don't know about all that, but my college major *is*
Child Psychology, so I guess it's in my nature." I wink and
point at William.

I winked?! What the hell is wrong with me? I feel my cheeks burn under his scrutiny. Talk about being socially awkward. Quickly turning around, I face Ashley, trying to hide my embarrassment.

Ashley glances back and forth between William and I, narrowing her eyes. Something flashes across her face, but it's gone before I can ascertain the emotion behind it. "What college are you going to, Bella? Is it out of state or local?"

"It's local. Dad said he'd be finding care for the boys before I start this fall, but I still wanted to stay close. You never know when they'll need me." I play with a strand of my hair, thinking of the twins. "Frankly, I think I need those boys just as much as they need me. They were my anchor throughout the whole grieving process. They gave me a purpose to keep going and I could honestly say I'd be a different person today if it wasn't for them."

I wipe a rogue tear and apologize. "I'm so sorry. I didn't mean to be a downer and get emotional on y'all. If the schedule sounds good then I can be here with the boys Monday morning."

"You are not a downer, Bella," Ashley coos. "I think she's the perfect fit for Harper, don't you William?"

"Yes."

That's it. That's all I get. A one-word answer letting me know I have the gig. God, I hope the rest of our interactions aren't like this. *Awkward AF.*

After discussing pay and other logistics, we catch up on what little of my social life I'm willing to share, which isn't much. *Let's be honest, they wouldn't be thrilled to know the truth about my extracurriculars.* We quickly move on to Ashley's life back in Palm Beach. She apparently is dating some hotshot lawyer and is smitten. It seems there might be a wedding in the near future.

Realizing what time it is, I place my empty cup down on the island and step off the bar stool. "It's been so nice catching up, but I have to get back before the boys burn the house down on Dad's watch." I chuckle. "I'll be back Monday morning. Please call if anything changes between now and then." I wave goodbye to William and walk toward his sister on my way out. "Hope to see more of you, Ashley. It was so nice spending time together." With a hug and a squeeze, I'm out the door, ready to shake the awkwardness of this morning's encounter.

Chapter Three

WILLIAM

ANOTHER MONDAY, another cup of coffee. Popping a pod into the Keurig, I try and decipher the emotions running through me. Finally landing on a mixture of excitement and nerves, I try to explain the feelings away.

It's the first time I've ever left Harper with someone other than family or a professional facility, so that could very well be the source of my nerves, but where is the excitement coming from?

A vision of Isabella flashes in my mind's eye. *God, she is stunning.* I don't ever remember her being so damn beautiful. Her long black hair and piercing gray eyes are enough to bring any man to his knees. *But she's so fucking young.* Eighteen years young, to be exact. I give myself a mental slap, shoving any and all thoughts of Bella's beauty out of my mind.

Switching gears, I go over the schedule she texted me last night. It looks like they're going to the arboretum instead of the zoo. Harper will get a kick out of seeing all the pretty flowers and I wish I could be there to see her reaction.

I've never had any excursions with Harper before. I'm not good with planning that sort of thing and Heather was never one to plan activities for us or even establish a set schedule for our daughter, despite being the primary caregiver in our home. I don't think there was a motherly bone in that woman's body.

What in the hell was I thinking marrying her?

A knock at the side door brings me back to the here and now. I walk over and open it, seeing two spunky six-year-old boys and a smiling Bella.

"Morning." I clear my throat. "I forgot to give you a key on Saturday." After waving everyone inside, I move to pull out the spare key from the overflow drawer and hand it to Bella. "Feel free to come and go as you please. Treat this as you would your home." I go on to write all of the login details and instructions for the security system on a sheet of paper. "If possible, please try and memorize this information and then burn it when you're done. I don't want it floating around where someone could easily get ahold of it."

Just as I'm handing Bella the paper, Harper begins to babble through the baby monitor.

"Sounds like our little pumpkin is up." Bella beams, turning to face the twins. "Boys, sit at the breakfast nook. You get thirty minutes of screen time while I get Harper situated and breakfast started."

"Woohoo!" the boys cheer, as they pull their tablets from their packs, leaving me in awe of how easily she just took control of the situation. I'm about to tell her how impressed I am with her when I realize she's already left for Harper's room. *Right*, I need to be just as efficient and get ready for work.

"Matt, Max, I'm heading to my room. Holler if you need anything." I walk out of the kitchen donning the biggest smile. Things might just be looking up for the Hawthorne family.

Forty minutes later, I step into the kitchen and inhale deeply. The smell of breakfast sausage and maple syrup pull an audible groan from me. "It smells good in here. Is there anything left for dear old daddy-o?" Okay, that was weird. I've never called myself daddy-o before. Sure, I'm Harper's father, but it's not like the twins are mine and Bella their mother.

"Yes, I left you a plate on the counter. It's covered in foil to keep it warm. There are breakfast sausages and French toast," she replies without skipping a beat.

Maybe she didn't find that slipup as awkward as I did? *God, I hope not.* Day one and I've already had to reprimand myself *twice.*

"Thanks but you don't have to cook for me too, you know. I was just kidding."

"No worries. It makes no difference cooking one extra batch since I'm already making enough for four," she says as she begins to load the dishwasher.

Not wanting to make things more awkward, I grab the plate and sit at the table without further comment. I'm about to damn near lick the plate clean from how good everything is when Bella places a travel mug of coffee in front of me.

She's fucking perfect. Not only is she drop-dead gorgeous, she's also amazing with Harper, can cook her ass off, *and* she supplies me with coffee? *Clearly, I proposed to the wrong woman.*

Mentally smacking myself—again—I remind myself that not only is Bella eighteen, she is also my best friend's niece and partner's daughter. The thought of making her mine is not only off-limits, it's impossible. I have to keep my head in check and do something to break out of this Bella fog I'm in. STAT.

"You don't have to wait on me hand and foot. That is *not* a part of your job description." Grimacing, I continue. "I didn't hire you to play house. You're Harper's nanny. Nothing more, nothing less." Dick thing to say, but Bella needs to know from the start that there are boundaries which under no circumstances can be crossed. This isn't some romance novel where the single dad falls in love with the hot nanny.

"It's coffee, not a declaration of undying love." She rolls her eyes and shakes her head. "It's seriously no hardship and there is definitely no reason for the attitude, William." Bella circles a finger in my direction. "I should have put a little chill pill in that coffee of yours. Next time, I'll know better." With a wink, she turns her back to me and heads toward the mudroom.

Well lookie here, Bella has some sass to dish.

Seizing the opportunity to slip away without further confrontation, I move toward Harper's highchair and plant a kiss on top of her head. "Goodbye, pumpkin. I hope you have a wonderful day." Stepping toward the twins, I simultaneously ruffle their hair and speak loud enough for Bella to hear. "That goes for the rest of you too. Let me know if you need me to bring anything home." *Home.* As if this was their home too. Before I make this morning any more awkward, I step out into the porte-cochere and into my SUV, turning up the radio as I speed off to work.

As soon as I'm settled in my office, Aiden pops his head through the doorway. "Hey Hoss. How'd the first morning handoff go? Isn't Isabella amazing?"

She's amazing, alright. Not sure I want to share just how amazing I think she is with her father, though.

"She's perfect. I'm just worried we're monopolizing too much of her time." I slowly run the palm of my hand down my face. "She's eighteen. Shouldn't she be going out with friends, getting into trouble, doing all sorts of things kids her age do? I remember eighteen and I was nowhere near as responsible as Bella."

"Bite your tongue, man. My Bella has always had a good head on her shoulders. I think losing Lucia only solidified that even further. I suppose she could have gone either way, rebellious teenager or what she is today." Aiden lets out a sigh as he runs a hand through his blond hair. "I'm truly blessed she turned out to be as strong as she is. I honestly don't think I could have handled a hot mess teenager on top of the twins while grieving the loss of my wife. No fucking way."

"What about friends? Surely she needs some sort of release. She can't take on all of that responsibility without letting loose every once in a while," I wonder out loud, not sure if the concern is purely an altruistic one. "I'm afraid I'm just adding more to her load and that it'll become too much for her to handle."

"She unwinds," Aiden huffs out while rolling his eyes. "We're having a get together next week and some of her friends are coming over for the barbeque. I sent an invite to the group via the email chain. Are you coming?"

"I must have missed it with everything we've had going on. Of course, I'll be there."

"Great. You'll get to witness firsthand that Bella does, in fact, let loose. Man, you make it sound like she's our servant and we don't let her go out or have fun." Aidan places his hand on his heart in mock indignation. "During the school year, I would take the morning shift with the twins and Bella would pick them up from after school care. She was only in charge from four to seven and was only on full-time duty when I had to go out of town for work. Otherwise, she's been free to do whatever she wants—within reason, of course."

"I didn't mean anything by it, I swear. I was just saying she's a lot more grown-up than I was at her age. That's for sure." I shift in my seat, suddenly becoming extremely uncomfortable with this topic. "So, you ready for the Cicily contract? I hear she's one tough broad to handle."

"Yes. That's actually why I came in here this morning." Aidan flashes me a megawatt smile and leans forward in his chair. "I've got her security team briefed and ready to go. Just needed you to go over the contract one last time. Her manager made a couple of changes and I want to run them by you beforehand."

"Of course." I take the file from his hand and shoo him out of my office. "I'll look it over now and get back to you within the next hour. Let's see what crazy demands they've come up with now."

As soon as the door closes behind Aiden, my phone dings notifying me of an incoming text message. It's from Bella. After unlocking my phone and opening the messaging app, I see a picture of Harper trying to pick a tulip.

BELLA: Don't worry. She didn't actually pluck the flower. The Arboretum police would have chased us out 😶! It did, however, make for a perfect photo op.

I quickly type out a reply.

WILLIAM: Thanks for sharing. It made my morning.

I tuck my phone back into its charging cradle and smile. It feels good to know Harper is having fun and being cared for with genuine concern. I'll have to remember to thank Bella once more when I get back to the house tonight and maybe apologize for being such an ass earlier.

It's six o'clock when I make my way up the steps and into the house, tulips and chocolate in tow. As soon as I step inside, I hear commotion in the kitchen and the sweetest sound to ever bless my ears, Harper's giggles, courtesy of the two boys sitting on either side of her. Matt and Max are making silly faces at Harper while slurping spaghetti noodles and making noises reminiscent of an elephant in distress.

"Looks like I've been missing out on all the fun." I laugh wholeheartedly. "I come bearing gifts. Tulips for the ladies, and chocolate bars for the gents. That is, of course, if it's okay with Bella. Not sure what the rule is on sweets before bedtime."

I know I'm laying it on kind of thick, but I kept feeling like a piece of shit the whole day. Bella is so damn sweet, going out of her way to make Harper's day fun— even sending me update photos—and how do I thank her? By being an asshat, implying she wasn't taking her job seriously.

"They're allowed a sweet treat after dinner, but you really didn't have to bring us anything." Bella's cheeks turn the prettiest shade of pink as she puts down another place setting at the table. "Will you be joining us for dinner, or will you be eating later?"

Before I can answer her, both boys turn to Bella and assault her with the biggest puppy dog eyes I've ever seen. "Bo Bella, can we eat the chocolate now, pleeeease?" I chuckle and quietly mouth *sorry*, hoping I didn't just create a nighttime tantrum for her.

"You both can have some chocolate after dinner as long as you thank Mr. Hawthorne for his kindness." She looks up at me through her long thick lashes and smiles. "Thank you for the flowers. They're beautiful."

"Thank you, Mr. Hawthorne," the boys say in unison.

"No problem. It was my pleasure. I was inspired by the photo you sent earlier and didn't see why my beautiful Harper couldn't have some tulips of her very own." I smile, remembering Harper trying to pick the flower at the arboretum. "Besides, I wanted to thank all of you for giving my daughter such a fun day."

Unable to help myself, I move behind Bella and gently place my hands on either hip, digging my fingers into the material of her leggings. I'm asking myself what the fuck I'm doing when her body responds with a sharp intake of breath. *My touch affects her.* I smile to myself as I breathe her in. She smells of amber and vanilla—the sultry scent such a stark difference to what I'd expect from someone her age.

Leaning in even closer—I hover my lips just above the skin behind her ear—and softly whisper, "Sorry for this morning."

As if my voice was the key and her body the lock, goosebumps begin to rise along the contour of her neck and her once steady breathing turns ragged. *Instantly, I envision her breathing like this, writhing underneath me while I slowly lick my way down her body.* Realizing I've crossed a line, I take one last moment and squeeze both hands before releasing my grip on her hips.

I shouldn't have done that, knowing full well touching her like that is off-limits. So much for not crossing boundaries.

Tomorrow. Tomorrow I'll be better.

ISABELLA

I TOSS AND TURN but sleep eludes me. My body is still humming from the contact with William earlier today. I have never experienced anything like that before. Sure, I've been attracted to other men and my body has done the typical indicative of arousal, but never to the extent of what happened with William. My whole body came alive under his touch, reacting as if it were a live wire and his hands the conductor.

Why? Why does my body want someone so completely off-limits?

Unable to sleep, I decide I need to scratch the itch William has spurred on. Making sure the boys are asleep and Dad is in his room, I begin getting ready for a night out and shoot my friend Cassie a text.

BELLA: You down for the hunt tonight?

Not two seconds later, Cassie replies.

CASS: You know it, *biatch*!!! Whoop Whoop! 🐎

I can always count on Cass to be my wing woman. She is no drama and always down for fun. Opening my closet, I survey the options, selecting a tried and true little black dress paired with a slim black clutch and a gorgeous pair of Jimmy Choo stilettos.

Moving on to my hair, I take it down from the sloppy bun that is my signature hairdo, and add in some fresh waves with a styling wand. Spraying the roots with dry shampoo for volume, I fluff and tease until I've reached the desired height. *The bigger the hair the closer to God.* Though I'm pretty sure God wants nothing to do with my activities tonight.

I decide on a smoky eye, soft blush, and glossy nude lips to finish off my look. I'm ready. Ready to get rid of this burning need within me and get over whatever it is I feel for William.

Looking down at my phone, I see Cass texted she was on her way to Uptown and would meet me there in ten. *Perfect.* I grab my keys, stick them in my clutch, and tiptoe out to the car.

Spotting Cass up at the bar, I make my way toward her, surveying the crowd as I walk.

"Hey, hot chica. I'm so jealous of your hair. I wish I hadn't chopped mine off." Cassie reaches out and tugs at the ends of my long black hair.

"Shut it. You know your long bob is hot as fuck." I roll my eyes and wave my hand toward her face. "And don't they say blonds have all the fun?"

"Whatever. You know that between the two of us it's *you* who's having more fun." She swirls her index finger in her martini glass, fishing out the olive. "*So,* are you going to share what has us out on a Monday night? Kind of early in the week to get a fix, no?"

I call out to the waiter and order a glass of bourbon, neat. "Long story short, an interaction earlier left me wanting, and the man who caused it is off-limits."

"*Innnnteresting.* Do I happen to know who this gentleman is, or is that information off-limits too?"

"No, you don't. It's my uncle's best friend, my dad's business partner, and the father of the little girl I'm nannying." I take a slow sip from the tumbler placed in front of me and hand the bartender cash, telling him to keep the change.

"Holy shit!" Cassie whisper-shouts. "Talk about cliché, Bella. No judgment here, though."

Closing my eyes, I take a deep breath and nod. "I've had a crush on him for as long as I can remember, but he's always been just that—a crush." Turning toward the room, I scope out the scene once more. "Until today... he hadn't touched me. I swear there was something there. It was pure electricity when he grabbed me by my hips... but what do I know? I could have just imagined the whole thing."

"When was the last time you hooked up with someone?" Cassie's brows furrow inquisitively.

"It's been about a month. The boys starting summer vacay has really put a kink in my extracurriculars, and not the good kind." I see a guy sitting in the VIP area, making an obvious point of checking me out. "I think I've found tonight's tribute," I sing-song. "Don't look now, but he's sitting to the right of the VIP section, white button-up, black slacks, and blond hair."

Cassie waves a cross in front of me, sending me off with her version of a blessing. "Vaya con Dios."

I throw my head back and laugh, reminding her God wants nothing to do with my clandestine activities.

William

My mind is far away, reliving the memory of having Bella between my hands. The memory of her skin coming alive at the slightest touch leaves me wondering what else

I could make her body do. *Would she be a responsive lover? Would she taste as sweet as she smelled?*

Enough. I'm sure my recent obsession with Bella is nothing more than just having a thirst that needs to be quenched. I haven't gotten laid in six months. I'm no cheater, and things with Heather stopped being physical when I suspected she was letting someone else take a dip in what was now a communal pool. I'm not a jealous man but there was no way I was risking a venereal disease just because Heather was convenient and I was horny.

My boy Ren snaps his fingers in front of my face. "Earth to William. Where the hell'd you go?"

Slowly blinking my eyes, I turn to face him. "Yes, I'm here, asshole. Just have a lot on my mind."

"Mmhmm. Well, like I was saying, there is a hot blond at the bar. I'm going to head over if you don't want to call dibs."

"She's all yours. Not my type."

"Since when are blonds not your type?" Ren rolls his eyes as he steps toward the bar.

Since your hot little niece walked into my home.

Gazing back toward the other side of the VIP area, a flash of long black hair catches my attention. I've found my girl for the night, and she is perfect. Wavy black tendrils cascade down to a juicy round peach of an ass—an ass I'd love to bite—long defined legs peek out from under her little black dress—I can picture those legs wrapped

45

around me as I... *wait...* that *is* my girl. The very girl I came here to escape.

What in the hell is she doing here? Is that a drink in her hand?

Before I know it, my feet are carrying me toward her. Just as I'm about to reach her, a man who looks to be about my age reaches out and pulls her toward him. As if in slow motion, the man wraps his arms around Bella's waist and causes her to stumble into his chest.

I. See. Red.

"Get your filthy hands off her." I growl, barely sounding human.

Immediately, Bella spins around and stares at me with wide eyes and a perfectly pouty mouth shaped in an O of surprise.

"Hey man, she came up to *me*. Why don't we let the lady decide who she wants to go home with tonight?" A sleazy smile spreads across the man's face as he squeezes Bella's waist tighter.

I've seen enough.

Reaching out and taking a fist full of the man's shirt, I pull him toward me, effectively breaking his hold on Bella. "She's off-limits and if you value your life, I suggest you turn around and forget you ever saw her." I push him off me and toward a booth where he sits his ass down, like the coward he is. Grabbing Bella's hand, I turn us around and steer her toward the rear entrance of the bar, not stopping until we've reached the valet.

I hand the attendant my ticket and we wait in silence as he pulls up my SUV. Both of us are clearly in shock, neither of us wanting to be the first to break the silence. As soon as the car pulls up, I move to open her door, closing it once she's inside and rounding my way to the driver's side to tip the valet.

Once we're in the car, we sit in silence. Not knowing what to do, I pull out onto the road and drive. About five minutes into our self-imposed silent stand-off, the floodgates open and words come pouring out of both of us.

"What the hell were you doing there, Bella?" I say at the same time she speaks, "Don't tell my dad."

Nervous laughter follows what could only be described as an awkward moment.

"Before I promise you anything, you need to answer my question first. Last time I checked, you were eighteen and clearly not old enough to get into that bar. How in the hell did you get in?"

"Fake ID. Are you going to tell my dad?" Bella looks up at me with those gorgeous gray eyes I can't say no to.

"I won't tell him as long as you promise you won't do this again. How long have you been doing this, and what were you hoping to accomplish?" I pull over into the parking lot behind Buzz Brews, an all-night diner.

"That's two questions." She raises an eyebrow and smirks. "I've been doing it for a little over a year. What were *you* looking to accomplish tonight?"

"You smell like you bathed in whiskey." I redirect her last question, not wanting to answer the real reason I was there tonight.

"I spilled my drink on myself when you pulled that guy off of me. It's my drink of choice, and nice try but you can't change the subject. You still haven't answered my question and now you owe me two. Why were you at the bar and where is Harper?"

"I was looking for something you can't offer, and therefore shouldn't concern yourself with."

Bella audibly sucks in a shallow breath upon hearing my words, but I continue, needing to make this invisible line that much clearer.

"Harper is with Hudson and his girlfriend. They stopped by after you left and offered to babysit." I chuckle, remembering how Hudson awkwardly held Harper. "Angie, Hudson's girlfriend, has baby fever. She thinks that spending time around Harper might make him see the light. Besides, who am I to deny free childcare with someone I trust."

"That was nice of them." Her sweet smile slowly transforms into a wicked one, making those perfect plump lips all the more tempting. "How funny... I was also there for something you can't offer and therefore shouldn't concern yourself with. Now that we've cleared that up, we can both go our separate ways."

She starts to open the car door, but I grab her wrist and pull her toward me. I must have pulled harder than I thought because suddenly she's up against me, both palms splayed across my chest. My gaze drops to where her body meets mine, watching her hands rise and fall in sync to the beat of my desire. I wrap my arms around her and notice Bella's half-lidded eyes are searching mine, for what, I don't know. Perhaps the answer to whatever the hell it is we're doing here.

As if she's heard my thoughts, she whispers, "What are we doing?"

I raise one hand, cupping the back of her neck and bring her face closer to mine. Light shines through the window, illuminating her face and causing her eyes to turn the most mesmerizing shade of silver—a gray so pale it resembles the moon's surface. Absolutely stunning. My eyes flicker back and forth between the two magical orbs and I lean in a fraction closer, hovering my lips over hers as I whisper, "What we shouldn't..."

Mustering every ounce of willpower I possess, I breathe her in one last time and gently push her back into her seat. Reaching over her warm little body, I pull on her seatbelt and click it into place. "I'm taking you home, where you should be at this hour of night," Bella begins to protest but before she can say anything I brush the pad of my thumb across her lips and continue, "Don't worry about your car. Someone from the team will be picking it up."

Bella nods in agreement while I quickly place both hands on the steering wheel in an attempt to keep them off of her. Having her this close and alone is almost too much to bear and having my hands anywhere near her is asking for trouble.

Willing my cock to stand down, I shift my car out of park and pull back onto the road. *It's time to take little miss temptation home.*

Chapter Five

WILLIAM

IT'S BEEN A WEEK since the incident with Bella at the bar. Things have been tense around the house, but I've been doing my best to avoid her and any potential confrontation.

Today, however, that will be impossible. It's her dad's cookout and there is no way anyone could miss Bella in her neon pink bikini. It's like one of those old cartoons where all the flashing arrows point to the main character. -> *Tightest body up ahead* -> *Next turn, Heaven on Earth* -> *Hot babe right here* -> All signs pointing straight to God's gift to mankind, Bella.

She's sitting poolside in a lounge chair, sipping on a pink drink, face hidden behind large black shades—obscuring her gorgeous eyes—her long black hair is in a sloppy top knot, with wavy wisps cascading down her face. *She's absolute perfection.* My gaze follows the curves of her body and land on her dainty feet when a blond plops down on the edge of her chair, whispering something into her ear.

"Whatcha lookin' at?" Titus shoves my shoulder, a wide grin splaying across his face.

Ren appears to my left. "Oh man. You've got that same look you did at the bar last week. Too bad the ladies by the pool are off-limits. Especially my niece." He chuckles, not realizing how his words hit too close to home.

"You're off your rocker, Ren. I'm not interested in Bella or her friend. I was just in my head, thinking of a new contract I'm trying to pull in."

"Sure. That's what that look of desire was all about. Your desire for a new contract." Ren rolls his eyes and shoves a cold beer into my hand.

"They have tight little bodies. I wouldn't fault you for looking." Titus lets out a low whistle. "But Aidan would straight up chop your balls off if you came anywhere near Bella or her friend. Price is too high if you ask me."

"Nobody asked you because nobody is interested. Quit stirring up trouble where there is none." My blood is boiling at the thought of anyone else laying their eyes on Bella—anyone but me—so I try to change the subject before I go all caveman on Titus and Aidan figures out what we're all talking about. "Speaking of the bar, how'd it go with the blond you set your sights on, Ren? I haven't heard you talk about anyone since. Has the eternal bachelor finally settled down?"

Ren's eyes narrow as he looks over toward the girls, spitting out his beer in the process.

"Whoa there, buddy." I tap Ren on the back. "What happened?"

"Beer went down the wrong pipe... I think big bro might need some help manning the grill. See y'all later." Spinning on his heels, Ren heads toward the outdoor kitchen without so much as a backward glance. *That was weird.*

"What was that all about?" Titus points a thumb toward Ren.

"No clue, brother. No clue."

As I take a long pull from my beer, Bella gets up from her lounge chair and starts to head toward the house. I have to find a way to talk to her. This awkwardness between us needs to end, if only for Harper's sake. I'm sure she'd benefit from having Bella and I being on talking terms again.

"Gotta take a leak." I motion toward the house with my bottle and make my escape.

Making sure Aiden is occupied, I slide in through the French doors and into the kitchen. *Where did you run off to, little moon?* As if on instinct, my feet carry me toward the right and up the stairs, where Bella's room is located.

As soon as I turn down the hallway, I see Bella entering her room. *Gotcha.* I lightly tap on the door frame, not wanting to enter her space without consent. Things between us are strained enough as it is and I sure as hell don't want to add more fuel to that fire.

Bella lets out a gasp as she whirls and clutches her chest. "You scared the shit out of me. What are you doing up here?"

"I wanted to talk... privately." I run my fingers through my hair, unsure if this is such a good idea.

"What is there to talk about? Everything is fine. I'm fine." Bella spits the words out a mile a minute, a clear indicator things are *not* fine.

"Look, I don't want things to be weird between us. I want you to know you can always count on me if you ever need anyone to talk to. I know you take on a lot of responsibility and must need an outlet—"

Bella cuts me off before I can finish my sentence. "Right. I'm going to talk to my dad's friend who also happens to be my boss about what I do for stress relief." She rolls her eyes, sarcasm rolling off her in waves.

"Stress relief? Is that what the deal at the bar was?" My eyes narrow and brows drop as I look at her, waiting for an answer.

"Keep your voice down," Bella whisper-shouts, worrying her bottom lip. "And yes, it's something like that. Between being the perfect student, perfect sister, perfect role model, and perfect daughter... I just need something for me. Something that's solely mine. For my pleasure, regardless of what anyone else thinks or feels." Bella's gaze shifts back and forth between me and the door, letting me know she's finding this topic of conversation about as comfortable as I am.

Sensing her distress, I move closer in an attempt to soothe her. With the back of my hand, I reach out and caress her face. "Don't play a role with me, Bella. You're perfect the way you are."

At my words, Bella squeezes her eyes shut and inhales deeply. "You don't understand. You couldn't possibly."

An overwhelming sense of protectiveness comes over me and I'm flooded with the urge to shield her from any and all harm—which is ridiculous. She's not mine to protect, and even if she were, there is no way of protecting someone from absolutely everything.

Pushing my errant thoughts aside, I pull her in for an embrace, wrapping my arms under hers and holding her tightly against my bare chest. I bury my nose into her neck, smelling that delicious mixture of amber and vanilla I've grown to crave. "Let me in. Let me understand," I whisper, gently nuzzling her ear.

I feel her shudder beneath me, but before she can respond, we hear Aidan's distinct voice down the hall. I quickly release her, putting some distance between us, just in time for Aidan to appear in the door frame. "Bella—"

"Hey, Dad. Just came up to find some aloe gel. William is turning into a lobster and I thought I had some left over from our week at the lake." Bella waves the tube of aloe gel she managed to procure from thin air and throws it to me.

I catch the tube and make a show of squirting some into the palm of my hand before liberally applying it to my face and chest. "Bella. Always a lifesaver," I say with an awkward chuckle.

"Right. Well, I was actually coming up here to see if you knew where William was hiding. I wanted to introduce him to your aunt, Mariana." Aidan motions to the woman standing behind him.

I'd only met Mariana once, at Lucia's funeral. From what I recall, she travels constantly as an agent for the Federal Bureau of Investigation, only visiting once in a while to see her sister's family.

"Hello, Mariana. It's nice to see you again, and under much better circumstances." I wave the tube of aloe in my hand. "I would reach out and shake your hand, but I wouldn't want to get you dirty."

"I wouldn't mind getting dirty with you one bit..." Mariana's gaze turns predatory as she reaches out her hand, placing her palm on my bicep.

Bella clears her throat. "Well if you all will excuse me, Cassie is waiting downstairs."

I'm not interested in Mariana but blowing her off and chasing after Bella would be a massive indicator to Aidan that Bella and I are hiding something. I'm not ready for Aidan to know anything, especially since I don't fully comprehend what the hell is going on between his daughter and me.

Having no other choice, I play the part of the available bachelor and go along with Aiden's ambush of a setup. *What a clusterfuck.*

Isabella

My stomach churns as I make my way down the stairs. An odd sense of jealousy overcame me when I saw Mariana place her perfectly manicured hand on William. I was so flustered I didn't even manage to say a hello before storming out, not that anyone noticed. I'm sure the two lovebirds are already busy making plans for an official date—something I could never have with William.

This is so stupid. I have no right to be jealous. The man is thirteen years my senior, my dad's friend, and my boss. Even if for some reason he were interested in me, it would be a cold day in hell before us being together would be a possibility.

Regardless, my stomach is still in knots at the idea of him with Mariana.

"What's that face all about?" Cassie raises her brows in question as I approach the lounge chairs.

"Remember what happened at the bar with William? Well, he just confronted me in my room and it was the first time we really talked since Uptown." I say in a hushed tone, taking the drink she's offering up in solace. "Long story short, we talked, I got upset, he hugged me—it was amazing—we almost got caught hugging by my dad, and then my dad tried to set him up on a date with my aunt Mariana."

"Holy shit." Cassie urges the drink to my lips. "Drink up, chica. It's fortified with booze and Lord knows you can use it right now."

"Ha! I really shouldn't. It will give me the liquid courage I need to go yank Mariana away from William." Sighing, I lay my ass down on the lounge chair. I have no right to claim William, and I know it.

"Bella?" I hear William call my name, concern evident in his tone.

Turning around to face him, I wonder how much of my conversation with Cass he heard. "Hey. What's up?"

"The girls who are watching the kids today, do you trust them?" He nods toward the kids' area where all the party-goers dumped their offspring upon arrival.

"Yes. They're our backup babysitters for when neither Dad nor I can watch the twins. I thought we needed a childcare station for the cookout, knowing all the adults would be too busy to keep a proper eye on the kids. I sure as hell didn't want a repeat of the baptism shenanigans." I give a half-hearted chuckle. "Why do you ask? Did one of them do something wrong?"

"No. I was thinking I would ask one of them to sit for Harper sometime this week, so you and I could go out and talk." He's describing what could very well pass off as a date.

"That sounds lovely," Cassie chirps in, reminding me she's been here the whole time. "I could watch Harper if neither of the girls are available. I have tons of experience seeing as how I'm an auntie six times over." Cass raises her brows as she takes a sip from her drink. "My siblings have been very busy."

"How does Monday at six sound?" William looks toward Cassie expectantly.

"Perfect! Harper and I are going to have the best time." Cassie smiles as she shoos William away. "Now go and give us some space so we can gossip about you behind your back."

"Cassandra Marie Martinez!" I squawk in disbelief.

Chuckling, William brings both of his hands forward, palms up in a pacifying gesture. "Sounds good, ladies." And with a wink, the man I've been lusting after turns around and leaves.

Chapter Six

ISABELLA

THOUGHTS OF MY PSEUDO date with William have been all-consuming for the past forty-eight hours. So much so that it's been difficult to get the simplest of tasks done—even the twins have caught on to the fact that something isn't normal.

"Bella Bo Bella, the doorbell is ringing. Aren't you going to go get it?" one of the twins asks as he pulls on the hem of my dress. It's a gray sleeveless Victoria Beckham midi dress—made out of stretch knit material so it's casual enough to pair with flats but easily dressed up with a pair of killer heels for tonight.

"Bow-chicka-wow-wow," Cassie sings as I pull the door open. "That dress hugs you in all the right places, sister. Please tell me that's what you're wearing tonight."

I walk Cassie back to the playroom where the twins are playing with Harper. "I sure am. I'm switching up the flats for a pair of my black suede Manolo Blahnik BB pumps. I was hoping you could watch the kids a little earlier than expected so I can do my makeup."

"Of course chica. You know I've got your back. But to be honest, all you really need is a little smoky eye and some nude gloss. Just bring your makeup bag to the playroom and you can do it while we chat."

I do as she says, dropping her off in the playroom and running into the mudroom for my makeup bag. Before I step back into the hall, I notice a small earring—It's a gold leaf with a black pearl in front of the stud backing. *Hmmm. Must be Ashley's.* I place it on the counter and mentally remind myself to shoot Ashley a text. I would hate for her to throw out a perfectly good earring just because she thought she was missing the matching pair.

I walk to the playroom, and straight into a scene out of a modern day Mary Poppins. Cassie has the boys playing the 'clean up' game while rocking Harper back and forth.

"You're a natural." I clap my hands and grin. "It never gets old watching you in action."

"I have so many nieces and nephews. They've been my trial by fire for as long as I can remember." Cassie rolls her eyes as she keeps the twins' pace by tapping her foot on the hardwood floor. "Come on boys! Let's see who's going to win the clean up game. First one to finish gets dibs on the coloring books."

Cassie places Harper down in her enclosed play area while I take out my eyeshadow and brushes. "You know, one day it's going to be you with a ton of kids. I see how you look at babies."

"Hush your mouth, Bella. I'm the youngest of five siblings and I'm in no hurry to further populate the Martinez family." Cassie makes a sign of the cross with her thumb and forefinger, kissing her thumb at the end.

Laughing, I pull out my compact and start on my eyes. "Whatever you say, Cass."

"So where is Mr. Hot Stuff taking you tonight?" she asks while laying out the coloring books and crayons.

"Tao for sushi. I wonder if he's planning on taking Mariana there too." Blowing a raspberry, I continue. "Ugh, this isn't a date, so I shouldn't even be placing myself in the same category as my aunt."

"Hey, if it walks like a duck and quacks like a duck..."

"It's probably something relating to Harper. Nothing more. I definitely don't want to build this up to be something it isn't and then be totally crushed when the reality of it all hits." I apply two generous coats of my favorite mascara, placing the tube back in my makeup bag.

Just as I'm about to pull out the gloss, my phone chimes. "It's a text from William." I unlock my phone and read the message, summarizing it for Cassie. "He's running late. Said I should drop off the boys with Dad and meet him at the restaurant for dinner."

"Speaking of your father, are you going to tell him who you're meeting for dinner?" Cassie's hazel eyes widen to epic proportions.

"Um, no. What kind of question is that? It would be all kinds of awkward if he found out I was meeting up with William after hours."

"So what are you going to tell your dad?"

"Nothing. He doesn't really ask me anything. Ever. Since the accident with Mom, he never talks about anything personal, and that includes my social life. I don't know if it's the guilt from laying so much responsibility on me or if it's just too much for him to handle— imagining what a teenage girl is up to in the middle of the night." I sigh deeply. "I couldn't tell you. All I know is that he treats me differently since Mom's death. It's as if I stopped being his little girl and somehow became his employee."

"Shit, Bella," Cassie whispers low enough for it to elude little ears. "I'm so sorry."

"It is what it is. I lost both of my parents the day my mother died... and the worst part of it is, it's all my fault." I blot my eyes with a tissue, not wanting to smear the work I'd just done. "I really can't blame my father for disappearing on me when I was the one who took his wife away."

"Isabella Moretti, don't you dare say that. It was a car *accident.* Keyword being *accident.* You cannot blame yourself for such a loss and you most certainly cannot make excuses for your father because of it." Cassie's eyebrows knit together as her gaze pierces through me, seeing into the depths of my self-inflicted torment. "He is your father, you are his child. That means you're supposed to come first—always. That's what parents do. They are the ones who teach you the meaning of unconditional love."

"Unconditional love. Is that even real?" I chortle, the sound tainted with bitterness. "If it is, I can tell you right now that I've never experienced it."

"Only because you've never allowed yourself to. You know I love you, but you need some truth shoved in your face. You've built these walls around yourself. Only hooking up with one-night stands, nothing more; and now I find out about this whole thing with your father? It's no wonder you're so jaded when it comes to love."

"Okay, I get it. I promise to make more of an effort in that department. Now can we get off the topic?"

Sniffling, I pick up my bag and kiss Harper on the cheek. "I don't want to be all blotchy and red-faced when I see William later."

"See, that's where you should start. William would make perfect practice." Cassie claps her hands together excitedly.

"For the last time, this is *not* a date." I roll my eyes and let out a slow breath before turning to look at the twins. "Speaking of my non-date, I'm going to be late for dinner if we don't get going. Boys, finish coloring your pictures. We're picking up fried chicken on the way home."

The boys cheer and quickly start stowing away their crayons. I shake my head and laugh. "They *love* fried chicken. If you ever need to bribe them, just offer them food."

Chapter Seven

WILLIAM

THE WAITRESS DROPS off a rocks glass with my favorite whiskey—much-needed after the day I've had. We have a new contract which is pulling Bella's dad out of state for two months, at the very least, and he's asked if I could keep an eye on his kids until his return.

I take a long sip, feeling the warmth of the amber liquid as it travels down my throat. *If he only knew what he was really asking.* I can barely keep my hands off Isabella as it is. Inviting further opportunity to be around her is just a recipe for disaster.

As if my thoughts have conjured the beauty herself, Bella walks into the restaurant looking like a vision in gray. Her dress hugs her in all the right places, and I could easily see myself ripping that dress off after a night of dinner and dancing. Hell, forget the dinner and dancing, I can see myself ripping the dress off *right the fuck now*.

I want to wrap her long black hair around my fist and pull her head back—exposing the elegant column of her neck—allowing me to nip my way down to her collarbone, licking the hollow beneath with a wet stroke of my tongue...

"William." Bella's sweet voice pulls me out of my fantasy. I would normally stand to pull out a lady's chair—manners and all—but doing so now would only serve to expose the throbbing hard-on I've got going on under the table.

"Bella. Thanks for agreeing to meet me for dinner. We have an unfinished conversation I would like to get out of the way." Her face falls and I get the feeling I must have said something wrong.

The waitress approaches the table and I order for us. "We'll have the tasting menu tonight, with two glasses of my usual." I motion toward my glass, remembering Bella's drink of choice is also whiskey.

"Of course, Mr. Hawthorne, I'll put your order in immediately." The waitress nods and spins on her heels, heading toward the kitchen.

As soon as the waitress is out of earshot, Bella reaches for my glass and takes a slow sip. "Mmmm, delicious." She licks her lips and smiles. "You remembered my favorite drink."

With the amount of money I drop here on a weekly basis, the waitress didn't bother asking for Isabella's ID— not that she looks under twenty-one tonight. *Jesus.* That tight little body has my hand twitching in restraint.

"When did you start drinking, and why whiskey? It's not exactly a woman's go-to drink."

"Well, that's very sexist of you. And to answer your questions, fifteen after the car accident." She takes another sip, licking her top lip as she slowly puts the glass back down on the table. "And shortly thereafter, I was introduced to whiskey. I was at a party and the guy behind the bar offered to pop my whiskey cherry. I let him, and we've been a thing ever since. *The whiskey, not the guy...* though he did pop more than one cherry that night."

I swallow hard and my dick twitches in my pants. The thought of Bella and sex has me reeling as naked visions of her flit across my mind.

All that comes to a quick halt when it hits me how old she must have been during her first time. Rage consumes me and I do my best to temper my emotions. "Who was he? Your first? So help me God, he better have been a minor or I will find him and castrate him where he stands," I whisper-shout. *So much for keeping my cool.*

"It's none of your business who I choose to sleep with, William." Bella closes her eyes and sighs out a breath of frustration. "But I'll tell you if you promise to answer one of my questions. Tit for tat."

"*Fine,*" I hiss.

"I was sixteen and he was a senior at the public high school. I knew our paths would most likely never cross again and we both knew it was just a one-night stand. Not a big deal. None of them ever are." She looks off to the side, avoiding my eyes.

"Bella..." I reach over and clasp her delicate hand in mine. The contrast of her slender fingers in the palm of my big calloused hand denoting the stark difference between us. "I'm not even sure how to broach that response. First of all, let me make it clear that I'm not judging nor will I ever. I get that we all cope differently and sometimes we do things we wouldn't otherwise do to self-medicate our internal struggles... I just want to know one thing, what exactly have you been doing to self-medicate?"

"It's pretty obvious, no? You've seen me drink and attempt to pick up a random man at a bar." Bella's face flushes a deep shade of red. "I really don't think it's that big of a deal. I have to be so perfect in every other aspect of my life, I deserve to let loose in my private time.

Especially if it's not hurting anyone else." She takes a long sip of my drink before continuing. "It's not like I'm getting shitfaced every day, but even if I were and it were during my private time, whose business is it anyway."

"It's *my* business," I growl out.

"Why?" Bella laughs in disbelief. "I'm not your problem."

Oh, little moon... but you are.

The waitress interrupts, bringing us an amuse-bouche, effectively cutting off a premature declaration and giving me a minute to gather my thoughts. *Thank fuck.*

"Well? Why am I your business, William?" Bella cocks an eyebrow, pressing me to answer.

"Because you are my employee and my friend's daughter. I care about your well-being and want you to resolve whatever internal issues you have in a healthy, safe, and positive manner." *Who the fuck am I? Mr. Rogers?*

Bella scoffs at my response, hell, I would have too. "That's rich. Coming from the biggest playboy of them all. Isn't your licentious behavior what landed you with Heather in the first place?"

"Yes and I don't regret it because it led me to my beautiful daughter. Although, my personal scandal should serve as a warning to those who partake in casual sex." I tug at the collar of my shirt and smirk. "You never know if your no-strings partner is batshit crazy and will haunt you for the rest of your life."

"So what you're saying is that instead of going in blindly, I should fully vet my partners and stick to them exclusively? That sounds a lot like a relationship, completely rendering the point of 'no strings' useless."

"It's not a relationship if both parties have a mutual understanding that it's only about sex." *Mayday, mayday, I'm going down.* This conversation sounds an awful lot like a sexual proposition. A very inappropriate sexual proposition. I need to turn this ship around—*fast.* "Besides, sex isn't the only source of stress relief. Taking up hobbies or exercising are two very good examples of healthy outlets." *Though, neither quite as fun.*

"I have a hobby and I also workout regularly. Neither of those things should be a preclusion to doing something I love."

It's my turn to cock an eyebrow as I nearly choke on my own saliva, lingering on her admission. Naturally my mind hones in on her declaration of loving sex, but there is no way in hell I'm even touching that. Doing so would lead us farther down this bizarre rabbit hole of sexual frustration. Something neither of us is free to explore.

Before I can respond, the waitress sets down our first course and explains the dish, quickly retreating. No doubt she sensed the tense nature of our conversation.

"I didn't know you had a hobby. Please share." I wave my hand, motioning her to continue.

72

"I write children's books and illustrate them myself. I know... me, of all people, writing children's books." Bella laughs self-deprecatingly. "I promise, none of the books teach children how to engage in acts of loose morality. Quite the opposite, in fact. The books revolve around coping with life's curveballs in a healthy and positive manner. Hypocritical, right?"

I stare at her in wonder. "Isabella, that's amazing. Who better to teach children how to slay their dragons than someone who's actually battled her own." Without realizing it, I've reached for her hand and begun to slowly caress her wrist back and forth with my thumb. "Maybe one day you can share those dragons with me. You don't always have to fight them alone."

In that moment I see her—the real her—past all the layers of bravado and right down to her very essence. The battered and scarred beauty, who—despite life's tragedies—has clawed her way to the surface the only way she knew how. *Damn, it's alluring.* I'm truly and utterly captivated, blown away by her willingness to be vulnerable, shedding all pretense and showing me her true self.

With a clearing of her throat, the moment is gone. Bella erects her walls once more and does a complete one-eighty on our conversation. "So, are you bringing my aunt here on a date?"

As if I'd just been bitch-slapped, I sit there in silence trying to comprehend what just happened.

"You *are* dating Mariana, right?" Bella's wide eyes look at mine for answers.

"I'm not sure what gave you the impression I was dating your aunt. I can assure you I have no intention of doing so."

"Right. Okay. Good." Bella lifts her glass, only to find it's empty.

Just in time, the waitress approaches the table with two fresh glasses and a waiter in tow with the second course.

"Right. Okay. Good," I repeat Bella's words, a smirk evident on my face. It's clear she's embarrassed by her little display of jealousy. "Enough serious conversation for tonight. Let's talk about college. Are you looking forward to starting this fall?"

Bella shoots me a grateful smile, gladly avoiding any further discussion of dating, sex, and dragons, keeping the rest of our conversation pretty tame. *The way it should have been to begin with.*

On our way out, I notice she didn't valet. "Let me walk you to your car. It's late and you never know who's lurking around."

"Sure. I parked this way." She motions toward the corner of the parking garage, but as we get closer to her SUV, I sense something's off.

"Wait here," I instruct her to stay put as I survey the area and take a closer inspection of her vehicle.

The entire driver's side of the Tahoe is vandalized—its windows have been smashed in and the side panels have been spray-painted with the word 'Whore' across them. Upon further inspection, two of the tires have been shot at and are completely deflated. I'm about to crouch down when I hear a loud gasp behind me.

I turn toward the sound and see Bella's eyes filling with tears. I rush toward her, instinctively closing the space between us and wrapping her protectively in my arms.

"I told you to stay put. You need to listen to me and do as I say." My words come out as a harsh growl.

"Who did this?" Isabella's voice is muffled as she murmurs into my chest.

"I don't know, but whoever it is, I'm going to find them and make them pay. I promise, little moon." Stroking her hair, I place a kiss on the top of her head. "We need to call this in and let your father know what's going on. He's leaving town and there is no fucking way you're staying alone with the twins while that lunatic is out there."

If I was feeling protective before, it's nothing compared to how I'm feeling now. All of my senses are pulling me toward Bella, urging me to shield her from the outside world. I quickly come up with a plan that will allow me to keep her safe and close, the only problem will be getting her father to go along with it.

Chapter Eight

ISABELLA

SHIT. SHIT. SHIIIIIIT.

Dad is on his way and I'm not sure how we're going to explain a) why we were out to dinner alone, and b) how I ended up with alcohol on my breath.

"Here. Chew on this. Your dad will be here soon." William shoves a mint into my hand.

Thank you, mind reader.

Not two seconds later, Dad's car comes swerving around the corner. William, sensing my anxiety, wraps his arm around me reassuring me everything is going to be okay. "Trust me, Isabella. I've got you."

"Thank you," I manage to whisper back. Despite the circumstances, his affection brings me a deep sense of security. Whoever did this to my car has no way of reaching me when I'm tucked safely in his arms. I could stay like this forever.

Beside us, a car door slams, effectively breaking the moment and causing us to take two steps back from each other. Looking up toward the sound, I see my father, worry and rage warring across his face. "What in the holy hell happened here?" He walks around the vehicle, taking in the vandalism for himself. "What were you doing here so late?"

Before I can respond, William steps in. "She was meeting a girlfriend for dinner and called me when she found her car like this." He shoves his hand through his hair, tugging at the ends. "I was apparently the last person on her car log, otherwise I'm sure it would have been you whom she called. I'm glad I was close by and could make it here as quick as I did."

Wow. I'm floored by the ease in which the lies just pour out of him.

Dad stares at William with narrowed eyes. "Did any of the parking attendants see anything or anyone suspicious?"

"I've talked to the staff, but nobody saw anything and the vehicle is parked in a corner where the perp's actions would have been obstructed in the video. It's a major security deficit on their part if you ask me."

I take in a deep breath. If there's no reason to see video footage of the garage, then Dad won't see William and I walking toward my car together.

Dad takes two steps toward me and pulls me into an embrace. "I'm glad you're okay. I don't know what I would do if something happened to you. You're my baby girl."

At the words 'baby girl', William makes a choking sound. When I look over Dad's shoulder, I see that his face has turned a deep shade of red. I'm glad Dad isn't facing him at this moment. There's no doubt he'd be questioning his sudden aversion to that particular term of endearment.

William clears his throat and raises an eyebrow. "With you leaving town tomorrow, I don't think it's wise for Bella and the twins to stay at your house, alone." William's eyes flicker back and forth between my father and me. "Since they're spending so much time in my home already, it would make sense for them to stay there. I have a full security system and I'll be there in the event anything else were to happen."

Hold your damn horses. Is he suggesting what I think he is?

I already have a hard time keeping my emotions in check. Living with him twenty-four seven is just asking for trouble. "It's okay. I'm sure we'll be safe at Dad's. There's a full security system there too."

William's eyes shoot straight through me, the intensity in them burning holes into my soul. "Bella, a system can only do so much. It's always best to have someone on the premises to act in defense. If you don't feel comfortable in my home then I suggest we post someone from our team at your place."

"Nonsense." Dad waves a hand in the air. "The original members of WRATH are the only ones I would entrust my kids to, and it makes sense it be you, since Bella is already caring for Harper and is practically living in your home as it is. I fly out at zero eight hundred hours, so I'll bring them over to your place tomorrow morning before I leave." Dad kisses the top of my head. "Keep me posted on any developing information, regardless of how small you think it might be. We need to find the son of a bitch who did this and skin them alive. Nobody messes with my family. Nobody."

"Ten-four. I'm opening a file for Bella and will be handling it personally. I'll also be working from home as much as possible, and I'll send someone from the team to watch over everyone if I can't be at the house for some reason."

My knees threaten to give out at the idea of so much interaction with William. Dad mistakes this as my reaction to the vandalism and reaches out to comfort me.

"Everything is going to be okay, baby girl. I trust William to watch over you, and he'll be there around the clock until we find whoever did this." Dad squeezes my shoulder in a reassuring manner. "We will make them pay. I promise."

We drive up to what will be our home for the next couple of months. I've been here many times before but seeing it today is conjuring all types of new emotions. It appears a family of butterflies have taken residence in my belly since finding out I'll be sharing a roof with William. *Every. Single. Night.* Talk about an exercise in self-restraint. Staying away from that sexy man will be damn near impossible.

My thoughts drift back to the night before where I swear he was borderline propositioning me with a no strings attached scenario. I could be totally off base, but I swear I saw hunger in those cerulean eyes of his.

"Welcome to your new home." William greets us in the foyer, raising both arms wide in an all-encompassing gesture. "Please treat it as if it were your own."

"We will!" the twins chime in unison as they head back toward the playroom. No doubt they are heading straight for the gaming consoles William installed last week.

"Where's your father?" William looks behind me and into the front yard. "I would've thought he'd want to deliver the precious cargo himself."

"He had to fly out earlier than expected, so someone from the team met us at the house and followed us here. They're stationed outside until further notice from you." I awkwardly bounce on the balls of my feet, not knowing where to go from here. "So... where should I place our bags?"

"In your rooms, of course." Without further elaboration, William picks up all three bags—as if they weigh nothing—and makes his way toward the stairs.

Does he want me to follow him?

I catch up and quietly trail behind him, my eyes roaming over his body as I unabashedly take advantage of the view. His dark brown hair is damp from a shower and his white dress shirt is pulled taut across his back—his broad shoulders taper into the V of his waist and lead my hungry eyes straight to his ass. *Oh, that ass...*

"Bella?" William's voice pulls me from my trance and I immediately feel my cheeks flush with embarrassment. He's standing a few steps ahead, staring at me expectantly, no doubt having caught me in the middle of my ogling session. "Did you hear me, or should I repeat myself?"

Needing to wipe that smirk off his face, I try to feign innocence, though I'm pretty sure it's pointless. "I was just running through my mental to-do list for the day. Can you please repeat your question?"

"I was saying that Harper and the boys have rooms on the second floor. You could also have a room on this floor if you'd like, but none of the remaining rooms come with an en suite." He walks us into a large room with a bay window looking into the back yard. "If you'd rather have an adjoining bathroom, we could set you up downstairs next to my office. It's ultimately up to you but that room is larger and boasts an amazing tub, so I've been told. With all that said, where would *you* rather sleep?"

William fails to mention that the guest room downstairs is also close to his room. Something that should be a deterrent. *Totally a deterrent.* It also doesn't go unnoticed that he is definitely selling the downstairs bedroom over the one on this floor. *Ulterior motives, maybe?*

"It would probably be best if I stayed close to the kids in case they called out in the middle of the night," I quickly say while depositing the boys' bags onto their twin beds.

A glance around the room lets me know William took the time to turn this space into a welcoming environment for the twins. The whole room is decorated in dark blues and varying shades of white, the shelves are lined with children's literature, and a toy box full of goodies lies at the foot of each bed. "When did you have time to do all this? This is beyond thoughtful."

"Seriously not a big deal. I messaged my assistant last night and had her pick this stuff up." He runs the back of his hand along his stubble, pausing at his chin. "Your room has been set up downstairs. You can hear the kids through the monitor we've installed in here as well as the one already set up in Harper's room. There's no excuse that should keep you from enjoying your own bathroom and the privacy that room provides." Without accepting further argument from me, William picks up my bag and makes his way downstairs.

Not wanting to give him the last word, I quickly hurry behind William and land a verbal jab—dripping in sarcasm. "If you were going to decide for me, then why even bother giving me an option? Just spare me the illusion of having a choice next time, and by all means, decide what you think is best."

At my words, William comes to a halt—dropping my bag and slowly spinning around to look at me. "My apologies, *little moon*." A wicked glint shines in his eyes and the corner of his mouth lifts into a smirk. "Next time I'll be sure to just tell you what I'd prefer. It's good to know you'd be amenable." William picks up my bag with a wink and turns back around, heading toward my new room.

I'm left with my mouth ajar, shocked at his blatant disregard of the sarcasm I was dishing out. He can't possibly think I was being serious. I'm so not okay with doing everything he says and wants. Last I checked, this wasn't the 50s.

It takes me a minute to reach the guest bedroom but when I do, I'm left speechless. It's bright and airy, done up in a pale blue and white. The room boasts a sitting area in front of a bay window and beside it a vanity fit for a queen. Chanel cosmetics are strewn atop it, and a matching jewelry armoire—which seems to be fully stocked—sits beside it for easy access during dressing. Directly opposite the vanity sits a king-size bed, framed by two large windows. The bed looks as billowy as a cloud, with its excessive amount of pillows and what I can assume is the most luxurious of down comforters. I seriously want to throw myself onto the bed and never get up.

William emerges from the adjoining bathroom, his lips turning up in a sly smirk. "From the look on your face, I can assume you find the room adequate."

"Yes. Thank you. You really didn't have to go to all this trouble. The cosmetics and jewelry are a bit too much, don't you think?" I wave my hand toward the vanity.

Suddenly his face morphs from playful to something I can't quite put my finger on. "No, It's not too much. You deserve this and more. Let me take care of you... until we've caught whoever's harassing you, that is."

My body shudders at the thought of last night and how it could have been so much worse. In a flash William is in front of me, embracing me in his strong arms. "Don't worry, little moon. I won't let anyone hurt you."

I tilt my head up, looking into his bright blue eyes. "Why do you call me little moon? It's not the first time you've done it."

William moves one hand up my back, resting it at the nape of my neck and gently squeezes. "Your eyes. They're just like the moon. Both the palest shade of silver and continuously pulling me in with their beauty."

"They are?" I ask breathlessly, wondering if my response was even audible.

William slowly brings my lips to his, gently caressing with the slightest of contact. "Mhmm. They are."

The vibration of his words against my mouth causes me to gasp, allowing William access inside. Without hesitation, he seals his lips over mine, taking my mouth without mercy—the sensation of his soft velvety tongue so at odds with the forceful pressure of it moving against my own causes my knees to buckle.

Sensing my need for support, William places his forearm below my ass and lifts me up until my face is parallel to his, pulling my legs to either side of him.

William's mouth seals over mine once more. Our tongues swirling together, as if doing a dance they've known all their lives. I can feel his hunger. *His need.* His kisses are far from sweet or gentle. No, they're sheer carnal desire and I can't help but give in.

I return his kiss, matching it with the hunger that's built up deep inside me. Nothing I've ever experienced has felt like this before. This, whatever this is, it's all-consuming. It's like a fire that's been lit within my soul, and the only possible way to sate it is to give it more.

I want more. Need more.

Tugging my hair back, William nuzzles his nose below my ear and breathes me in. "So. Fucking. Good. You smell *so fucking good.*"

A noise escapes me, something between a gasp and a mewl. The noise seems to spur William on and he continues his delicious assault on my exposed neck—he nips, licks, and sucks his way down from my neck to the dip below my collarbone and onto the swells of my breasts.

William cups a breast in one hand, the nipple visibly erect through the cotton of my top. A wicked smile spreads across his lips as he takes it between his thumb and forefinger, squeezing it and tugging it hard. The sensation causes me to groan in pleasure, making me want more.

I need more.

I slowly and forcefully grind my core against William, trying to relieve the ache in my throbbing clit.

It feels sooo good.

I can feel the head of his aroused cock pressing against my entrance and it causes me to groan with desire. William must be on the same page because he grabs my waist in both hands and starts to grind me up and down the length of his arousal.

"Fuuuuuck," he growls out. "If this is how good you feel with clothes on, I can't even imagine how amazing it will be when I—"

His words are cut off by a high-pitched wail from the monitor. Harper is awake and ready to be out of her crib.

"Duty calls." Panting heavily, I lay my head on William's chest.

"This isn't over, little moon. Not by a long shot." William gives me one last kiss before depositing me on the floor, accepting defeat... for now.

Chapter Nine

WILLIAM

IT'S BEEN A WEEK since Bella and the boys moved in and I've done my best to stay away from her after that stunt I pulled in her room. I swear that shit came out of left field—I was like a man possessed. The way her eyes kept roving over my body paired with her scent and close proximity pushed me over the edge. I couldn't hold back if I tried.

I don't know what I was thinking putting her in a room just down the hall from me. *Fucking masochist.*

The kiss we shared keeps playing in my mind on repeat and I'm walking around with a perpetual hard-on.

Thank fuck I'm working from home. There haven't been any additional attacks on Bella and I'll have to head into the office this week—so I'll need to get this tenting issue under control before then.

Either I completely walk away from her for good or I let myself give in. *Just once. Just to get her out of my system.* So far walking away hasn't been very effective. It's just made me miserable and unable to focus.

The more I think about it, the more it seems okay to have just one taste... just one sweet dip into her delicious honey and I'll be over whatever this is.

I've been with quite a few women in my life and none—absolutely none—have made me crazy with desire like Bella. This is seriously worse than being a horny teenager. I can't escape her. Her scent is everywhere, reminding me of just how good she tastes.

A knock at the front door interrupts my thoughts of Bella. I wonder who it could be since I wasn't expecting any company and the security out front hasn't alerted us to any visitors. As I'm approaching the door, I see a familiar head of blond hair.

Hell. No.

"Heather, what the hell are you doing here?" I glower while pulling the door open with more force than necessary.

"I wanted to see you and Harper. Is that too much for a wife and mother to ask?" Showing no signs of remorse for walking out on us, Heather steps past me and into the foyer.

"You have some balls, Heather. We have a hearing on Thursday. Anything you want to discuss with me you can do it there, with our attorneys present. As far as your relationship with Harper goes, you're the one who decided to terminate parental rights. Or did you forget?" I move to stand in front of her, blocking any further access to the home.

"I didn't forget, but I've changed my mind. It would be crazy to cut all ties with my beautiful daughter. Such a well-behaved baby, and anyway, she is the spitting image of me after all." Plastering on a fake smile, Heather flips her hair as if Harper's accolades are all her doing.

"We can have this discussion in front of our attorneys. You've disrupted Harper's life enough, and at this point I'm not even sure she'd remember you." I know this is a low blow but I need to get this woman out of my house. "You being here isn't healthy for Harper. She needs stability and you showing up whenever you please is not going to work for us."

"That's why I came back. I can stay here until all this divorce mess is handled and my schedule with Harper is set. Besides, who better to watch our baby than her own mother. I know you can't be taking care of her all on your own." Heather moves to step around me but I'm able to sidestep her, denying her further entry.

"Stop trying to come into the house. You're not welcome here. Frankly, I'm not sure how you got around our security. I'll be sure to fire whoever let you in." I run my fingers through my hair, tugging at the ends—a nervous habit I've developed which leaves me looking like I've stuck my finger in a socket.

As if summoned by the she-devil herself, Bella pops in around me. "Hey, didn't know we had company. Just wanted to ask you about our outing tomorrow."

"Now's not a good time, Bella. I'll come find you once I've walked Heather out." I'm not trying to be rude but I need Bella as far away from Heather as possible.

"Oh, this is rich. Did you find a replacement for me already? Didn't take you long, did it? And a younger model too." Heather's eyes rake over Bella, studying her every detail. "Does she fuck as good as I do?"

"*Jesus.* It isn't like that with Bella. She's barely eighteen, my friend's daughter, Ren's little niece, *and* the help. I'm not interested in her like that and even if I were, she is completely and utterly off-limits."

Well, shit. I know I spread the denial on pretty thick but I need to get Heather off Bella's trail ASAP. That woman is volatile and as unpredictable as a magic eight ball. Surely Bella will understand.

"Yes. I'm *just* the help." Bella shoots Heather a saccharin smile before turning back to me. "Speaking of which, I need to check on Harper and make sure all this commotion hasn't woken her up." Before I can get a read on her face, Bella turns and walks away.

"Oh, I'm so sure all she's doing is taking care of Harper." Heather rolls her eyes as she puffs out a breath. "Bet she likes to stay after hours and take care of you too."

"Enough, Heather! You don't get to come here and tell me who I can and can't hire to take care of my daughter when I have papers saying you wanted to terminate parental rights. Please leave this house or I'll have you escorted by security."

"Fine. You and that homewrecker can play house all you want. I'm not going to stand by and let her take everything that's mine." Heather shoots me a look that could kill a lesser man, flips her hair once more, and turns to leave—slamming the door behind her.

What a clusterfuck.

Isabella

If he thinks he can talk about me like that, he's got another thing coming. *Screw him.* Technically I am his employee, aka the help... and thirteen years younger... and his friend's daughter... and his best friend's niece. But the kiss must have meant something, right? It was mind-shattering, earth-shaking, game-changing, all of the 'ings' and then some. I can't be alone in feeling all that from our one kiss. *Not. Possible.*

Although it has been a week since it happened and he hasn't so much as grazed me while walking by. It's evident he's been putting in extra effort to stay away from me—maybe that's his way of telling me he thinks the kiss was a mistake?

Ugh. This is too much. I already have a psycho to worry about, I sure as hell don't need to be worrying about a grown-ass man who has made his feelings as clear as day. He doesn't think of me in a romantic capacity and I'm totally fine with that. *Totally.*

It's not like I'd be open to a relationship either. I know I promised Cass I would try to open myself up to the possibility, but the one thing this whole experience with William has taught me is that this isn't meant for me.

I simply need to keep myself busy with work, the twins, and preparing for college.

"Bella, we're done with our workbooks. Can we go outside and play now?" Matt asks while jumping up and down like a little jumping bean.

"My, oh my! Don't we have a lot of energy today." I laugh as I check the boys' worksheets. "Okay. It looks like you both completed today's learning activity, which means—"

"We get to go plaaaaay!" the twins shout in unison, their cheery little faces pink with excitement.

"Okay. Let me get Harper's sippy cup and we can all head outside."

I'm moving around the room trying to gather Harper's cup, binky, and Jellycat Bunny—Lord knows we can't go anywhere without that bunny—when I hear the deep baritone voice of the devil himself. "Would you mind if I tag along?"

I turn toward his voice and see that he's changed into gray sweats and a V-neck T-shirt. Why must he look so good in everything he wears? Doesn't he know I'm trying to be mad at him?

"It's your house. You can go wherever you'd like." I don't mean to sound bitchy, but I need to distance myself in order to protect my heart. I need all the help I can get with him walking around like a Greek god straight out of a romance novel.

"Is everything okay?" William's furrowed brows only serve to infuriate me further. He must know that his words would have some sort of effect on me, and not a positive one.

"Everything is fine. Why wouldn't it be? Now if you'll excuse me, *the help* needs to get the kids outside to play." I walk past him with Harper on my hip and the boys trailing behind.

Before I can reach the door, William shoots out his hand and grabs me by the waist, pulling me into him. "Hold on. Are you upset about how I described our relationship to Heather?" The corner of his mouth begins to lift, forming a smirk. "I didn't mean it."

"It sure sounded like you meant it—but it doesn't matter anyway. Everything you said was true, which makes this conversation pointless. And even if it weren't, this isn't the right time to talk about it." I step away from him and yank the door open, calling for the boys as I step outside.

I've just put the boys to bed and I'm exiting their room when my phone goes off. *Damn it. I hope it didn't wake them.* I close the door as quietly as possible and pull my phone from my back pocket.

WILLIAM: Meet me in the guest house. I have a surprise for you.

What in the world is this man up to?

BELLA: Okay... I'm bringing a monitor with me.

I quickly swipe a monitor off of the kitchen counter and make my way out the side door and back toward the guest house. Its exterior matches the Cape Cod style of the main house but it's one-tenth the size.

Not knowing what to expect, I hesitantly open the front door and am completely blown away by what I see. *It's absolutely gorgeous.*

The suite is also decorated in a coastal farmhouse style—my favorite—but it's been done up as an art studio with an office situated in front of huge panoramic windows overlooking the garden. The large desk is made from distressed wood and is accompanied by a cozy white chair. *I could totally see myself writing in that chair for hours at a time.*

William steps out from what I can only assume is the suite's bathroom or bedroom. "Do you like it? I had it set up as your writing cave. You can come back here whenever you like and work on your children's books." He moves toward the large easel in the back. "You can do your artwork here or there's a graphic design program installed on the laptop on the desk if you'd rather use that. I wasn't sure what medium you preferred, so I got both to be safe."

"William, this is all too much. I don't even know how long I'm going to be staying here, and I definitely won't be staying past the summer." I put a hand to my heart, overwhelmed with gratitude but confused as hell as to what this all means. "Why did you do all this? I'm just the help, remember?"

"Don't throw that in my face again. I just said that to get Heather off your back. I didn't want her catching whiff of us or it would make things exponentially more difficult when it came time to finalize our divorce."

That does make sense...

"Okay, I get that. But you could have clued me in so I wasn't blindsided." Like a dog with a bone, I can't let these hurt feelings go.

"When was I supposed to do that? Right in the middle of my conversation with Heather? That would have defeated the purpose, and it's not like I could have predicted her showing up after all this time. I came to you as soon as I got rid of her but you weren't having any of my attempts at explaining."

That also *makes sense...*

"Okay. I get it. But what does all that have to do with the guest house? I still don't understand why you did all this." I open my arms wide, gesturing at all the changes clearly made for my benefit.

"I want you to feel at home here. Help you pursue a dream you're passionate about and maybe get you to stay for longer than just the summer."

"You know I have to go to college in the fall." I start moving toward him, as if pulled by an invisible tether.

"The school you're attending is local so you could commute from the house. You were planning on moving into an apartment off-campus anyway, so this is just an extension of that plan. You have a private entrance, bedroom, kitchenette, and workspace. Plus, you wouldn't have to pay rent. The only request I have is that you watch Harper whenever you're able." William's eyes are pleading, searching mine for an answer. "She will miss you when you start college and this way she can easily transition into being away from you as opposed to cutting you out of her life cold turkey."

"I'd never leave Harper like that, you should know that. I love her and I'll always be a part of her life if you'll let me."

William grabs me by the waist and pulls me into him. "So you'll stay?" His eyes shift back and forth between each of mine as he squeezes me tighter. "Past the summer?"

My breathing becomes labored at the sheer proximity of him. William's kind gestures mixed with all this physical contact has me feeling drunk on emotions.

I breathe him in, taking in the manly scent of cedar and sandalwood—a heady combination that has me forgetting his question. Unable to stop myself, I pull myself closer and lean in for a kiss.

Wrong move, apparently.

William pulls away from me immediately, leaving me more confused than ever.

"That isn't a good idea, Bella." William wears a pained look on his face.

"You thought it was a good idea last week." I know it sounds like I'm whining, but I can't take this back and forth with him. One minute he's hot and the next he's cold. It's like he's two different people. One of them wants me and the other doesn't want to be anywhere near me.

"That was a lapse in judgment. It would serve us well to keep that where it belongs—in the past." William turns to walk out the door, but before stepping out, he looks back one last time. "I hope that won't affect your decision to stay."

And just like that, he leaves me alone in the beautifully redone guest house, feeling all sorts of whiplash from the hurricane of a man that is William.

Chapter Ten

WILLIAM

IT'S THE DAY of the hearing and I'm ready to get this circus over and done with. Because Heather had a change of heart, our attorneys thought it best to meet beforehand to try to resolve any preliminary issues before bringing our case in front of the judge.

We're at my attorney's office, sitting in a conference room waiting on the she-devil herself. The woman who allegedly wants to renege on her termination of parental rights is running late. *Figures.*

"We're giving her ten more minutes and then we're heading to the courthouse. I don't give a flying fuck if she's now claiming to be the next Mother There—"

Interrupting me mid-sentence, Heather walks into the conference room—acting as if she didn't have a care in the world.

"Good of you to grace us with your presence, Mrs. Hawthorne," my attorney, Daniel Mathers, chides. Not receiving the desired response, Daniel turns to her attorney of record and gets down to business. "Now if we could please tend to the issues at hand. It is my understanding that your client is wanting to withdraw her request for termination of parental rights."

Heather's attorney, Samuel Martin, tsks at Daniel. "You should know better than to address Mrs. Hawthorne directly when she is represented by counsel."

"Save it, Martin. I was merely extending my salutations. Now, stop trying to get off base and answer my question."

"Well, yes... in a manner of speaking, Mrs. Hawthorne would like to withdraw her request for termination of parental rights. I say this because Mrs. Hawthorne is withdrawing her petition for divorce, therefore making the termination of parental rights moot."

"That's fucking bullshit!" I roar loud enough for the entire building to hear. Daniel tries to calm me down but I'm shaking with rage, making his effort pointless. To make matters worse, I make the mistake of looking across the table at Heather's smirk of utter satisfaction, which only serves to make me angrier.

Realizing any attempts to calm me are futile, Daniel turns to Heather's attorney. "Martin, you know as well as I do that she can't just withdraw her petition. You'll have to petition the judge and ask them to dismiss the case without prejudice. The fact that your client walked out on a one-year-old child and has been missing from her life for the past couple of months makes it highly unlikely the judge will do so without prejudice."

"I know the process, Daniel. Thanks for the refresher on civil procedure though." Martin chuckles.

Yes. The motherfucker chuckles like he hasn't just dropped the craziest bomb on us.

Daniel keeps on as cool as a cucumber. "If you are in fact aware of the process and procedure for requesting dismissal, then please enlighten me as to the purpose of this meeting."

"It was Mrs. Hawthorne's hope that we would approach the judge with a joint petition for dismissal."

"You've got to be goddamned kidding me!" I slam my fist on the table in frustration. "That's got to be the most idiotic idea she's had yet. I can tell you right now, there is no way in hell this will be a joint petition."

"There you have it, Martin. We will not be agreeing to your requests." Daniel moves to stand and I follow. "We'll be seeing you in court."

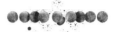

We've just left the courthouse and the judge has ruled in Heather's favor, dismissing the case without prejudice. To say that I'm shocked would be an understatement. "What in the hell happened in there? I thought you said it wouldn't be likely for the judge to rule in Heather's favor."

Daniel shakes his head while narrowing his eyes as if deep in thought. "I have never in all my years of practice encountered anything like that. Are you sure there is no connection between Mrs. Hawthorne and the presiding judge?"

"What are you saying? Like, does she know him?"

"Yes. Does she know him or have any familial relation to the judge? Anything that would make the judge biased toward Mrs. Hawthorne."

"Not that I know of, but you bet your ass I'm going to be looking into that. So where the hell do we go from here? You know I don't want to be married to that woman a minute longer than I have to." I pull out my phone to see if I've missed any calls from Bella. If I'm being honest, she's also a major reason I can't stand being tied to Heather any longer.

"I'll head back to the office and prepare a petition for divorce and custody agreement. Hopefully the next judge assigned to your case has a better head on his shoulders." Daniel shakes his head before continuing. "This does make the whole custody situation trickier, but in the meantime I can set up an emergency hearing seeking an injunction against Heather. This would keep her from doing certain things like accessing funds or making decisions that involve Harper." Daniel pulls a card from his coat pocket and hands it to me. "This has my personal number on it. Call me if she tries anything crazy."

"Of course. Thanks for your help with this crazy-ass bullshit." I place my hand on Daniel's shoulder, attempting to convey my gratitude before heading off toward my car. I need to put as much space as possible between the courthouse and myself.

Just as I'm about to reach my SUV, the bane of my existence steps out from behind a van parked next to me. "Hello dear husband. Do you want to give me a ride home?"

"Fuck. No."

This woman really is crazy.

"Oh, come on. You heard the judge. We're still married in the eyes of the law." Heather sneers at me while flipping her hair. "So technically, the house you've been shacking up in is community property and half of it is mine."

"Stop trying to act like a lawyer, Heather. The house was purchased before the marriage and we weren't married long enough for you to have made any substantial improvements that would qualify as marital equity. All of this was already outlined in the prenup, which would have left you with nothing had your initial petition for divorce gone through. Is that the real reason you wanted the case dropped?"

"Careful, William. You don't want to take that tone with your wife. It's abusive and we wouldn't want that getting out, now would we?"

Not only is this woman crazy, but she's also delusional.

"Heather, you're wasting my time. If you have any more insane demands, you can direct them to my attorney. You're getting served with another petition for divorce, and I *won't* be petitioning for its dismissal. Now if you'll excuse me, I need to get back to the house."

"I wouldn't do that if I were you..."

"Do what, Heather? Try and get my life back from the crazy train you've hijacked it to?"

"You're only filing for divorce because of that homewrecker you've been shacking up with. It would be such a shame if she discovered what stock you really came from." An evil smile spreads across Heather's lips. "I'd watch my back if I were you. You never know when the past will come back and bite you in the ass."

At her words, a deep sense of foreboding seeps into my bones. *She couldn't possibly know, could she?*

"I have no idea what you're talking about, Heather. How about you stop playing games you know you have no chance of winning." I open the door to my SUV and get in, not wanting to give her another second of my time. Whatever the hell she's scheming, she can do so on her own time.

I'm in my home gym trying to shake the sense of dread Heather's infused into my soul, but so far nothing is working. After running five miles and hitting the weights, I still can't rid myself of this nagging feeling.

I've replayed past conversations trying to figure out if I ever said anything that could have clued her in on our family's history. But nothing comes to mind. If she knows something, she sure as hell didn't learn it from me.

Serving as a reminder, her threat is further incentive to keep her away from Bella. Not because Heather might actually know something, but because it proves she's set her sights on Bella and could try to harm her. This cements my resolve to keep her at a distance. She doesn't need this kind of drama in her life.

I step out into the hall and toward the sauna housed in my private quarters. *Maybe a good steam will get rid of the deep chill that's overcome my body.* Lost in my head, I don't watch where I'm going and crash right into the very person I've been trying to avoid.

"Pay attention when you're walking, Bella. We wouldn't want you hurting someone because of your carelessness." I raise an eyebrow at her knowing full well that it was totally my fault.

"Seriously? *You* are the one who ran into *me.*" Bella narrows her eyes and purses her perfectly pouty lips. *She's fucking gorgeous when she's mad.* "Besides, if you hadn't insisted on me taking the room right down the hall from you, I wouldn't even be in your way."

Well if I wanted her to dislike me, I think I'm doing a pretty damn good job of it. "It's safer this way. Keeping you close, that is. Which reminds me, do you have an answer on moving into the guest house?"

"You've got to be kidding me." Bella rolls her eyes and lets out an annoyed breath. "You've been avoiding me like the bubonic plague, and if you do happen to run into me, you treat me as if I were a nuisance. Why in the world would I want to live anywhere near you?"

"So that's a yes then. Should I call a mover to get your stuff from Aiden's?"

"Are you deaf? That was a no. N. O."

"Right. We'll talk about this later, when you're not acting like a child." Not waiting for a response, I walk past Bella and into my room. *No* is not an acceptable answer. The best way to keep her safe is to keep her close, regardless of whether or not I can have her. She's living on my property—*end of story.*

Chapter Eleven

ISABELLA

THAT MAN IS infuriating! He gives me the illusion of choice but then refuses to accept my answer if it's not one he likes. I'm definitely not moving into the guest house. I don't care that I'd have the hottest landlord *ever*, or that the guest house is decked to the nines with every single amenity I would want. It isn't worth it if I have to put up with his mood swings and alpha tendencies. Okay... so not all of his alpha tendencies are bad, some of them are damn hot. *I would totally put up with those.*

Ugh! I really need to get out of this house and blow off some steam before I do something I'll regret. I take my phone out of my back pocket and message Cassie.

BELLA: Hey chica, you down for the hunt tonight??? 🥃 🍸

I head to check on the boys. Harper is still napping and I left the twins with watercolors before stepping away to retrieve my backup brushes. That's when I ran into William and got totally sidetracked. *I hope they haven't destroyed the playroom.*

My phone beeps in my hand as I reach the boys. All is well, and there are no paint casualties—that I can see.

CASS: You know it, babe. I'm always up for some fun. Just let me know when and where. 🐱🐾♀

BELLA: You're the best! Let me double-check with William so I know one of us will be home with the kids tonight.

CASS: Look at you sounding all domestic 💋 💋 💋

BELLA: It's not like that, Cass. But I'll fill you in on how it is later...

CASS: Ooooo! I can't wait to hear all about it!

I put my phone in my back pocket and ask the boys if they're ready to help me start dinner. I like to give them little tasks to keep them out of trouble while I get food ready. It's a dangerous thing to give these two unsupervised time—I'm surprised I didn't walk into a mess with the watercolors.

We've just settled down with our kitchen duties when the monitor goes off and Harper starts to fuss, waking up from her afternoon nap. I'm about to go get her when William's deep voice cuts through the monitor.

"Hey, princess. You ready to go play with the boys and see Bella?" At the mention of my name, Harper squeals. "Yes. I'm excited to see her beautiful face too. She's something special, isn't she, my little princess?"

A blush spreads across my face at the realization that he finds me beautiful *and* special. He'd been acting like such an ass this past week, I could have sworn that the exact opposite was true. But if his conversation with his daughter is an indicator, then that broody man *does* like me... *so why has he been such a giant dick to me?*

At that moment, William enters the kitchen with Harper on his hip. "She's got a fresh diaper and is ready to party." Placing her down on the floor, he closes the baby gate behind him. "What's for dinner?"

"Breaded pork chops with roasted potatoes and Brussels sprouts."

"That sounds amazing. I'm going to miss your cooking when Chef returns from maternity leave. We might have to give her a couple of nights off just so we can have some of your delicious dinners."

Was that a compliment? "Umm, yeah. She'll be back before I leave in the fall, right?"

"You're not leaving in the fall. You're staying here. On my property. But yes, Chef will be back by then, so you won't have to worry about cooking with your busy schedule."

I take in a deep breath, trying to calm the rage building up inside me. "If the kids weren't here I would have some choice words for you... but this is not the time." I whisper-shout while shooting him a death glare. "Anyway, I need to know if you're okay with keeping an eye on the kids tonight. I haven't had any free time since moving in and I would like to go out with Cass to blow off some steam."

"What exactly are you planning on doing with Cass?" William narrows his eyes into thin slits. "See, I know what you like to do to 'blow off some steam' and I can't say that I'd want you doing that tonight."

My mouth hangs open, shocked at his audacity. "I thought you said you would never judge me? What happened to that, huh?"

"I'm not judging you. I'm simply telling you that from now on you need to find another way to blow off steam. One that doesn't involve a one-night stand."

The boys have clued in to the fact that our conversation is a tense one and have apparently been all ears. "What's a one night stand?" Matt asks.

"It's when someone stands all night long." My face reddens with a mixture of anger and embarrassment.

"Why can't Bella Bo Bella stand all night if she wants to?" Max asks with true innocence in his eyes.

"Ummm, well..." William struggles to find a response, giving me the perfect opportunity to take control of this awkward as hell conversation.

"There's no reason I can't stand all night if I want to." I wink at William and give him a soft smile. "So William will keep an eye on you, and I'll go stand all night long with Cassie."

The boys quickly lose interest in our conversation, now that we've resumed a friendlier tone. William, however, has no intention of dropping the subject.

He walks directly behind me, placing his hands on my hips and his face in the crook of my neck, before whispering in my ear. "You are free to go out with Cass, but I'm letting you know right now that if anyone so much as breathes on you—they will have to answer to me." William slowly runs his nose along my neck and places a soft kiss below my ear. "You'll also have a full detail on you tonight. And that's not up for debate, *little moon*."

His not so stealthy assault on my body has left me shaking and speechless. My chest is visibly rising and falling, and I have no words. *No. Words.*

William chuckles behind me. "Good. I'm glad we're on the same page." Giving my hips one last squeeze, he finally drops his hands and walks away.

I cannot believe he just touched me like that in front of the kids. I'm pretty sure my panties are soaked and my face is visibly flushed. *The freaking nerve of that man!*

Cass and I decided on going to The Blue Door, an upscale martini lounge with an impressive whiskey collection. The place is decked out in dark blue velvet—it's everywhere, from the cozy wingback chairs to the curtains lining the walls. Crystal chandeliers are strewn throughout and the tables situated between the seating areas are all Lucite. It's the epitome of *chic*.

I've ordered whiskey and Cass her usual dirty martini. I'm taking in the opulent room when the bartender places a silver dish in front of us containing stuffed olives, mixed nuts, and delicate crisps. *I'm in love and I never want to leave.*

"Good call on picking this place tonight." I sip my scotch and raise my brows at Cass.

"Totally. I thought we would need something a little quieter so you could dish all about Mr. Hot McBroody Pants."

"*Ugh.* That man drives me crazy. One minute he's hot and the next he's as cold as the iceberg that sank the Titanic." I shake my head, unsure if I should fess up about the kiss. "Okay. So no judgment. We sort of had a super hot steamy kiss last week."

"Oh. My. Gawd!" Cass whisper-shouts. "Why didn't you tell me about this sooner?"

"Things have sort of been hectic lately. But it doesn't matter anyway because right after that he went all McBroody Pants on me and avoided me the entire week." My face flushes at the memory of this afternoon. "Well, up until earlier today when he kissed my neck... right in front of the kids."

"He what?! That is so freaking hot. He totally wants you, Bella. He wouldn't be all over you if he didn't." Cass pops an olive into her mouth.

"He doesn't want me. Or if he does, it's not all the time." I blow out a breath of frustration. "I don't have time for games. That's why I've only given in to one-night stands. Each party gets what they need and then they are on their merry way. No drama."

"Speaking of one-night stands... do you see anything you like?" Cass slyly looks around the room.

"That reminds me, there will be no random hookups in my foreseeable future." I purse my lips and shake my head.

"What? Why? I thought that was the purpose of 'the hunt' tonight." Cass furrows her brows in confusion.

"Mr. McBroody Pants *forbids* it. Plus, he's put a full detail on me tonight. See those guys over by the door? That's my security detail." I lift my head toward the tall men dressed in all black. "William gave me no choice. *Again.* He's always so damn controlling. I swear, he's worse than my father."

Cassie gasps in mock horror. "I seriously cannot believe he is having you followed. The balls on that man." Typically, I would be in total agreement with her, but the sarcasm in her tone lets me know she didn't really mean that. I roll my eyes at Cassie but she continues despite my not being amused. "Sure there's probably some psycho out there who clearly thinks you're a whore..." Cassie sucks in her lips and tries not to giggle. "Sorry, I couldn't help it. You know I don't think you're a whore. Screw society and their double standards. If men can have one-night stands, so can we. But honestly, I do think the security detail was a good call. At least until they've caught whoever did that to your car."

"I know. You're totally right. But I still don't like William dishing out orders like he owns me."

He sort of does though.

William has taken over every part of me. I spend every waking moment with him somewhere in my head. Either at the forefront actively taking part in some fantasy, or in the background as I subconsciously make decisions that always manage to turn out in his favor.

"So what are you going to do about it?" Cassie pulls me from my thoughts.

"He's asked me to move in permanently. Well to the guest house. He redid the whole thing and it's absolutely—"

One of the men from the security detail has made their way over to us and cuts me off. "Excuse me miss, Mr. Hawthorne would like to speak to you." The burly man hands me a cell phone and I begrudgingly press it to my ear.

"Yes, William. I put my phone on silent so I wouldn't be bothered on my night off. But by all means, please tell me what is so urgent it couldn't wait until I get home?"

"Bella, there's been an incident with your father. He was shot—"

The phone falls from my hand and everything around me starts to move in slow motion. *Shot. My father was shot.* This can't be happening. I've already lost one parent, and now... I choke on a sob as an image of my father laying on the cold ground, covered in a pool of his own blood, flashes through my mind.

My breathing becomes labored and I feel my knees begin to wobble, unable to support my weight any longer. Reaching out, I try to keep myself upright, but it's pointless. I start to fall, and as soon as my knees hit the ground, my vision blurs and everything fades to black.

Chapter Twelve

WILLIAM

AS I WATCH Bella asleep on my bed, I try and think of how I could possibly deliver the news about her father without breaking her heart. Jacob brought her straight home after I'd talked to her on the phone earlier—apparently what little information I gave her regarding the incident was enough to make her pass out in the middle of a bar and I'm definitely not wanting a repeat of that.

I should've told her in person but I knew she wouldn't have come home without a good reason. *That woman is so fucking stubborn.* It's almost midnight and I'm thankful the kids have slept through all of the commotion. I don't know how I'd manage to care for them at the same time as handling the inevitable meltdown that will be Bella once she finds out everything that's happened.

I lift my shirt over my head and take off my jeans, leaving me in just my boxers. Lifting the covers, I slide into the bed and pull Bella close to me, settling her back to my chest. It's probably not the best idea, being half-naked this close to her, but I know she'll want answers as soon as she wakes. Therefore it makes no sense for us to be in separate rooms. Well, that's what I tell myself at least.

Taking in a deep breath, I close my eyes and bring my lips to Bella's neck, kissing it softly. *Mine.* My eyes immediately shoot open in surprise. *What the fuck?* That thought came out of left field, slamming into me like a Mack truck.

There's no way she could be mine, but apparently my traitorous subconscious didn't get the memo. It doesn't care that she's completely off-limits.

Shaking my head, I mentally chastise myself. Now is not the time to be having this internal debate. I need to be worrying about more important things, like the situation with Aiden.

"I'm sorry, little moon," I whisper into her hair, taking in the scent that is so uniquely her. "I promise I'll be here every step of the way, keeping you and your brothers safe."

Bella stirs at the sound of my voice. "William?"

"Yes, beautiful?"

"Oh, thank god. For a second there I wasn't sure where I was. The last thing I remember was being at the bar..." Her chest begins to rise and fall rapidly, no doubt remembering the phone call that brought her here. "Oh god. My father. Please tell me that it was all a nightmare. Please tell me he's okay."

I sit up and turn Bella slowly, making sure to keep my hands on hers—letting her know that I'm here. "Bella, I want you to know that everything is going to be okay. Regardless of whatever happens, you will get through this."

"No. This can't be real. Everything is fine. Dad will be back home soon and everything will go back to normal. The boys will go back home and I'll go to college." Bella's eyes bounce in their sockets, unable to settle on any one object in the room.

Trying to give her a focal point, I cup her face with both hands, and wait until her eyes fall on me. "Bella, your father is in a coma. There was a mix up on the schedule and your dad's backup didn't show. Aiden was left with only Marcus as his partner. Marcus noticed a suspicious delivery vehicle on the property they were monitoring and immediately tried reaching out, but he got no response from Aiden's radio, despite the multiple calls he placed. A sweep of the area later discovered Aiden's radio had been smashed prior to the shootout. There was no way he could have received the warning."

"But those things are their satellite phone and radio all in one. They are sturdy as fuck. How in the hell did it get smashed?" Bella's brows knit together in confusion.

"The radio breaking was without a doubt intentional. Based on what time his receiver went off-line, we can safely say that it was damaged prior to the arrival of the delivery vehicle. Unfortunately, there was no way he could have gotten notice of the attackers."

"What happened after the attackers got onto the property?" Bella's eyes are closed as she asks the question.

"Are you sure you want the details?" I ask, softly pushing back a rogue strand of hair. I know this is a lot to take in and I don't want her getting too overwhelmed.

Bella answers after a long pause, "Yes."

"Aiden was walking down a flight of stairs when the bullets started flying. He lost consciousness after taking multiple shots to the body, and tumbled down two flights of stairs, sustaining severe trauma to the head along with more gunshot wounds." Bella lets out a pained cry as she falls into me. "I'm so sorry, little moon."

Bella's entire body trembles against me. "I need to see him. I need to know he'll be okay."

"He's currently stable and being seen by one of the best neurologists in the country. He's very hopeful and can explain the prognosis when you see him tomorrow." Bella lets out a sigh of relief and allows herself to sink into my chest. "We can fly out in the morning, once the kids are up. I didn't want to wake them and cause any unnecessary trauma. They're too little to understand, and bringing them to the hospital in the middle of the night won't change anything. The doctors don't expect there to be a change in Aiden's status within the next couple of hours, so I think it's best if we try and get some rest before heading out there with the whole crew."

Bella tightens her hold around me. "Thank you for handling all of this. I'm a mess and I wouldn't even know where to start." Unbridled tears fall down her face and onto my bare chest. "I keep thinking of my mother and how we lost her, and now we're at risk of losing Dad too. The boys shouldn't have to go through this twice. They're too little to be without their parents."

I cup her face, wiping away her tears with the pad of my thumb. "This is just a fucked up situation, little moon. But I promise we will get through this. I'm here and you don't have to go through this alone. Whatever you need, you just tell me and I'll make it happen." Sliding my hand to the nape of her neck, I pull Bella closer and press my lips to her forehead—silently vowing to take away all of her worries.

Isabella

Soft kisses on my neck, shoulder, and back pull me out of slumber. Somehow I managed to fall back asleep after my conversation with William last night. I'm sure it had something to do with the fact that I was being held in his arms, his warmth cocooning me in much-needed comfort.

The mental fog of sleep starts to lift and I slowly begin to remember the details of last night. Once the reality of the situation hits, I immediately sit straight up in bed. "Oh my god! We have to get going! I have to get the kids ready. Have you called the pilot? I assume we're taking the company jet, right?"

William runs his hands up and down my arms in a soothing gesture. "Shhhh. Calm down, Bella. I don't want you to worry about anything but yourself right now. Ashley flew in yesterday and has agreed to go with us to California for the trip. She is up and has the kids eating breakfast at the moment. I've gone ahead and packed your bag, along with some toiletries. If for some reason I forgot something then we'll just buy it once we land."

I wrap my arms around William, unable to convey my gratitude any other way. *Where did this man come from, and what has he done with Mr. McBroody Pants?* It's moments like these that confuse the hell out of me. Is this the real William—a kind and thoughtful man? Or is he the arrogant and controlling man I've seen so much of lately?

William kisses the top of my head, gently running his fingers along the exposed skin of my back. It's then I notice I've somehow changed into a camisole and sleep shorts.

"How did I end up in my pajamas?" I hesitantly ask.

"You kept tossing and turning, pulling at the dress you were wearing. It must have been uncomfortable, but you wouldn't wake up to change. After about an hour of restlessness, I took the liberty of changing you. You still have on the panties from last night, but you weren't wearing a bra so you can't blame me for having seen your gorgeous tits. That's all on you." William shoots me a devilish grin. "Fret not, I didn't touch the goods. I don't take advantage of unconscious women. I might be an ass, but I'm not *that* kind of an ass."

My cheeks flush in mortification. Sure, I'd been naked in front of men before but I hadn't known any of them well, and I certainly didn't have mixed emotions about them either. I try to turn the tables in an attempt to regain control. "You didn't touch, but I bet you got enough of an eyeful for the spank bank."

"Little moon, you've already given me plenty of material for my spank bank. I didn't have to see you naked for that. It *was* a sweet bonus though." William's wicked smile is accompanied by a wink. "Would you like to know which fantasies you star in?"

Flushing once more, I turn and walk toward the bathroom. "What I would like is to get to California as soon as possible. I'll meet you in the kitchen when I've showered and changed. It'll only take a minute."

Shutting the door behind me, I hear William's muffled voice. "Don't get all pissy, Bella. I knew you were worried and was only trying to lighten the mood."

"See you in ten!" I shout back and start the shower, hoping to douse the desire his teasing has ignited. *Talk about inappropriate timing.* At least he did manage to take my mind off of my father's situation, even if it was just for a little while.

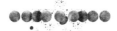

Beep. Beep. Beep.

Deep in thought, I zone out to the melodic tempo of Dad's monitors. *How in the hell did this happen? He always knows what to do. He always comes home safe. He's untouchable.* Oh, how wrong I was. There's nothing like a bitch-slap from reality to make you realize how delusional you've been. No one is invincible. Not even my father. He's just a man. Just as susceptible to injuries as the next guy.

William walks in with two cups of coffee. Sitting in the chair next to me, he holds one out for me to take. "Here. You didn't sleep much last night and we've got a long day ahead of us."

"Thank you. Any word from the neurologist?" I take a sip of the dark bitter liquid, taking comfort in its warmth.

"Yes. He said there hasn't been any change since we spoke earlier this morning." William turns his whole body to face me, taking the cup of coffee from my hands and placing it on the floor next to his. "Isabella, he doesn't think there will be a change in his condition any time soon."

A strangled sob escapes me as my body crumples against the seat. *We can't lose him. The boys need him. I need him.*

William pulls me into him, holding me tight. "The doctor wants to try a couple of experimental procedures but needs your permission first. Aiden never filled out his advanced directive and you're the first in line to act as his surrogate, so that means you get the final say in his care. I know this isn't going to be easy, but I'll be by your side through it all."

"Why me? Isn't it company policy to let you know what he wanted? I mean this job isn't exactly the safest in the world. I can only assume you guys would prepare for this type of thing," I ask in disbelief.

"Either Aiden didn't fill out his directives or they're lost somewhere. We can't find them on the company server or anywhere in his office. We've looked everywhere but since he was one of the founding members, it's likely his records didn't transfer over when we upgraded our network a couple of years ago. That, or he felt he was invincible and didn't need them."

"This is so unreal." I place my hands over my face, overwhelmed with emotions.

"Good morning. I've come to check on my patient." The neurologist, Dr. Ansley walks in and picks up Dad's chart. "I see that there has been no change in Mr. Moretti's condition."

"Dr. Ansley, I'm Aiden Moretti's daughter. I'm sorry I missed you earlier this morning. I was seeing to my brothers." I stand to shake the doctor's hand. "Thank you for your help with my father. We really appreciate you flying out from New York for us. Is it possible to ask you a couple of questions regarding my father's condition?"

"Of course Ms. Moretti. What would you like to know?" The doctor's warm smile reaches his eyes, bringing a sense of peacefulness to a situation that is anything but.

"How long is he expected to remain like this? Is there anything we can do to help him wake up?"

"Mr. Moretti's CT scan showed there was widespread swelling of the brain due to the head trauma he sustained in the fall. We believe that this is what caused his coma. You see, when the brain swells and creates pressure on the reticular activating system, the body is unable to wake." Dr. Ansley fidgets with his pen, as if bored with the speech he's probably given a million times. "Although his RAS is impaired, his brain is showing signs of certain brainstem functions which could be promising. In short, I think his coma should last two to three weeks, until the swelling subsides. It is only then that we will be able to truly see what damage has been done."

"Does that mean he'll be able to come home in less than a month?" My eyes widen in anticipation of his response.

"I'm sorry to disappoint you Ms. Moretti, but that outcome would be extremely rare. Many times the process back to full consciousness is done in baby steps, if at all. It isn't completely impossible though, so it's good to maintain optimism."

"So in this instance, what is a likely outcome?" William's voice booms from behind me.

"Well, regaining full consciousness from the onset of waking is a possibility, just not a very likely one." Dr. Ansley attempts to smooth over his bluntness upon seeing our stricken faces. "It has happened in the past, so he very well could be the exception. On the other hand, Mr. Moretti could enter into a vegetative state, this could be temporary and a precursor to being in a minimally conscious state, and then full recovery. Like I said, you never really know until the swelling subsides and we can see the extent of the damage he suffered."

"In other words, we have a long road ahead of us." I close my eyes and sigh.

"Yes. But he is in very good hands. I would like you to sign off on a couple of forms, allowing me to treat Mr. Moretti with certain procedures. They aren't commonplace with this facility and they require your authorization as his default surrogate."

"Of course. Whatever he needs." I blindly sit on a chair, coming close to missing it altogether.

"Great. I'll send the nurse in with the forms." Dr. Ansley nods once before walking away.

"Everything will be okay, little moon." William walks toward me and kisses the top of my head. "We'll keep the rental property until your father wakes, then decide whether we want to transfer him closer to home or stay out here. I can continue to work remotely in the meantime. Fuck, with all the business we do out here, it's probably a good idea to set up a satellite office in California."

I'm so grateful for William right now. Not only does he make things easier, but he also makes them bearable. The sudden urge to feel his warmth all over me takes over and I bolt up to standing. Without hesitation, I wrap my arms around his waist and press myself into him, needing to get as close as possible. "Thank you, William," I whisper into his chest, hoping he feels the gratitude pouring out of me. I know my words are insufficient, but they're all I can muster.

Chapter Thirteen

ISABELLA

THE PAST WEEK has been a blur. Dad's condition remains the same and we're still living in the rental property. The twins have a birthday coming up next week and I don't want them to miss out because of everything that has happened. Not wanting them to suffer more than necessary, I resolve to make their day special despite the shitty situation we all find ourselves in. Besides, I know Dad wouldn't want it any other way.

I'm sitting at the kitchen island working in Photoshop when Ashley walks in.

"All of the kids are down for a nap—*at the same time.* Can you believe it?!" Her eyes open wide in a mixture of awe and excitement.

"Ha! You've managed to bag a unicorn." I laugh while patting her on the shoulder. It's then I notice her beautiful pendant earrings and remember the one I'd found back at William's house. "I've been meaning to tell you I found one of your earrings back at the house in Dallas. It's really pretty and I'm sure you've missed it. It's a gold leaf with a black pearl in front of the stud backing."

"Huh, that doesn't sound like anything I own." Ashley's eyebrows scrunch together in thought.

Duh, Bella. How could I be so naive? William is a grown-ass man. A man with needs. It probably belongs to someone he's been seeing, or saw. *What if that someone was my aunt?! Don't be stupid, Bella. He already told you he wasn't seeing her. So then who does the damn earring belong to?*

"Bella? Is everything okay?" Ashley pulls me from my thoughts, and the look on her face tells me I wore my neurotic inner dialogue on my proverbial sleeve.

"Yeah. Sure, of course. Why wouldn't it be? I was just thinking about the boys' birthday coming up. I'm designing some of the party decor as well as the invites. Do you think the other members of WRATH will come out for their party?" I put on a fake smile and hope my change of subject is enough to throw Ashley off my scent.

"I know Titus will be out here by the end of the week... visiting Aiden, of course." Ashley's cheeks flush red as she tacks on that last bit. "I'm sure they'll all be coming out here at one point or another, so why not just make it one big scheduled visit as opposed to various individual ones. That way we can pen in the boys' party."

Before I can ask Ashley what that flush was all about, William walks into the kitchen and heads for the fridge.

"Hey." William's deep voice rumbles in greeting.

He looks absolutely delicious in a fitted long sleeve Henley—sleeves pulled up, exposing his forearms—and a pair of dark washed jeans that hug his tight ass just right.

I'm pretty sure Ashley just caught me ogling her brother, and now it's my turn to flush beet red. *Time to get the hell out of Dodge.* "I'm beat. Going to see if I can lay down for a bit while the kids are down." I jump off the bar stool and scurry out of the kitchen, not giving either of the Hawthorne siblings a chance to say a word.

William

Well, that was odd. Bella couldn't get out of here fast enough, which makes me curious...

"What were y'all talking about?" I pin Ashley with an accusatory gaze.

"The twins' birthday party and whether or not the team will be able to make it out here." Ashley purses her lips and raises an eyebrow in suspicion. "She did, however, get really weird when she asked me about a missing earring she'd found at your house. She got this strange look on her face when I told her it wasn't mine. It almost looked like jealousy."

I try to school my face as much as possible, but Ashley is like a bloodhound. If she catches a whiff of any secret, she doesn't relent until she's got the other party divulging all of their deepest and darkest. *Not today, Fido. Not today.*

"I wonder what that was all about." I shrug my shoulders and take a gulp from the orange juice container in my hand. *I don't even like orange juice.*

"Hmmm." Ashley looks at the orange juice carton and then back at me. "You know it would be a terrible idea for you to hook up with her, right? She's thirteen years younger than you. *Thirteen.* Not to mention she's your best friend's niece and friend's daughter. A friend who is in a coma. Oh, and let's not forget that you have a deranged ex who won't let you go. Do you really want to bring her into that mess?"

"There's no bringing her into anything because there is nothing going on between us." I try and remain stoic but Ashley keeps busting my balls.

"And all of those reasons don't even come close to touching what the real problem would be. The whole situation between our parents is the big whopper and what should be your biggest deterrent. Does she know about our dad? That's all sorts of fucked up." Ashley shakes her head and closes her eyes, displaying a look of horror on her face. "If Bella were to find out, she may never want to speak to you again. Do you really want to risk building a relationship only to have it fall apart on you? You'd have that big secret looming over you at all times. Waiting for the other shoe to drop."

"What big secret?" Bella asks as she steps back into the kitchen.

"I thought you were going to take a nap," I snap at her, my voice coming out high pitched like that of a prepubescent boy.

"I forgot my charger." She raises a brow as she picks up the laptop charger attached to the outlet under the island. "So... what's the big secret?"

Unsure of how much she really heard, I decide to err on the side of caution and share the minimum. "My father's death. As you can see, it's none of your concern; and if it's all the same to you, I would rather not talk about it." My tone is cold and sarcastic, not actually seeking permission but rather being dismissive. I can feel Ashley's eyes boring into me but I don't bother looking over at her. She can try and guilt me all she wants, but she isn't getting shit out of me. *Deny. Deny. Deny.*

"I- I'm so sorry. I had no idea."

I instantly regret taking that tone with Bella. She doesn't deserve my treating her like this, especially with what she's got going on right now.

"Mhm." I nod and walk past both Bella and Ashley. "I'll be in the study."

I've only been in the study about two minutes when the door swings open. "There's nothing to tell, Ash—"

"It's not Ashley." Bella's soft voice flows into the room, causing my heart to clench with guilt. "Can I have a minute?"

"Yes. Of course," I quickly respond, praying this has nothing to do with what Ashley and I were talking about—if only I were that lucky.

"You've always been there for me. Through all of the sorrow..." Bella's voice trails off as she looks out the window. "I don't know if you remember this, but you were the one who held me during Mom's funeral. Dad was a mess, unable to care for himself, much less his children. Uncle Ren was all about the twins, trying to comfort them the best he could. The boys didn't understand what was going on and needed Uncle Ren to rein them in. Lord knows those two were more than a handful. And me? I was caught somewhere in the middle. Left in limbo to deal with my pain and grief alone."

Tears start falling down Bella's beautiful face and she does nothing to wipe them away. I go to move toward her but she stops me, lifting one hand in the air. "No. I need to get this out."

Not wanting to break her train of thought, I sit down and let her continue.

"I was fifteen, scared, alone, and confused. I didn't understand how such a tragedy could strike our family. I *needed* Mom. The boys *needed* Mom... Dad *needed* Mom." Bella's eyes squeeze shut, as if trying to block out a memory. "I felt hopeless. Surrounded by a shroud of darkness and lost in a sea of loneliness where every man was out for themselves. My father, the twins, and even my uncle. But then you came in like a shiny beacon of light, my own personal life raft. You saw me standing by myself, walked up to me and took me into your arms, whispering words of comfort." Bella's eyes look deep into mine, a multitude of emotions shining through them: anguish, sorrow, gratitude... and *love*? "I will never forget what you told me that day. You pulled me into the crook of your neck and whispered into my ear."

Like stepping back into a memory, Bella and I speak the words together. "When you feel alone, I'll be here.

When you feel sad, I'll be here. When you feel scared, I'll be here. I will *always* be here."

Holy shit. I remember.

I'm paralyzed with overwhelming emotion as I try to remember the day of the funeral. Sure enough, it all starts coming back to me.

Aiden was a mess, barely able to hold himself upright as he sobbed audibly. The twins were wailing uncontrollably as their mother's casket was being lowered into the ground. They didn't understand why she was leaving them. Ren tried his best to comfort the boys, but it was short of a miracle how he managed to keep them from running into the ground after their own mom. Shifting my gaze, I finally noticed Bella. Tears ran down her cheeks, but the overall look on her face was vacant. Like she'd checked out. Given up on everything.

In that moment as I watched my friends grieve, I thought of when I'd lost my own parents. Recognizing the look on Bella's face, I knew I had to step up. I couldn't bear the thought of her going through such a loss on her own.

"I remember," I manage to croak out.

Bella walks behind my desk and lifts her hand to my face. "And now, with my father... you're here. Again."

My body comes alive at her touch, the need to feel her in my arms once more is overpowering. Giving in to my emotions, I pull her down onto my lap, squeezing her waist with both hands and kissing my way down her neck.

"William, wait..." Bella's squeak of surprise does nothing to mask the desire I see in her eyes, but I stop my ministrations and let her continue. "I shared all of that with you so you would know that *you* are not alone. Whatever happened with your father, I want you to know that I'll be here. I'll *always* be here."

My chest tightens and a lump forms in my throat. Bella's words have rendered me speechless. This girl. No, *this woman...* amidst her own grief and sorrow has somehow found the strength to be there for me. *God, if she only knew.*

Chapter Fourteen

WILLIAM

WHAT THE FUCK is wrong with me? I have a
gorgeous woman sitting on my lap, baring her soul to me,
offering herself up despite her own misfortunes. Fuck if
I'll let the past keep me from enjoying her. I refuse to taint
this moment with guilt. If that makes me a monster, then
so be it.

Pushing all of those thoughts aside, I relent to the
insatiable need of tasting her once more. I run my fingers
through her hair and pull her lips to mine, coaxing her
mouth open with my tongue, delving into what surely

must be heaven. As if she were the most delicious cookie, notes of vanilla and spice assault my senses. *She tastes so fucking good.*

I suck her juicy bottom lip into my mouth and bite it gently, eliciting a whimper of need that has my dick twitching in my pants.

"William..." Bella moves one of her legs over my lap, effectively straddling me in the chair. "Please..."

"Please what, little moon?" I mumble into her skin as I run my hands up her back, peppering her neck and chest with kisses. "What do you want?"

Bella's hips start to grind into me, her pussy rocking back and forth against my cock, seeking relief. "I need—" A gasp leaves her pouty lips as I lower her camisole, exposing the hardened bud of one nipple. It's pink and perfect, beckoning my mouth to suckle it. "—you. I need you." Bella's words come out part mewl as I take her nipple into my mouth and suck hard, lapping my tongue over it in a wavelike motion.

"Oh, yes. Do that again." Bella's hands shoot up, she runs her fingers through my hair, coaxing my head to her other breast.

"If you liked that, just wait until I get my mouth on your clit." I chuckle in satisfaction, knowing full well what's in store for my little moon.

Lifting Bella up, I lay her on the desk and leisurely kiss my way down her stomach. Making my way down to her jean-clad pussy, I place one last kiss on her mound before gently biting down on it—locking eyes with her—letting her know she's mine. *That pussy is mine.*

"Did you... did you just bite my pussy?" Bella asks in mock indignation. *She isn't fooling me. I can practically smell her sweet honey, begging me to eat it up.*

"Yes, little moon. And now, I'll be licking it." Her whole body shivers at my words. *Fuck yes, she wants me.*

"Lift your sweet ass for me, baby." I guide her hips up while lowering her shorts and panties with one hard pull, because who has time to peel off layers?

Not me.

I need to taste her.

Now.

She lies bare in front of me, and if there were ever a time to stop, it would be now. I know once I've placed my lips on her flesh there will be no turning back. I pause for a moment, but the fact that she is so goddamn young and is completely off-limits does nothing to assuage the need inside of me.

Unable to find any fucks to give, I spread her knees wide, taking her legs and placing one on either side of my head, leaving me with the most amazing view between her thighs.

"Fuuuck, you're perfect." I groan, my voice thick with desire.

I've never seen a more beautiful cunt. Her pink velvety folds are glistening and swollen with arousal—ready to be devoured like the ripest of peaches.

"William, please—" Bella squirms in anticipation.

"Patience, baby." I chuckle as I grab my rocks glass and hold it above Bella's beautiful pussy. "A good girl knows to do as she's told. Now hold still." Lowering my mouth to her slit, I lathe my tongue over her once, twice—"Mmmm. You taste *so fucking good.*"

Bella's half-lidded eyes open wide in surprise as her gaze lands on the glass hovering above her entrance. "Wha— What are you doing with that?"

With a mischievous wink, I tilt the glass as I lower myself onto her once more, allowing the amber liquid to spill over her heated folds. Bella sucks in a sharp breath and lets out a squeal as I lick up her soaking slit, catching every last delicious drop.

"Mmmm. Delicious." A wicked grin spreads across my face as I watch her chest rise and fall rapidly with yearning.

Wanting to give her the release she so desperately needs, I lower my mouth and latch onto her swollen clit. Bella moans on contact, lifting both hands to keep my head right where she needs me the most. *As if I'd ever fuckin' leave. She tastes like home and there's no way I'm giving her up.*

Unintelligible words leave her mouth as she grinds her pussy down on me, letting me know she likes what I'm doing. I lift my gaze to hers and smirk. "This, little girl, is what it's like to be eaten by a real man."

Bella whimpers and her face becomes pained. "Don't stop, please don't stop."

"My greedy baby wants more?" I lift an eyebrow as I run both hands up her thighs, letting them land on her ass before squeezing hard and pulling her closer to the edge of the desk.

Bella nods wordlessly. Knowing she's ready for more, I take two fingers and insert them into her heat, slowly plunging them in and out. Feeling how wet she is, I circle her clit with my thumb and insert a third finger into her. Bella gasps at the invasion and I know in that moment, there is no sweeter sound. "Do you like taking my hand, little moon?"

"Mmhmm. So. So good." Her breathy voice sounding like the filthiest of porn has my dick so hard it's about to break off.

Bella's greedy little pussy rocks into my hand, wanting more, taking more. Being the gentleman that I am, I deliver, roughly rubbing her inner wall and placing unrelenting pressure on her G-spot. As if on cue, Bella's breath quickens, becoming more and more ragged as she starts to climb into ecstasy, letting out a string of incoherent babble. "Oh. God. Oh, my. Oh my, fuck."

Her legs quiver against me as I gently clamp down on her swollen nub with my teeth. The unexpected sensation taking her over the edge and causing a guttural groan to rip through her.

I watch in awe as her body is overcome with glorious satisfaction. *Yup. I'm fucked.* Watching her unravel—tasting her heady release on my tongue—it's my drug, and I can't get enough.

She looks absolutely stunning—head thrown back, hair splayed across the desk, skin flushed pink and glistening with a slight sheen of perspiration, all of it adding to the overall glow radiating from within.

"You're perfect. Fucking perfect," I whisper into her skin as she comes down from the ultimate of highs. Once her legs stop shaking, I lift her to her feet and right her, kissing her on her temple.

"That was... I didn't know it could be like that." Bella's eyes begin to water.

"Shhhh, baby. Everything is okay." My heart clenches at the sight of her tearing up. I have no fucking clue why she's about to cry and can only hope that I didn't push her too fast. "Tell me why you're upset."

"It's my fault. It's all my fault." Bella moans. What was a light sprinkle now becomes a torrential downpour of sobs. I can barely understand the words that are coming out of her mouth.

"What's your fault?" I pull her into a tight embrace, stroking her hair from behind.

"Mom. She died because of me. We were arguing." Bella pulls away from me and I let her, sensing she might need some space to get whatever this is off her chest. "If I hadn't been yelling at her, she would have seen the other car. She would have been paying attention. She wouldn't have died. She's gone and it's all my fault."

"Bella, there's no way you could have known what would happen. People argue all the time in cars and live to tell about it. Sometimes shit just happens. There's no reasoning behind it. The only one at fault was the other driver who hit you. That's who you need to be blaming, not yourself."

"No. It's my fault. I'm the reason she's not here, raising the twins. I don't deserve to ever feel what you just gave me. I have no right." Bella stops pacing and glares at me.

"Is that what brought this on? Oh, god. Bella, you deserve the world. You are a beautiful, brilliant and kind young woman. You've practically devoted your life to the twins, only reserving a very small portion of your free time to yourself. If your mother were here, she would be so proud. You can't live your life like this, thinking her death is your fault."

"*I can* because *it is.* This is my atonement, my reparation. This is how I right my wrong." Bella walks toward the door. "I deny myself this type of pleasure, this type of joy. This is too good. You're too good."

"Bella, wait..." I hurry toward her, grabbing onto her waist and preventing her from walking out.

"No. My job is to fill her shoes the best I can. Helping the boys in whatever way I can. I'm the perfect student, perfect sister, and perfect caregiver. The only thing I ever allow myself is a little release. I've ensured that it's always been just that, a release. Nothing more. I don't deserve anything more." Bella turns her head, unable to look me in the eye. "This. What just happened here, was so much more than just a release. You see me. The real me. Broken and battered. What you just did... it made me whole. And I can't let it happen again."

"That's where you're wrong." Lifting both arms above her head, I pin her against the door, grinding my hips into her. "I'm going to make it happen again and again until it gets through your pretty little head that you are worthy of acceptance, joy, and love. You think you need atonement, little girl? Let me be your salvation." I lick up Bella's neck, watching goosebumps rise in my wake. "I'll give you your redemption—" I whisper into her ear, taking the lobe into my mouth and releasing it with a pop. "—one orgasm—" I hover my lips above hers. "—at a time."

Bella releases a pained whimper before her lips attack mine. I can feel her hunger, her need, and I'm more than happy to satiate it. I grind my hardened length against her, letting her know just how much she affects me.

Bella presses herself against me as she slides down to her knees, her gunmetal eyes never leaving mine. Shaky hands reach for my belt and I stop them. "Baby, wait." Bella's brows furrow in confusion as I lift her back to standing. "While I would love nothing more than to have those juicy lips wrapped around my cock, I want to make sure you aren't doing this out of some fucked up sense of obligation or guilt."

Bella's eyes sparkle as a slow smile overpowers her frown. "I want this. I want to show you..."

"What? What do you want to show me?" I waggle my brows and grin. "I know now isn't the best time to be a perv, but what can I say? I'm a dirty old man at heart."

Bella purses her lips and cocks a brow. "You're a dirty old man, alright."

I'm about to pull her back down when there's a knock at the door. "Just a minute," I shout as I right myself quickly.

Just missing my disheveled appearance, Ashley flings the door open and looks back and forth between Bella and me. "The tiny terrors are up. Thought I'd give y'all a heads up since I'm heading to the grocery store."

"Thanks. I better go find them before they get themselves into trouble. Those two could find mischief

even if it were hidden behind a leprechaun's pot of gold."
Bella shakes her head as she walks out.

"Ashley, could you hold up a minute? I would like a
word with you before you leave."

"Sure." Ashley steps into the room, closing the door
behind her. "What's on your mind, big bro? Well, other
than fucking the teenage nanny."

"Don't look at me like that. You have no idea what
you're talking about." Shooting her a death stare, I motion
for her to sit.

"Oh, I don't? So I didn't just walk in on you two about
to fuck? Come on, William. I'm not stupid." Ashley rolls
her eyes and shakes her head. "It's your funeral when her
father and uncle find out. You know that, right? You also
know she could very well leave you once she finds out
about our dear old dad."

"Enough, Ashley. You don't have to remind me of that
every time you see me."

"My apologies. I shouldn't fault you, it's probably
genetic. Hawthorne men just can't seem to keep their
hands off of Moretti women." Ashley scowls, the look of
sheer disgust evident on her face.

"This is not the same and you know it. Our dad might
have slept with her mom, but he was a married man with
a family." I run a hand over my face, realizing what I've
just said.

"Ummm, wake up, big bro. You are a married man and last time I checked, you have a family. Not only is that an issue, you still have to worry about her family and how she will take the news when she finds out about our parents."

"She won't find out unless you tell her. Dad's been dead for three years and Mom's been missing for just as long." I point a finger in her face. "So don't you dare ruin this. I mean it."

Ashley rises from her chair and walks toward the door. "Don't worry. I'll keep my mouth shut, but remember this—the truth always comes out in the end."

The door slams and I'm left alone with my dark thoughts. Knowing Ashley will keep our family secret should bring me some sort of comfort, but instead, her words end up sounding more like an ominous prediction of doom, chilling me to my core.

Chapter Fifteen

ISABELLA

IF THERE'S A silver lining in all this, it's the weather.
Instead of having to endure a triple-digit heat wave, it's a
beautiful seventy-five degrees with clear blue skies and a
gentle breeze. *God bless California.* I'm making the best of
our situation and bringing the kid train outside. There's a
swing set, sandbox, and treehouse so I know they'll be
entertained for hours.

I'm at the sandbox with Harper when the patio door opens and William steps out. "Heading to a meeting. Won't be back until late tonight, so don't wait up."

"Okay." I scrunch my brows, curious as to what's brought on this change in mood. "Is this meeting the reason for your scowl? If it's causing you to be in such a foul mood then maybe you should cancel."

"I'm not a child, Isabella. I deal with matters straight on, regardless of whether they're enjoyable or not." William kisses Harper on the nose and waves goodbye to the boys who are up in the treehouse.

"You don't have to be a donkey about it." I roll my eyes at his rebuke. "We'll save you some pizza. It's movie night and we're ordering in from that place down the street."

"Don't bother. I'm eating out." And with those parting words, William slams the door behind him.

Well shit, who pissed in his Cheerios?

Whatever. I'm not going to let his dickish attitude ruin my day. I look down at Harper's big beautiful eyes and smile. "We are going to have so much fun, aren't we pumpkin?"

It's that moment Harper chooses to release *the* loudest fart, causing giggles to erupt all around. I can't help but join in on the laughter as I see the proud smile on Harper's face. Drying my eyes, I pull her in for a hug.

"Yes, sweetheart. You should be proud. Such a tiny thing making such a big sound."

The laughter helped ease the darkness William's mood left behind, but I can't help but feel that this cloud was just the beginning of something worse to come.

The kids and I are snuggled up on the couch as the end credits to *Finding Dory* roll in the private theatre. There's a huge projection screen, snack bar, and comfy lounge chairs along with a fluffy sectional, perfect for cuddling. Harper is asleep on my lap, while the boys are passed out on either side of me. *Movie night was a hit.* I'm debating moving them to their rooms when the phone in my pocket vibrates. I pull it out as gently as possible and see that it's an unknown number.

Choosing to ignore it, I get up and take Harper to her room. If they want to reach me badly enough, they'll leave a message. It isn't a local number and anyone else I'd want to talk to has already been programmed into my phone.

I've made my way back to the media room when my phone starts vibrating again. *Hmm, it's the same number.* Not wanting to wake the boys I step out into the hallway and answer the phone. "Hello?"

After a long pause, a woman's voice comes through the line. "Hello, Isabella. You'll never guess who I've run into, all the way out here in California."

The woman's voice sends prickles up my back and has my hairs standing on edge. "Look, whoever you are, I don't give a flying fuck who you've run into. Just do us both a favor and lose this number. Either that or I can easily block you."

"Poor Isabella, I wouldn't do that if I were you. How else would I be able to send you pictures of William and Mariana sharing an intimate meal together."

Suddenly my mouth goes dry and the room starts to spin. *Did she just say William and Mariana, my aunt?*

"Cat's got your tongue, sweetie?" The woman cackles, her words causing bile to rise up my throat. "Looks like whoring yourself out didn't work out so well. By the looks of it, William is moving on." Her tone goes flat and loses all amusement. "Keep an eye out for the photos. I'll be sending them shortly."

The line goes dead before I even have a chance to ask her anything else. Not that I'd even know where to start with my questioning. The whole conversation was surreal.

My phone vibrates twice, notifying me of an incoming text message. I unlock my phone and freeze. Staring back at me are grainy images of William and Mariana huddled close to each other. The room they are in is dimly lit but there is no mistaking those broad shoulders or great head of hair. That's *my* man... with *my* aunt.

William is placing his hand on Mariana's while she shoots him a coy smile. *Yeah right. As if there were a shy bone in that woman's body.* I scroll to the second picture and have to refrain from throwing the phone. William's face is obscured while Marianna whispers into his ear, her hand visibly pressed into his leg.

This is the meeting he had to go to? The one keeping him out late? *Hardship my ass.* I can tooooootally see he's not enjoying himself.

I know we aren't officially together but I thought our time in the study meant something. I opened up to him. Told him I was there for him. But instead of him coming to me, being open with me, he chooses to share himself with Mariana. *What a fucking joke.*

Seeing him with her, like that, sends a piercing shot of pain straight through my chest. He clearly didn't want me to know who he was meeting up with. Otherwise he would have told me. And if there wasn't anything nefarious about it, he would have shared the purpose of the meeting.

But nope. Instead he was a total jerk.

In that moment I remember his words. *"Don't bother. I'm eating out."* My stomach revolts and I run to the bathroom just in time to hurl. Did he mean he was going to eat *her* out like he'd done to me earlier today? *Rein the crazy train in, Bella.* I'm sure he just meant he was eating dinner out.

There has to be a logical explanation for all of this. There just has to be. Whoever sent these messages did so with the intention of ruining whatever I have with William. Which begs to question, who knows about us and why would they want to break us apart?

Lifting myself up to the sink, I splash cold water onto my face and resolve to confront William about this as soon as possible. I can only hope that he had a good reason for keeping this from me.

If he doesn't, the mystery woman might just get what she wanted.

William

Guilt has my steak tasting like sawdust. I shouldn't be keeping things like this from Bella, and wondering what her reaction to this would be has my stomach in knots. My phone vibrates alerting me to another incoming text message, but I silence it and divert my attention back to the woman next to me. *I just have to get through this dinner.*

"Mariana, you said you had news for me?" I take a gulp of water and try to wash away the horrible taste in my mouth.

"Yes. We know we've run the details of your father's murder with you before but there was a new development and we wanted to question you about it." Mariana's coy smile seems extremely inappropriate in our conversation. Here she is talking about my dead father and she can't stop blushing like a schoolgirl.

"I've talked to y'all about this countless times. Nothing has changed."

I was away on business when I received a call from Ashley. She was hysterical. Wouldn't calm down no matter what I said. After minutes of attempting to soothe her, she managed to mumble that she had walked in on my father's body and my mother was nowhere to be found.

That's when I placed a call to 911 on three-way, telling her to get out of the house and into her car. I wanted her as far away from there as possible.

Once the police arrived, I called the guys. Titus and Ren showed up first. The scene they walked into was straight out of a horror movie. Blood was everywhere and my father's body was splayed out front and center, serving as a warning.

The team looked for my mother but couldn't find her. Forensics later confirmed that the blood soaking the room was from both of my parents, leading us to believe she had been attacked as well. Signs of a struggle were evident and it appears that she had been dragged out of the house based on the blood streaking the floors and doorway.

Forensics also uncovered the extent of brutality my father had endured while dying. Sure, there was no love lost between my father and me, but I would never wish for his death. Especially not one as sick and twisted as his was. Whoever mutilated him wanted to send a message. He'd been castrated and amputated after being shot. The sick fuck that did this cut off all of his appendages, including his balls and dick.

"William? You listening?" Mariana's voice cuts through my thoughts, bringing me back to the present.

"No. Sorry. What were you saying?"

"We have evidence from a new crime scene matching that of your father's." Mariana looks at me expectantly, continuing when no questions follow. "Forensics sent us the information from a crime scene involving Isabella—"

"What?" Mariana had my attention now, and if she noticed the reasoning behind the change in my demeanor she didn't mention it.

"The local police department contacted us when they noticed the bullets recovered from the scene matched those of the murder investigation for your father. Whoever shot at Isabella's tires the night her car was vandalized used the same gun as the person who shot your father." Mariana's eyes soften at my concern and she reaches to touch my hand in comfort. "We will find whoever did this, William."

Ignoring her attempts to soothe me, I press her for more information. "How certain are you that it's the same gun?"

"As you well know, almost every gun barrel is rifled when being manufactured. The rotating grooves imprint a mirror image of the markings onto the bullet once it's been fired, creating unique striations." Mariana purses her lips as she shakes her head. "We were able to match the bullets recovered from both scenes to test them against each other, and without a doubt, whoever shot at Isabella's SUV used the same gun as the one that was used on your father."

"I don't get it. Who would want to hurt both of our families?" My entire face twists as I try to wrap my head around this new information.

"That's why I asked you out tonight. I wanted to ask you personally before bringing the rest of my team into this. I know Isabella has been working closely with you as of late. Is there anything that would tie her to your father?"

My mouth goes dry and my whole body stiffens at the question. I need air. *Now.*

"Excuse me, Mariana. I need a moment to process all of this." I get up from the table and head toward the exit.

I'm standing by the valet when a small hand scratches down my back. Spinning quickly, I'm able to grasp the perpetrator's wrist.

"Hello darling husband. I see you've moved on from the teenybopper and are now screwing her aunt." Heather's cold and detached eyes stare back at me.

"What the fuck are you doing here? How did you even know where I was?" Trying to get answers, I squeeze her bony wrist tighter.

"I know lots of things, William." An evil cackle falls from her chapped lips. Upon closer inspection, everything about her seems unbalanced—her hair looks like it hasn't been brushed in days and her usually impeccable clothes are disheveled. It's clear that this woman is unhinged. "Lots of things I've shared with your whore of a mistress. Well, I guess she isn't your mistress anymore."

"Tell me what you've done," I command through gritted teeth. "I swear to God, if you've hurt one hair on her head I will—"

"Is that a threat?" Heather's lips rise in a half-smile. "That would be a bad thing, William. Can't have you threatening your poor distraught wife who's caught you in not only one, but two affairs."

"I'm not going to play games with you, Heather. Tell me what you've done. Now!" Losing my patience, I shout—not caring if anyone can hear.

Heather tsks while waving her phone in front of her. "I've sent Bella visual evidence of your tryst with her aunt. Surprise surprise, it didn't go over too well."

I don't hurt women but at that very moment, I want Heather to be the exception. Not trusting myself, I drop my hand from her wrist and take a step back.

Is this why my phone's been vibrating non-stop. Oh, god. I've ignored every single message. What must she be thinking?

I pull up my phone and sure enough, I have three missed calls and ten text messages, all of them from Bella. Needing to do some major damage control, I call Bella's number but there's no answer. *Of course.* I've ignored her all night so why in the holy hell would she pick up my fucking call now. I need to get back to the house and try to undo the damage my crazy ex has caused.

Speaking of which, I look to where Heather was standing a mere moment ago and see she's disappeared. *Dammit. I knew I shouldn't have released her.* I shake my head knowing this is not the time for self-reprimanding. What I need to do now is get to Bella.

Stepping back inside, I pay for a dinner I didn't eat and quickly explain to Mariana that something came up. I know it makes me look shady, but fixing this situation with Isabella takes first priority.

I have to get back to the house before Heather does something else, causing irreparable damage. I have no idea what's going on in that crazy head of hers but based on whatever 'visual evidence' she took, I have a lot of explaining to do.

# Chapter Sixteen

ISABELLA

I'VE MANAGED TO put all of the kids to bed and have commenced pacing palooza. Yup. I'm in the living area directly connected to the entrance and I cannot for the life of me stop pacing back and forth. I look like a worried mom on the lookout for their errant teenager coming home after curfew.

Sadly, the reality is much much worse. I'm on the lookout for my secret lover. A man who I shouldn't even be having intimate relations with. *God, if my dad or Ren found out, we'd be in a world of hurt.* To be honest, I don't even know if he owes me an explanation. It's not like we're officially together. He just gave me mind-blowing oral. Once. That hardly a relationship makes.

Whatever. I don't care if I'm entitled or not. He had dinner with *my* aunt after trying to hide it and acted like it was some sort of business meeting. He's giving me a fucking answer, whether he wants to or not.

The front door opens and closes just as I'm about to permanently mark the floors with all my walking. Quickly, I move to a wingback chair and act nonplussed, even though I'm anything but. "How was your meeting?" I bellow into the foyer.

"Isabella." It's funny how he only calls me by my full name when he has something serious to say. In this case, I can assume it's going to be seriously bad.

"William," I reply with an aloofness I can't even believe.

William's hair is tousled as if he'd either just had the dirtiest of sex or he'd been running his fingers through it in worry. I silently pray for the latter.

"I'm not sure what's running through your mind, but whatever you're thinking, I can assure you it's not what it seems." William walks toward me as he delivers the single most cliché line of all time.

Scoffing, I roll my eyes. "I'm not thinking anything, *William*." I utter his name as if it were the most vile thing on earth. If he thinks I'm making this easy on him, he's got another thing coming.

"Isabella." There's my given name again. "I spoke with Heather and know about the pictures she sent you."

So *that's* who the psycho caller was. Okay, this can be a good thing. That bitch is totally off her rocker. I mean, who walks away from William and an adorable daughter? I wouldn't put manipulating the truth past her. Maybe the photos are old. Or photoshopped. Or... *Ugh, stop making excuses and let William explain.* "Okay. So, are the pictures fake? Were you not having dinner with my aunt?"

William grimaces and looks at me apologetically. "No. They are not fake." Quickly, he puts both hands up as if trying to calm a wild animal. "But it's definitely not what she made it seem."

I take a deep breath in, trying to calm the nerves that have my body shaking with raw emotion.

"Explain." The word comes out clipped and forced through gritted teeth.

"Mariana had new information on my father's death. Since our families are close, she called me to run some questions before bringing her team in officially." William's face looks tired as if tonight's events had caused him to age dramatically.

I feel a pang of guilt at the thought of William having to deal with his father's death all over again but then it hits me. *Why was the FBI involved in his death?*

Noting the puzzled expression on my face, William explains further. "Your aunt is the lead investigator assigned to my father's murder case."

A gasp escapes me. *How had I not known? Here I was, complaining about my mother, when his very own father had been murdered!*

"Not many people know what truly happened in our home three years ago. We chose not to make the situation public in order to keep whatever sanity Ashley and I had left." William runs a hand through his hair before continuing. "I need a drink."

I silently walk over to the bar cart, and with shaky hands pour him a rocks glass of amber liquid. William walks to me, taking the glass from my hand. "Thank you," he whispers as he brushes the back of my hand with his thumb. After what seems like an eternity of silence, he takes my hand in his and sits us down on the chaise. "Ashley walked in on my father's murder scene while I was away for work. It was brutal, Bella. Fucking brutal."

Licking my parched lips, I run through the various questions popping up in my head, wondering what to ask first. "Is that why she moved to Florida? Because of what happened?"

William nods. "She was barely twenty-two. Fresh out of college. I didn't want to damage her further by keeping her in a city that served as a constant reminder of what she'd seen."

"What about you? How did you handle it?" I scrunch my brows together wondering how this strong and beautiful man has been able to walk around with this secret weighing him down all this time.

"I fell into a parental role with Ashley and fucked the rest out of my system as best I could." He chuckles sarcastically. "Despite all of the drama with Heather, I don't regret it one bit. Out of my poor judgment came the beautiful light that is Harper and I wouldn't change that for anything in the world."

His love for his daughter warms my heart, temporarily making me forget what started this whole conversation in the first place. As if by divine intervention, Ashley chooses that moment to walk into the house, effectively cutting into the middle of our talk.

"Hey, guys. What are you doing up so late?" Her face is flushed and her appearance is disheveled. If this were a betting game, I'd say Ashley had just been out for a booty call.

William either doesn't notice or chooses to ignore the current state of Ashley's appearance. "We were talking about Dad."

"Oh, so you finally decided to tell her about our cheating father?" Ashley blurts out, seemingly relieved to avoid any direct questions about where she'd been. However, the last part of what she said totally caught me off guard.

"Your father was a cheater?" I ask, scrunching my nose and narrowing my eyes.

Ashley's face turns ghostly pale. "I mean..." She turns to William and glares. "It's late, I should probably go to bed. Taking a monitor into the room with me in case the kids need anything. You two clearly need to have a talk."

William scowls in disapproval. "We *were* having a talk before you came home. And don't think you're off the hook regarding your whereabouts tonight. We'll be talking later."

William turns to look at me once Ashley has disappeared back into the hallway, his face painting the perfect picture of peace and serenity. You'd think he'd at least look a little guilty, seeing as he was just caught in an omission. *Wrong.* And if I were to base my theory off of Ashley's look of disgust, it was an omission that had been discussed ad nauseam between him and his sister.

"Oh no, mister. You aren't going to smooth talk your way out of this. What did Ashley mean by your father being a cheater?" I raise a brow, silently urging him to continue.

"My father was a cheater." William huffs, acting as if my question is annoying him. *Me* annoying *him.* "Want me to break it down for you? My father fucked other women while married to my mother. It's not earth-shattering information."

My mouth opens and closes like a fish out of water before I finally regain control of my vocal cords and find my ability to speak. "How dare you say it's not earth-shattering? Cheating on your partner *is* a big deal," I blurt out in disgust. "Is it not a big deal to you because the apple doesn't fall far from the tree? Is that what you were doing tonight—*cheating*?"

William's face is unreadable, showing nothing that would betray his emotions. "First of all, we are not together so I couldn't have cheated on you even if I tried. Second of all, as I've told you before, there is nothing going on between Mariana and me. I'm not interested, nor will I ever be, in having a romantic relationship with your aunt."

Out of everything he just said, one thing stood out as clear as day. *We are not together.* His words feel like a knife slicing straight through my heart, rendering me speechless.

Holding my head up high, I school my emotions and try to mask the pain he's inflicted. "If there's nothing going on between the two of you then why hide the fact that you were meeting up for dinner?"

"Discussing my father's murder is not something you should be privy to. I simply shared this information with you to spare any hurt feelings Heather's little stunt might have caused."

My eyes begin to water. Unable to keep the first tear from falling, I turn my face to shield it from his view. Despite my best efforts, a treacherous sniffle gives me away.

"Bella." William's voice comes out as a gentle whisper. "I'm sorry if I've hurt you. It was not my intention."

Here we go with the emotional whiplash again.

"No, it's okay. I get it. We aren't together. You don't owe me a damn thing." Wiping the tears away, I turn to look at him. "I guess that means I don't owe you anything either. You'd totally be fine if I went out for some quick release, right?"

I know my words are extremely petty, but I can't help it. My wounds are so deep I want nothing more than to lash out in anger.

Looking into his eyes, I see that I've hit my target and struck a nerve. *The playboy doesn't like to share.* "Don't look at me like that. You can't have your cake and eat it too. If you want to go on dates and act like licking my pussy was no big deal, then so be it." A devious smile forms on my lips as I see his face tighten in anger, allowing me to regain control. "This goes both ways, and since I'm unattached, I can go out on dates too. You aren't the only man who knows how to use his tongue just the way I like."

A low rumble emanates from somewhere deep within William's chest. "*You are mine.*" His hand shoots out to the nape of my neck, bringing my face closer to his. "*Your lips are mine.*" He brings his other hand up to my face, his fingers softly caressing my parted lips. "*Both, these*" — William taps my mouth before pulling his hand down onto my pussy, clenching it over my mound— "*and these.*"

Unwittingly, a moan escapes me. *How? How can I be so infuriatingly mad one second, heartbroken the next, and turned on in another?*

William's low chuckle breaks me from my inner struggle. "My little moon likes it when I touch her." William's fingers move back and forth across the exterior of my heat while his palm applies firm pressure to my clit. He might try and act as if he's in control but his half-lidded eyes tell me he likes touching me too.

It takes all of my willpower but I manage to rip myself from his grasp. "If you ever want the privilege of touching me again, the parameters of our relationship need to be set."

William wordlessly stares at me with an intensity that would cower a lesser woman. He might think this unfair, but I'm not putting my heart on the line for a nanny with benefits situation. "Look, it's clear you don't think of me as anything more than a convenient fuck, so I'll do us both a favor and pretend whatever happened in the study was just a figment of my imagination."

Without saying another word, I stand to leave and retreat to the safety of my room. Just as I think this night couldn't possibly get any worse, my phone rings. My whole body stiffens as I read the Caller ID.

"H-Hello?" My voice shakes as I answer, silently praying that the caller isn't the bearer of bad news.

"Yes, is this Ms. Moretti? This is Dr. Ansley. I'm calling regarding your father..."

Chapter Seventeen

WILLIAM

IT'S BEEN ABOUT ten minutes since Bella went to her room, yet I'm still rooted in the same spot as when she left me. I want to show her how I truly feel, but doing so would only bring on more complications. Complications we don't need right now. *Talk about being stuck between a rock and a hard place.*

I know I was a total dick to her, but in my defense I had to be. A relationship with Bella isn't possible and filling her head with dreams that could never be is ten times worse than my being a cold-hearted bastard every now and then.

The truth of the matter is that I would love nothing more than to make Bella mine in every way possible. Hell, if it were solely up to me, I would marry her and lock her in my bedroom, only letting her out for sustenance when necessary. *Okay, I'm exaggerating... but only by a little.*

Bella makes me feel things I've never felt with anyone else. No matter what I do or how much I remind myself that she is completely off-limits, I find that my thoughts always wander back to her. I haven't even been able to fuck anyone else, nor had the desire to since she started nannying for Harper.

Harper. Another reason why I wouldn't want to be without her. Bella is loving and patient, always putting my daughter's needs first, something Heather never did. Deep in my heart, I know that Bella would be an amazing mother to Harper, and when the time came, to any children we had together.

I have no idea how I'm going to manage without her when she starts college in the fall.

The idea has my stomach in knots, bringing forth unbidden visions of her in the arms of some college punk. The scene changes and in vivid technicolor I see Bella dancing at a college party with some random jock.

Squeezing my eyes shut, I try to push the visions out but it's impossible. I grind my teeth as the scene in my mind progresses to Bella making out with the random guy. *Fuck that.* My vision turns to red as I remember her threat from earlier: *You aren't the only man who knows how to use his tongue just the way I like.*

"Over my dead body." I hear myself say out loud.

The only way another man will be putting his hands on what's mine is if I'm dead and gone. And even then, I'd come back and haunt their asses from my grave.

The visions, though horrible, serve to spark a fire under my ass. It's just what I needed to see things clearly and give me that necessary push into action. To hell with the obstacles and impropriety, Isabella Moretti is mine and it's about fucking time the world knew it.

Decision made, I rise from my seat only to be stopped at the sight of Bella entering the formal living room. Her face is pale and her eyes glossy.

"What's wrong?" I close the gap between us and pull her against me.

"It's my father." Her voice trembles against the fabric of my shirt. "They said we need to come in right away."

"Let me go tell Ashley we're leaving and then we can head out." I squeeze her hands, trying to give her as much comfort as possible.

Bella looks up at me and nods, eyes full of sorrow and confusion. This woman has endured so much in her short years, and I refuse to be someone who adds to the long list of suffering. If I could somehow crawl deep inside her soul, where all the darkness and pain reside, I would steal her afflictions making them my own and prevent her from feeling any more sadness.

The streets are barren as we make our way to the hospital, adding to the ominous mood. Now is probably not the best time to let Bella know of my intentions with her but I want her to know that I'm here for her, in any way she needs me to be.

Reaching across the center console, I place her hand in mine, intertwining our fingers and squeezing. "Bella, I'm here." Lifting her hand, I place a soft kiss onto her open palm. "I'm sorry for the things I said earlier. I didn't mean them."

Bella's eyes narrow and her lips turn down in disapproval. "*Now*? You choose to do this *now*, on our way to see my father?"

I take my hand from hers and move it to her nape, stroking the racing pulse with my thumb as if trying to tame a wild horse. "I'm telling you now so you know you're not alone. Whatever happens with your father, I want you to know that I'll be here. I'll *always* be here."

Bella's eyes open wide and I see the moment it clicks.

"You remember," she breathes out. "I thought what I said in that office meant nothing to you. That I'm nothing to you."

"You could never be nothing, little moon. Since the day you walked up to my house driving that monstrosity of a mom-mobile, those silver eyes and your sweet as pie nature won me over. I was officially mesmerized by all that is you." Taking advantage of the red light, I pull her face close to mine and nip my way up her jaw. "Everything after that has been a sad attempt at trying to stay away, all based on a damn sense of impropriety." I place a wet kiss to the soft skin below her ear and growl. "*No more.*"

"William." Bella's breathy voice comes out part moan. "The light is green."

Okay... that's not what I was expecting her to say.

"Look, I understand if you aren't ready to hear this. I just need you to know that I'm here and I'll be here for you in any way you need."

"You mean because of my dad." Bella's tone is ice cold as her gaze focuses straight ahead.

Releasing my hand from her nape, I nod and let out a sigh, realizing she isn't going to make this easy. I should have known a simple apology wouldn't have done the trick. "I'm dropping this conversation because of the timing, but don't mistake it for a lack of interest. This talk is far from over."

Isabella

After the callous way he's treated me, he has some nerve to think we'll just fall into whatever version of a relationship he wants whenever he wants. *He's lost his damn mind.* I plan to make him sweat this out as long as possible.

"Dr. Ansley said we're to go straight to the nurses' station instead of Dad's room. Someone there will notify him of our arrival." I quickly exit the car before it's even rolled to a stop.

We're almost to the hospital entrance when I hear William's laughter behind me. "Are we playing a game of cat and mouse now?"

I look behind my shoulder and glare. "No game. You've just decided to spring your change of heart on me at the worst possible moment, that's all."

William catches up to me, wrapping one arm around my waist. "Okay, little moon. Whatever you say."

He might have been playful and teasing a moment ago, but as soon as we step foot inside the hospital our entire dynamic shifts.

The nurses seem to be expecting us because as soon as we step into their line of sight, there's a mad dash to alert Dr. Ansley of our arrival.

"Ms. Moretti?" an auburn-haired nurse calls out to me.

"Yes. I got a call from Dr. Ansley telling us to come to the hospital as soon as possible." With steely resolve, I begin walking toward my father's room.

"Ms. Moretti, you have to wait!" the nurse shouts for me to stop but I keep moving forward.

My body momentarily shuts down upon opening the door to my father's room. *He's awake!*

"Daddy!" I whisper-shout as I break into a sprint, needing to be by his side as quickly as possible. But the joy is short-lived, making my smile fade just as fast as it began. "He isn't moving. Why isn't he moving?" I ask in a panic to anyone who will listen.

Looking up, I see Dr. Ansley walk in with the nurse rushing closely behind. The look on his face coupled with William's strong hands on my shoulders lets me know that I need to brace myself for whatever news he's about to share.

"Ms. Moretti, I do wish you would have waited to speak with me first," Dr. Ansley scolds. "Your father is technically awake but not quite aware. This is called Unresponsive Wakefulness Syndrome, previously known as a vegetative state."

"You're saying my father is a *vegetable*?" I shriek, unable to contain my horror.

"Shhhh, Bella. Let the doctor explain," William whispers from behind me, rubbing his hands up and down my arms.

"We don't use the term *vegetable* anymore, Ms. Moretti. Your father possesses a fully functioning lower brain stem. Furthermore, several studies have shown that many patients in this state are responsive to emotional triggers as evidenced by the use of an fMRI."

"What does that mean? Can he hear us? Does he know we're here?" I ask in rapid-fire succession.

"Like I said, your father is awake but he isn't aware. He doesn't possess reasoning or understanding and any physical movement is purely reflexive." Seeing my face fall, Dr. Ansley quickly tries to add in his version of a positive spin. "However, it's extremely difficult to diagnose the difference between Unresponsive Wakefulness Syndrome and a Minimally Conscious State. Thus far, we can only say that he is unaware of his surroundings but we will continue to monitor him for any sign of conscious awareness."

"So what now?" William asks when the silence extends beyond comfortable.

"We wait. He can either progress into a persistent state or move forward to a minimally conscious state of awareness. We are hoping for the latter and will be performing several exercises and tests to ensure he receives the best care and treatment possible."

"All of these big words to say my dad isn't really here. He's gone. Just like our mother." My face contorts into an ugly cry and I'm no longer able to keep the tears at bay. "I'm sorry. I need a minute."

Pulling myself from William's arms, I rush into the adjoining bathroom and shut the door. Once inside, I let myself fall apart.

Granted, sitting on a toilet seat is not the most ideal environment for mourning, but it's private and allows me to hide from any onlookers. I couldn't stand listening to Dr. Ansley one more second and I know William will try to tell me everything is going to be alright when it really isn't.

Our father is gone. *How fucking cruel can this world be?* His body might be here but his mind is not. And after having endured the loss of our mother, I refuse to let myself get sucked up in false hope.

Once I've finished crying out all of my tears, I step to the sink and look at myself in the mirror. My hair is disheveled, and my gray eyes are red-rimmed and bloodshot. I look like I've been crying for days.

Opening the tap, I allow the cool water to slip through my fingers before cupping it with both hands and splashing my face. Not sure it'll help much but it's definitely better than nothing.

I'm about to open the bathroom door when I hear the timbre of William's deep voice. "I know. I know. I'm sorry, but it couldn't be helped."

William is talking to my father? Is he conscious? I open the door as quietly as possible and see William at my dad's bedside with his back to me. My dad, however, is staring blankly at the wall. I guess nothing has changed. Curious to hear what else William has to say, I stay rooted in place and remain quiet.

"I didn't mean for it to even go there, I swear. You know me, always swearing off relationships. Who knew your daughter would be the one to tame my fucked up heart." William chuckles as he runs a hand through his messy hair. "She means the world to me."

His words throw me off-balance, literally. I lose my grasp on the door and it flies open, causing me to fall flat on my face.

"Bella? Oh my god, are you okay?" William's worried voice hovers above me. "I swear I'm going to stick you in a padded ball and roll you everywhere for your own safety."

I finally get the courage to look up at William from my mortifying vantage on the floor. "Ha. Ha. Very funny. You can wipe that smirk off your face now."

"Okay, but... did anybody teach you it's bad manners to eavesdrop?" William's lips rise into a half-smile.

"Oh, so you didn't mean what you were saying. You just said those things because you knew I was listening." I try to act as nonchalant as possible, but I'm not sure I'm fooling anyone.

"Are you fishing, Miss Moretti?" William's previous half-smile turns into a full-on predatory grin.

I'm pretty sure my face is now beet red. "Thank you. I appreciate what you're trying to do. The mood in this room has definitely been lifted, Mr. Hawthorne." Making my way toward the bed, I allow myself to brush against William's hard body and I swear I hear him suck in a sharp breath. "So you told my father about us? Does that mean you want to make us a thing?"

"I would love nothing more than to make us a thing. Once your father is fully awake, we'll tell him together and I'll announce it to the team." William's tone is unwavering, as if he's given this a lot of thought.

"Is that what the doctor said? That he will eventually become fully aware?" I know I said I wouldn't hang on to hope, but the sound of having my father back is way too enticing.

"Not in those words exactly. He said it could go either way, but he doesn't know your father like I do. I know Aiden and he's a fighter. He will come out of this. For you. For the boys. I know I would if I were in his shoes."

Thoughts of William lying on a hospital bed assault me, making my legs wobble and threaten to give out. "Don't you dare say that, William. Don't you fucking dare." Panic rises through me, allowing the darkness to envelop me in its dread. "I couldn't take it if you left me too." The words tumble out of me before I can stop them.

I know they make me sound weak, but it's the goddamn truth.

William is my rock.

Like a splash of cold water, it hits me. My feelings for this man have been developing since the time he held me at my mother's funeral. I allow myself to fall back into the memory of William clutching me tightly, promising he'd always be there.

From the age of fifteen up until this very moment, William has taken the role of my protector—whether it's shielding me when needed, or simply holding me up to give me the extra boost of support, he's always been there, helping me endure whatever sick and twisted gift fate has in store.

"Shhh, baby. I'm not going anywhere," William whispers into my ear. Apparently, amidst my inner freak out, he managed to pull me into an embrace, wrapping me up in his warmth. "I'll never leave your side. I promise."

I soak up his words, letting him give me what I need... *what I need...* I *need* William.

My breath catches in my throat as the sudden clarity of my feelings leaves me breathless, that one revelation letting me know how far I've fallen for this man—and if I were being honest, I don't ever want to get up.

Chapter Eighteen

WILLIAM

IT'S BEEN ALMOST a week since the visit to the hospital where Aiden was diagnosed with the syndrome that essentially mimics him being catatonic. Despite my trying to lift Bella's mood, the tone around the house has remained somber. I've given Bella some space and time to process the change with her father, but I'm now second-guessing if that was the right move.

I raise a mug to my lips, inhaling the robust aroma of roasted coffee beans before taking a much-needed gulp. I tossed and turned all week, not sure of how to move forward with the relationship between Bella and me. I've never cared this much for a woman and I don't want to fuck it all up before it's even started.

"Mmmmm, I smell the nectar of the gods and it's calling my name," Bella sing-songs as she walks into the kitchen.

"Well, if you're looking for nectar, I've got some for you right here." I smirk while pointing at my groin.

Bella laughs while smacking me in the abs. "You dirty old man. Couldn't resist, could you?"

"I'd say anything to make you smile like that." I raise my hand to her face, tucking a loose strand of hair behind her ear. *So fucking beautiful.* The sun is barely beginning to rise, its faint glow bouncing off of Bella's creamy pale skin and making her look like the goddess she is.

"Mission accomplished." Bella giggles while she moves to fill her mug. "Are you ready for the birthday party today? The whole team is going to be here along with the neighbor and his twin daughters."

"Hold up. First of all, how and when did you meet the neighbor? And second of all, why did you invite him to the twins' party?" The hairs on the back of my neck stand up, not liking the sound of Bella talking to some stranger. Especially when we don't even know who was behind the vandalism to her car. *Which reminds me, I need to reach out to Mariana about their new lead.*

"Relax, Rambo. Our back yard is right next to theirs. The boys kicked a ball over the fence and we had to knock on their door to retrieve it. Lo and behold, two little girls around the same age as the twins were the first to open the door, followed by a very flustered father. After he told them to never answer the door by themselves, we all introduced ourselves and set up a playdate for that afternoon. The kids have been besties ever since. So clearly, I couldn't not invite them to the party. That would just be rude."

"Okay. I'm just curious as to how this all went down without me knowing." I look at Bella over the rim of my coffee mug and ask myself if that's really all there is to it.

"You were out on a work deal. Something about talking to the team who took over Dad's contract."

"From now on, no more interacting with strangers unless absolutely necessary." I cock a brow, expecting her to argue.

But to my surprise, Bella simply salutes while shooting me a wink. "You've got it, *boss.* Now come help me set up the decorations before the kids wake up."

I knew there'd be a catch to her easy compliance.

Begrudgingly, I help set up the snack table while Bella sets up the selfie station.

"The twins are turning seven, not seventeen. Do they really need a selfie station?" I chuckle to myself, realizing how different things were when I was seven. We didn't even know what a selfie was, let alone a selfie station.

"Umm, yes, Grandpa. Besides, this isn't just for the kids. Most of the attendees are adults and we need to have activities for them as well."

"Ha. Ha. I'm not a grandpa, but I get it. You think I'm ancient. I guess that makes you a lover of ancient things." I walk up behind her, grabbing her by the waist and nuzzling her neck. Notes of warm amber and vanilla fill my nose, making my mouth water. I swear this woman sets off a Pavlovian response in me every time I'm near her.

Bella's breathing becomes shallow as she pushes her ass into me. "Oh, I do love ancient things. I love them very much."

I'm not sure if that was a play on words or if she's really confessing her love for me, but whatever it is, it has my dick twitching against her ass, begging to come out and play. "If you don't stop doing that, I'm going to fuck you right here and now—decorations be damned."

Digging my fingers into her hips, I thrust against her, letting my hard cock rub against the crease of her delicious ass.

"Finally ready to make me yours, Mr. Hawthorne?" Bella's breathy voice teases.

"Good morn—" Ashley steps one foot into the room only to swivel back around at the scene in front of her.

"My bad. Didn't know y'all were busy with that." She waves her hand in an all-encompassing motion with her back still toward us.

"It's okay, Ashley. You can turn around now. There's nothing to see," I say as I rearrange my package. "I was just helping Bella with the finishing touches for the party, but now that you're here..." I walk toward my sister, placing both hands on her shoulders. "You can help."

"Actually, both of you can help. I'm going to shower before the kids wake up and I need to get them ready for the day." Donning a Machiavellian grin, Bella wiggles her fingers goodbye as she walks out of the room.

"What the hell was that?!" Ashley whisper-shouts once we're alone. "You know her father and Ren would've murdered you if they were the ones to have walked in on you like that."

"Settle down, Ashley. I'm going to talk to them about it eventually. I'm just waiting for the right time." I try to sound nonplussed about it, but the fact that I've decided to date one of our friend's daughters, a teenager at that, is a little nerve-wracking, to say the least.

"Oh yeah? And how do you think it will go when you tell someone who is still recovering from a brain injury, or another specific someone who is extremely overprotective of their niece? I can't imagine it will go well, can you?"

"I get it, Ashley. It's a delicate situation and I promise I'll handle it with kid gloves," I huff out in frustration, only to realize the irony of my words after they've been said.

"Kid gloves." Ashley snorts. "How fitting."

"Quit talking and help me set up this damn table," I grumble, wanting to avoid any further conversation about Bella and me.

The house is packed and the party is in full swing. All of my brothers are here with the exception of Aiden. It's extremely sad that he couldn't be here, but I know he wouldn't want his boys to go without celebrating their birthday.

We visit the hospital on a daily basis and the twins could definitely use a distraction from their reality. With having lost their mother and now possibly their father, the twins deserve a little breather to just be kids.

My phone vibrates in my pants, alerting me to a text message. I wonder who it is since every one of importance is here at the party.

MARIANA: Sorry to miss the party, but something came up with that new lead. Let me know when you're free to meet up again and discuss.

Excitement runs through me at the idea of finally catching the asshole who destroyed our family and terrorized my woman.

WILLIAM: Understood. I'll get back to you as soon as I talk to the team.

"Who are you texting?" Bella asks as she comes up behind me.

"Your aunt. Said she couldn't make it to the party." I don't want to tell her about the possible connection between her attack and my father's murder until we've secured all of the facts.

"Funny how she decides to text you instead of me, her own flesh and blood." Bella's face flushes in what I think is jealousy and I can't help but smirk.

"Is someone getting possessive?" I tease. "You know there is no one else but you, right?" I want to take her into my arms but know that now is not the right time.

"How could I possibly know that when we've never really discussed the parameters of our relationship," Bella huffs out in a voice low enough for only us to hear. "Last I heard, you were labeling it a thing, and I'm not sure what a thing entails."

Before I can respond, Ren walks up engulfing Bella in his arms. "Hey Sprout. Everything looks amazing. I can't believe you put this together yourself."

"She did the illustrations on all of the invites and decorations too." I beam with pride.

Ren tousles Bella's hair. "Awe, my Sprout is so talented."

"Stop!" Bella squeals, batting away Ren's hands. "Unless you want me to mess up your hair too." Bella wiggles her way out of her uncle's arms and begins to walk away, calling out behind her, "If you gentlemen will excuse me, I need to refill the chip bowl."

Once Bella is out of earshot, I turn to face Ren. "Get the team together and tell them we have some things to discuss. We'll meet in thirty minutes."

"Got it."

I'm about to walk toward Bella when I see the neighbor approach her from the hallway. Deciding eavesdropping is the fastest way to decipher the stranger's intentions, I hang back and listen to their conversation.

"Thanks for inviting us. The girls are having a blast." The man's voice is cool and relaxed.

"Of course. It wouldn't have been the same without the girls. Matt and Max have grown very attached to them already. I know they'll really miss them when we have to go back home." Bella's tone went from happy to despondent at the mention of leaving. No doubt she wonders if it will actually happen.

"I'm sad to hear that you're leaving. Maybe you and I can go out for dinner before then. As a thank—"

The asshole doesn't even get the chance to finish his sentence before I'm inserting myself into their conversation.

"Dinner won't be possible," I answer, wrapping a possessive arm around Bella's shoulder. "She will be busy up until the moment we leave."

"I'm sorry, I don't think we've met. I'm Jackson, the neighbor. And you are?" Jackson raises a brow as he extends his hand in greeting.

"William. Now, if you'll excuse us. I have some things to discuss with Bella." Not caring that I've just left the man's hand hanging in the air, I turn Bella and I around and steer us into the study.

As soon as the door is shut behind us, I lift Bella into my arms and carry her over to the leather chesterfield sofa.

"It seems my little moon needs a reminder of who she belongs to." Guiding Bella's body onto her knees and hands, I run my right palm from the top of her head all the way to the curve of her ass, giving both cheeks a hard smack.

Bella's mouth hangs open and her breath grows ragged. "Yes, please. Show me I'm yours."

I widen the space between her knees, pulling up her sundress and exposing her lace-clad pussy.

"Has anyone ever spanked you here?" I ask as I bring down my hand onto her cunt, the loud thwack bouncing off the paneled walls of the study.

Bella moans, the sound music to my ears. "No. Do it again, please."

"My greedy little moon." I grin to myself, loving the fact that Bella likes to play rough. "Don't you worry your pretty little head. I'll do it again and again."

Needing no further invitation, I lower her thong with one hand while simultaneously running a finger up her wet slit with the other. I can feel her clenching against my touch, letting me know just how much she wants me.

"It's very naughty of you to lead the neighbor on, little moon. It's even naughtier to let him flirt with you in front of your man." I rub her pussy with the palm of my hand, stroking it in a circular motion. "For that, you get ten spankings. I need you to say you're mine after each one. Understood?"

Bella nods her head, signaling me to continue.

I stop stroking her and raise my hand before quickly slapping it back down onto her pussy. Bella gasps but remains quiet otherwise.

"Say you're mine, Bella."

"I'm yours." She pants.

I give her another open-handed blow, the sound of skin slapping against skin reverberating across the room.

"Say it again." I growl, my voice as hoarse as gravel.

"I'm yours," Bella whimpers.

I raise my hand and deliver another loud smack, noticing how she pushes herself back onto my hand. *Oh, she likes this. She likes this a lot.*

"I'm yours. I'll always be yours."

Thwack.

"I'm yours. Nobody else's."

Thwack.

"I'm yours. Take me, please."

Thwack.

"I'm yours. Please, William, please."

Thwack.

"I'm yours. Take me. Now!"

Thwack.

"Fuck! William. Please. I need you."

Thwack.

"I'm yours, okay? Now please just fuck me!" Bella's pussy clenches repeatedly against my palm, letting me know she's close.

On the last slap, I press my hand into her, finding her swollen bud with my fingers and applying firm pressure. Like a fuse reaching its end, Bella explodes, gushing her release onto my hand.

Needing to taste her, I lower my lips to her opening and lick.

"William," she gasps. "It's your turn."

I'm about to settle myself in front of her when there's a knock at the door.

"Fuck," I mutter under my breath. I pull up Bella's thong and lower her dress before yelling for whoever it is to come in.

I'm hit with an overwhelming sense of guilt as the door flings open and Ren walks in. "Hey, it's been thirty minutes and..."

Ren's eyes narrow as he takes Bella and me in. "What's going on here? Everything okay?"

"Yeah. I was just questioning Bella about the neighbor. He seemed to be flirting with her."

Bella's eyes widen before shooting me a death glare.

"Hell no. That man is way too old for you, Bella." Ren shakes his head vehemently, his words landing like a sledgehammer to my gut.

Bella gets up from the couch and walks toward the door. "Don't worry, Uncle Ren. Old men are overrated," Bella retorts, her eyes never leaving mine.

I narrow my eyes at her. "Don't knock it till you've tried it."

Ren's eyes flick back and forth between Bella and me, and I know I've overstepped. *Fuck it.* It was bound to come out sooner or later.

With a huff, Bella slams the door behind her, leaving Ren and me to the awkward silence of the room. Finally gathering the balls to look my best friend in the eye, I see that he's been staring daggers at me this entire time.

"There's a possible bullet match between my father's murder and the scene where Bella's SUV was vandalized," I say, completely ignoring Ren's death glare. He might have an idea of what's going on but I'm sure as fuck not going to give up any information willingly. At least not yet.

"Come again? Did you just say the murderer in your father's case is the same person who vandalized Sprout's car?" Ren's look of surprise lets me know we've moved on from Bella and me and onto the shit bag we need to find.

"Yes. Did you tell the guys about the meeting?"

"He sure did," Titus chirps as he walks into the room with Hudson following close behind. "Sounds like we have a killer to catch."

# Chapter Nineteen

ISABELLA

THE HOUSE IS deserted with random cups and plates strewn throughout, signaling it's cleanup time. I'm in charge of the food while Ashley picks up the back yard and William does the living areas. All in all, it's a smooth transition getting the house back to its normal condition.

I'm putting up the last of the leftovers when William walks into the kitchen.

"Hey, beautiful." His smooth voice cuts through the silence.

"Don't you 'hey beautiful' me. I haven't forgotten how you threw me under the bus with Uncle Ren earlier." I wave a finger in his direction.

"I had to tell him something other than the truth. Did you want me to tell him I'd just been slapping your pussy?"

"William!" I shriek before quickly putting my hand to my mouth. "Dammit. You're going to make me wake up the kids."

"They're out cold. Party wore them plumb out." William waggles his brows as he comes around the kitchen island, closing the distance between us. "That means they won't be able to hear your screams as I ravage your pussy."

My mouth hangs open at his boldness. "What about Ashley?" I manage to whisper as William snakes his arms around me, pressing his lower half into the back of mine.

"She went out with the guys." William pulls my hair to the side and trails open-mouthed kisses along the exposed skin of my back. Taking one end of the tie to my halter dress and pulling, William exposes my bare breasts to the cold air. "Said they were hitting up a bar in Malibu. Which means" —William turns me around slowly, biting at my chin before hovering his lips over mine—"they'll be staying out until well past midnight."

A moan escapes me as William flicks his calloused thumbs over my hardened nipples. "Mmmm. That feels good."

A delicious shiver runs through me. Needing to feel more, I grind myself on William's thigh as he continues his assault on my nipples.

"Not yet, naughty girl." William nips at my shoulder before hoisting me onto the counter, laying me down on the cold surface. Inch by inch, William lifts the material of my sundress, exposing my bare pussy.

"What do we have here?" William's greedy eyes stare intently at my naked flesh. "Looks like someone's prepared." His tongue darts out, wetting his lower lip and punctuating the action with a bite.

"Mmhhm." Actual words escape me, because who can formulate words at a time like this. *Not me.*

I arch my back as William's strong hands rub up and down my thighs, stopping only to squeeze and pry them farther apart. Settling himself between them, William pulls me closer, lowering his mouth to the flesh just above my knee and depositing a wet kiss. He kisses his way up my thigh until his full lips are hovering just above the apex.

"*Please,*" I whimper, unable to help myself.

William pulls away, a sultry smile dancing on his lips. He cups my bare pussy with his hand, squeezing it before quickly issuing a loud slap.

"*Mine.*" He growls as he lowers his lips to my aching cunt, teasing the folds apart with a flick of his tongue. "Every inch of you is mine. *Say it*," he demands before finally spreading my lips apart with his thumbs.

"I'm y—" My words cut off as he lowers his warm wet mouth to my pulsating clit, sucking it for all it's worth. "Holymotherfuckingshit." A string of profanity rips through me, every sense of propriety I once possessed *gone.*

Running my fingers through his hair, I grab hold, riding his face like he's my very own mechanical bull. He continues to suck and tease relentlessly, my body climbing to that peak of release where everything goes black and all else is forgotten.

My pussy clenches, grasping onto air, wanting to be filled, needing to be filled. At that moment, William thrusts three fingers into me at once, curling them up and reaching that magical spot he knows so well.

Instantly, my head falls back and my eyes roll as the most delectable warmth comes over me, leaving me shuddering in its wake. Moments pass as my body recovers from the sexual strike William just delivered to my pussy.

"Mmmmmm. So good." I pat William on the head and he chuckles.

"I'm not a fucking dog, though I'll fuck you like one if you'd like," he teases while lifting me off the counter and carrying me out of the room. "As much as I loved our impromptu kitchen session, it's time I take you on an actual bed."

William

I'm fucking her *tonight*, come hell or high water. The urge to take her in every way imaginable has consumed me to the point where all I see is her, and that shit needs to end *now*. I can't even go on a run without thinking of how good her pussy will feel as it strangles my cock.

Imagine me. Running down the street. Full hard-on in effect. *I'm scaring the poor neighbors.*

"What's so funny?" Bella scrunches her nose as she looks up at me, her big doe eyes full of wonder. Little does she know how thoroughly fucked she's going to be in a couple of hours.

I pull her closer to me before responding. "Just happy this moment is finally happening. I'm sick and tired of the universe interrupting us with baby monitors, nosy sisters, and concerned uncles. *Fuck all that.* Tonight, you're mine."

Bella giggles, her full tits bouncing in my face, tempting me to take them into my mouth. Laying her gently onto the bed, I do just that. Pawing her right breast, I squeeze, lowering my mouth to the pink little point and swirling it with my tongue. *Her soft skin tastes of sin and virtue combined, and fuck if I can't get enough.*

Taking the hardened bud between my teeth, I gently tug, eliciting a moan from the beauty beneath me. I run my hand along the curves of her waist, giving her gorgeous tit one last suck before making my way up to her neck and inhaling deeply. Her scent of amber and vanilla will forever remind me of home. *That's what she is, my home.* If I had any doubt whether or not the shit I feel for Bella is real, therein lies my answer.

I run my lips along the curve of her neck, savoring the feel of her soft skin against mine. Overcome with need, I take her flesh into my mouth and issue a bruising suck, wanting to mark her, needing to show the world that she's mine.

"William," Bella whimpers, rolling her hips into me as her hands travel south, sliding my briefs down and allowing my throbbing cock to spring out. Bella's eyes go wide and her mouth drops open as she takes me in for the first time. "*My god.* Are you sure you'll fit?"

I chuckle, enjoying her reaction. "Oh, it'll fit. And it'll feel damn good too." I take the head of my cock and rub it up and down her slit, teasing her.

Bella mewls as she follows my movement with her hips, chasing my dick like it's the last drop of water in the desert. Unable to withstand any more taunting, she grabs my forearm and pulls me down as she makes her demand. "Get inside me, *now.*"

My cock twitches at her plea, needing to please her just as much as it needs its own release. I move to grab a condom out of the nightstand but Bella's small hands stop me.

"No. I want to feel you. All of you."

I nod, unsure if this means she's on the pill or if she wants my baby, not giving a fuck either way. *I'd give this woman the moon if she asked.*

My dick bobs of its own accord, knowing it's just about to enter heaven. Taking it in my hand, I slap the head against Bella's beautifully bare pussy, swollen and glistening with her arousal. *She's ready.*

I slip my hands under Bella's ass and bring her to me, sliding her slick pussy right onto my throbbing cock.

Holy fuck.

It takes everything in me not to come at that very moment. Bella's pussy is the tightest wettest thing my dick has ever felt, and will ever feel for that matter. *I'm done. This is it. She's it.* Life after Bella does not exist as far as I'm concerned.

Bella's hands explore the ridges of my abs as she grinds herself on me, slowly sliding her delicious cunt up and down my shaft with every arch of her back.

"*Fuuuck.*" I grunt as I begin to feel that familiar tingle in my balls.

Needing to regain control, I pull out and place Bella on all fours, but the sight before me is just as gorgeous as the front.

"So damn perfect." I breathe as both hands land on either side of her hips, digging my fingers into her flesh.

Bella pushes herself back, wiggling her ass in response.

Thwack! "Your ass was begging for it," I tease before thrusting my cock into her without warning. I can tell I've hit her sweet spot because her whole body collapses into itself right as I slide over that magical bundle of nerves.

Keeping one hand firmly gripped on her hip, I run my other hand up her taut stomach and onto her nipple, rolling it between my fingers as I continue thrusting hard and deep into her.

I look down at my cock, sliding in and out of her, soaking wet with her arousal—and I swear I've never seen a more beautiful sight. "Come for me, baby. Show me how good I make you feel."

Grabbing her hips in both hands, I flip her over, needing to see her face as she comes. I tilt her ass up, positioning her just right, quickening my pace as I slam myself into her hard. Bella releases a string of curse words letting me know she's about to explode.

"Look at me, baby." I coax her into opening her eyes. "I want to see that gorgeous face of yours as you unravel for me."

Bella's channel begins to contract around my cock, milking it for all its worth and taking every last bit of self-control I had with it. Unable to hold back any longer, I come hard, spilling into her as our bodies meld into one, both of us shuddering from our intoxicating release.

Falling to the side, I roll her on top of me, wanting to feel her skin against mine and needing to know that this is real. Because, *holy fuck*, how could something this good be real?

We lie there in comfortable silence, reveling in the aftermath of our intense pleasure. This one moment of ecstasy gave me more clarity than any other sexual encounter ever has.

A year ago I would've sworn up and down that this, what I just felt, was not real. That nobody could experience a combination of love and lust so extreme that it left you wanting for nothing more.

"That was... exceptional." Bella looks up at me, her silver eyes glimmering in the dim light of the room. "I've never..."

"Me neither." I roll her over, peppering her face with kisses and pinning her body underneath mine. "So... are we going to be giving Harper a sibling, or are you on birth control and didn't tell me? Just so you know, I'm okay with either of those options."

"You're okay with getting me pregnant?" Bella's eyes go wide and her brows reach her hairline. "I'm so young and we just started this, besides, I'm on birth control."

I kiss her tenderly, slipping a hand behind her head. "Those things might be true, but I really don't give a damn. At the risk of sounding trite, I think I love you."

"You *think* you love me?" Bella swats at my chest as she arches a brow.

"I know I do—I love you, Isabella Moretti. There is no one on this earth I'd rather call mine. No one has ever managed to make me feel what you do. And trust me, I've been around the block."

Bella laughs a full-bellied laugh as she rolls her eyes and shakes her head. "Only you could ruin such a beautiful moment by reminding me of your previous man-whoring ways. It's a good thing I love you too."

My entire body warms at her words, feeling truly blessed to call her mine—even if it has to be a secret for now.

After another two rounds of mind-numbing sex, Bella and I fall asleep. I'm in the middle of a dream when a vibrating sound causes me to stir. Disoriented, I open my eyes and look toward the sound. My pants are at the foot of the bed with my phone illuminating one of the pockets.

I move to grab it, stepping out of the room as quietly as possible, not wanting to wake Bella. Looking down at my phone, I see that I've missed a call from Mariana as well as multiple calls from Ren.

Shit, if he only knew what I'd been doing when he called.

I bite the bullet and call Ren first.

"Hey," he shouts, the sound of club music blaring through the phone. "Hold on, let me go somewhere quiet."

After a minute, the music starts to die down, leaving only Ren's heavy breathing. "Okay. I got a call from the local PD back home. They pulled a car out of the river and think it's the same car that hit Isabella and her mom three years ago."

"Holy shit," I utter in disbelief. "Tell me everything they said. Word for word."

"They're still looking for the registered owner of the car, and get this... they don't think it was an accident."

A cold shiver of dread runs up my spine as the silence stretches across the line. Unable to say anything, I just stand there.

Without notice, a feminine voice cuts through the quiet. "Mr. Hawthorne, why don't you come back to bed? I miss you." Bella wraps her arms around me from behind, running her hands up my abs and onto my chest.

Fuck. I'm pretty sure Ren just heard that.

"What the fuck is going on, William? Was that Sprout?! What in the actual fuck! I'm going to fucking murder you!"

Yup. Ren definitely heard.

I clasp on to Bella's hands with my free hand while I try to calm her uncle. "Look, Ren, it's not what you think. I was going to talk to you about—"

"She's a fucking teenager, William. Have you lost your goddamn mind? For fuck's sake, her father is in the hospital right now. How could you take advantage of her like that?"

"Ren, it's not like that. I love her. I would never do anything to hurt her."

"You're just lucky I'm not in front of you right now. Your mouth wouldn't be able to spew out the bullshit it's spewing because I'd be beating it in. You're batshit crazy if you think you love her…. How, William? How can you love her? She's still a fucking child!"

"Bella stopped being a child the day she watched her mother die. In the blink of an eye, she went from being a carefree teenager to a surrogate mother of twins. We'd like to think that we've helped with their upbringing, but the truth of the matter is that those now seven-year-old boys are thriving—despite the shit life has thrown at them—because of Bella's care and attention." I can hear Ren's ragged breathing letting me know he's still there, so I continue. "Bella has continuously taken on copious amounts of responsibility that far exceed her physical age, without issuing one damn complaint. Open your eyes, Ren. She isn't a little girl anymore, she's a woman. A woman that I love and appreciate."

"I don't know, man. I can't fucking see straight right now. All you've said makes sense, but I just can't fucking see it." Ren's voice comes out choked, as if trying to stuff down the anger that's surfaced with this new revelation. "I need to talk to Sprout. Listen to her side of this sick and twisted thing y'all have."

"Do not talk about our relationship like that. I understand you're her family but I will not let you degrade what we have. It's real and I won't have anyone making Bella feel like we're doing something wrong."

"It *is* wrong, William. She's eighteen. One year younger and it would be punishable by law. I can't. I can't talk to you right now."

"Ren? Hello?" I look down at my phone and see that he's disconnected the call. Finally turning to look at Bella's face, I see she's gone pale.

"It's okay, baby. Everything is going to work out. Ren just needs a little time to process. It sort of caught him off guard."

Bella's face goes from ghostly pale to flushed. "It's my fault. I didn't know you were on the phone. You were so quiet, I thought you were just standing here."

"It's okay. I know your uncle. We've been best friends forever and I know that eventually he'll understand." I try to reassure her, but his last words have me questioning my own belief. "For now, let's just enjoy the fact that the kids are still asleep and get back into bed."

Bella squeezes her eyes shut and scrunches her nose. "God, I hope you're right. I couldn't bear it if I lost Uncle Ren too."

"I *am* right." Tugging her to the bedroom, I wink. "Now let me be the big spoon to your little spoon."

Chapter Twenty

WILLIAM

WE'RE AT THE happiest place on Earth, so the slogan goes. However, on this particular day, our motley crew is making it feel like the most awkward place on earth—thanks to the tension bouncing between Ren and I.

I gifted the boys passes to a local theme park and the whole damn team decided to tag along, Ren included, making things awkward as hell. Ren and I haven't spoken since our conversation last weekend and I'm sure as hell not about to hash everything out in the middle of a children's theme park. This is why I've been avoiding situations where I'd be alone with Ren all morning. I've been successful thus far, managing to do the impossible only because of Ashley.

My sister joined us under the pretense that she wasn't going to miss out on the fun, but I secretly think she knows what went down between Ren and me and decided to come along as a mediator. She's managed to insert herself between us several times today and we haven't even been here a full hour.

It's going to be a long day.

We're currently in the middle of her latest thwarting maneuver, and I have to say that I'm thankful for her assistance.

Bella took the twins onto the Buzz Lightyear ride, with Titus and Hudson following along, both vowing they were going to be the one to defeat the evil emperor Zurg.

Overgrown Man Children.

Had Ashley decided to join them, I would have been left alone with my one-year-old daughter and Ren. I highly doubt Harper would have been enough of a deterrent, unable to keep Ren from continuing the conversation from last week.

I don't think he would try to fight me here, but who's to say the conversation wouldn't escalate into something more if things got heated. I definitely wouldn't want my daughter exposed to that.

Harper begins to fuss in her stroller, letting us know she's ready to get out. I love this stage of development but I'd be lying if I didn't admit it turns me into a nervous wreck, constantly chasing behind her and making sure she isn't getting into anything she isn't supposed to.

Thankfully, Ashley takes pity on me and decides to take over. "Hey pumpkin. Want some ice cream?" She lifts Harper from her stroller and points toward the ice cream cart not too far away. "Ren, would you be so kind as to get your goddaughter and I a chocolate treat to share?"

"Of course." Ren smiles down at Harper, pulling on her pigtail before shooting me an icy glare. "I'll be right back."

Ashley doesn't waste a second, beginning her tirade as soon as Ren is out of earshot. "I know Bella's been sneaking into your room all week."

So this is why she tagged along... not because of Ren.

"Earth to William. Did you just hear what I said?" Ashley looks at me expectantly.

"Yes, I heard you. And yes, Bella and I have been sleeping in the same room. We're together now," I say nonchalantly, even though being able to say it out loud has my stomach doing somersaults.

"Does *he* know that?!" Ashley whisper-shouts as she points in Ren's direction.

"Yes. He found out last week. We still need to finish hashing it out, so I would appreciate you continuing to insert yourself between us, seeing as how this isn't the best location to have that sort of discussion."

"I'd say." Ashley snorts. "That would be a fu—" She stops herself, looking down at Harper. "I mean fudging disaster."

"Yeah. You could say that again," I mumble under my breath.

"You know what else would be a fudging disaster? If Bella were to find out about our parents from someone other than you," Ashley warns, cocking a brow and pursing her lips in disapproval.

"You don't need to beat a dead horse, Ashley. I'm going to tell her, I just haven't found the right time. There's been a new development in her vandalism case, and she's still dealing with her father's situation. Bella needs to decide if we're going to keep him here in California or if we're going to move him to a facility closer to home. Now is not the time to add to her ever growing pile of stress."

"Poor girl. I wouldn't want to be in her shoes." Ashley shakes her head and sighs, making me think she's done with her inquisition.

I'm wrong.

"So... how are things with your psycho ex? I'm sure that wouldn't add to Bella's stress, right?" Ashley snarks.

As if she's summoned the bitch herself, my phone begins to vibrate with Heather's number flashing across the screen. "Speak of the devil..." I groan.

"Are you going to answer it?" Ashley asks while rocking Harper side to side, trying to keep her from climbing down.

"Yes. She's still Harper's mother," I spit out bitterly before answering the call. "Hello. What do you—"

"You fucking son of a bitch. You actually filed for divorce!" Heather shrieks so loud I bet Ashley could hear her without me putting her on speaker.

"Of course I filed. I told you I would. It seems my attorney has finally managed to get you served. Now we just have to wait for the next available court date."

"Oh, you'd like it to be that simple, wouldn't you? Well news flash, William, over my dead body." Heather snarls, her erratic breathing becoming louder. "You think I'm this powerless insignificant little person you can walk all over. Well you're wrong." An evil cackle escapes her, causing the hair on the back of my neck to stand. "Just ask Aiden. He'll tell you how little and insignificant I am. I couldn't harm a fly, could I?"

At the mention of Aiden's name, my apprehension turns into rage. "What the fuck did you do, Heather? What did you do to Aiden?" Ashley's eyes go wide at the insinuation, quickly moving to get Ren.

"My dear husband, Aiden has always been good at his job, hasn't he? As an ex-Navy SEAL, he's never once allowed himself to get distracted. He's always been the best." Another cackle falls from her evil lips. "Well, he was the best until me, that is."

"Stop playing games and tell me what you did!" I shout, unable to control my temper any longer. "Tell me now or I swear…"

"What?" Heather snarls, her tone suddenly becoming eerily calm. "What will you do when you find out I told Aiden about *your* father and *his* wife?"

"You vile sick woman. Why on Earth would you dredge up the past like that? There was absolutely no reason for you to tell him that!" I shout in disbelief. "You're the reason he's in the fucking hospital, aren't you?"

"How was I supposed to know he'd lose focus because of little 'ol insignificant me? I'm powerless, remember?" Heather snidely adds, her sarcasm seeping through loud and clear. "Just imagine what little 'ol insignificant me could do if you continue with this divorce charade."

"Are you threatening me, Heather? I'd highly advise against it. And this is not a charade. We're getting a divorce." I look up to see Ren's narrowed eyes as he's trying to decipher our conversation. "I'm going to get to the bottom of what happened with Aiden, and if you're tied to his injury in any way shape or form—mark my words, Heather, you *will* pay."

I disconnect the call, unable to hear her vile bullshit any longer.

"What was that all about?" Ren asks, managing to put aside his anger toward me—at least for now.

"That was Heather. She isn't taking kindly to our divorce and I think she just implied she was the cause of Aiden's accident."

"How in the hell could she cause Aiden's accident? She's not even in California." Ren furrows his brows in confusion as he tries to piece everything together.

"About that... I saw her a couple of weeks ago and apparently she's bi-coastal." I take in a deep breath, trying to cleanse away the darkness Heather's call has left behind. "Based on what she implied, she distracted Aiden with information regarding his wife. Apparently this information left him so distraught he was unable to properly defend the client as well as himself."

"And what was this devastating information? Did she say?" Ren asks, his eyes narrowing in suspicion.

"Heather told Aiden that my father had an affair with his wife." Staring blankly into the crowd, I avoid Ren's gaze, not daring to look him in the eye. We're already on rocky ground and adding this bombshell of a secret could most certainly destroy whatever thin ice we've been standing on. "For now, we need to focus on preventing any further damage my psycho ex intends on causing. I have a feeling her next target will be Bella."

"Let me get this straight. *Your* psycho ex hurts *my* family as retribution against *you*, with something *your* family did to *my* family. And now, *your* psycho ex wants to hurt *my* family again, because of something *you* are doing?" Ren walks toward me until our shoes are practically touching. "Correct me if I'm wrong, but I think the running theme here seems to be *you*." Making an emphatic point, Ren shoves his index finger into my chest.

"Boys! Let's keep in mind that we're in a theme park—full of children." Ashley's high pitched voice manages to break through Ren's rage infused state, making him blink long and hard before he finally steps back.

Taking advantage of the momentary peace, I try to bridge the emotional gap between us. "Look Ren, I know you aren't my biggest fan right now, but we need to band together if we want to keep Bella safe. Heather has proven to be extremely unstable as of late and I wouldn't put much past her."

"For Bella's sake, I'll put our differences aside for now. But we still need to talk about what your intentions are with my niece. I swear by what I hold most dear that if you fucking hurt her, I will end you. Childhood best friend or not. I will fucking end you."

"Understood. I wouldn't expect any less from you," I add, trying to hold back the smile his acquiescence has caused.

"I'm gonna go find the rest of the team so we can come up with a game plan," Ren mutters as he begins to walk away. "Though I still think the safest thing for Bella would be to keep her the fuck away from you."

Full of remorse, I pull my gaze from him, knowing he might just be right.

Chapter Twenty-One

ISABELLA

THE KIDS ARE passed out in their respective seats, so I'd say today was a total success. This is despite the awkward tension we had to endure between the men of WRATH. Usually, they are full of nothing but jokes, always teasing each other and making everyone around them laugh. But today, it was as if they were all walking on eggshells.

I'm guessing it has something to do with the new security detail they've added to the already extensive one tailing us. I'll have to remember to ask William about it later.

William. Oh. My. Gawd.

The sex with him has been mind-blowing. Take the intense sex and couple it with our insanely strong connection and it's like a supernova explosion between us. I'm amazed we were able to keep our hands to ourselves today.

William is supposed to talk to the group about us, but I'm not sure exactly when that's going to happen. To be honest, I've been too busy floating on cloud nine to think about it.

We're finally alone since the kids and I are riding in William's Escalade, while Ashley is with the rest of the men in Ren's truck. Taking advantage of the privacy, I reach over and grab William's hand.

"Hey, hot stuff. You've been awfully quiet today. Is everything okay?"

"Of course it is. I've got you by my side." William shoots me a weary smile. "Though there is something I've been meaning to talk to you about."

"A 'though' is just as good as a 'but,' so you aren't fooling me. Just spit it out."

"Well, you see..." William hesitates which makes me worry even more.

"I see...?" I squeeze his hand, trying to reassure him. "Seriously. You could say the sky is falling and it wouldn't change how I feel about you, so go on with it."

"It's about my father." William chances a glance over at me, as if trying to gauge my reaction.

"Okay," I say after a long pause. I'm about to urge him to keep going when my phone rings. Pulling it out of my bag, I see that it's the hospital and quickly answer.

"Hello?" I ask while placing the phone on speaker.

"Yes. This is Nurse Jackson calling for Ms. Moretti," a familiar voice cuts through the line.

"This is she. Is my father okay?" I ask, holding my breath for her answer.

"Dr. Ansley would like you to come in as soon as possible."

It doesn't escape me that the nurse avoided answering my question. Though her calm and even tone *does* bring me some measure of comfort, I still don't trust it. This is what she does for a living and could totally be an expert at delivering heartbreaking news, even with the calmest of voices.

Needing to know either way, I ask again. "Can you at least tell me if my father is okay?"

"There's been a change in your father's condition and Dr. Ansley would like to discuss it with you before you step in to see Mr. Moretti tonight. Just as before, please come directly to the nurses' station upon arrival."

Finally accepting the fact that I'm not going to get a full answer from this woman, I drop the question. "Okay. I'll be there in about an hour."

I hang up the phone without thanking her or saying goodbye. The woman couldn't even answer my damn question, I sure as hell wasn't going to be cordial.

"Don't worry, Bella." William's deep voice cuts through my thoughts, acting like a balm to my soul. "We'll leave the kids at home with Ashley and one of the guys. Once they're settled, we'll head to the hospital and see what Dr. Ansley has to say."

I don't answer, I simply keep looking out the window, focusing my vision on the full moon beginning to glow through the darkening night. *How fitting.* It seems the moon has always been my companion on nights of significance, whether good or bad. Hopefully on this night, it's good.

William

Well, shit. I'm fucking glad I didn't tell her about our parents' affair. That would have been a disaster. Tonight is stressful enough as it is and giving Bella any additional information, information that is not good, could be debilitating for her.

We're walking up to the hospital and I can feel the anxiety radiating off of Bella in waves. She's been going through cycles of calmness followed by miniature meltdowns. Right now we're in the middle of the calm before the storm, and I'm afraid Dr. Ansley's news will throw Bella into a fit of hysteria.

Wrapping an arm around her waist, I try to comfort her. "Bella, I can see the wheels in your head turning. Everything is going to be fine. Let's just stay positive and wait to see what Dr. Ansley has to say."

"Okay, you're right. I've just been conditioned to expect the worst and that damn nurse wouldn't tell me anything over the phone."

"That damn nurse isn't *allowed* to give any medical information over the phone," Nurse Jackson teases from behind her station. Though her words are meant to be chastising, her tone is kind.

"I'm sorry. I didn't mean to be rude." Bella stares blankly at the nurse.

I'm pretty sure she *did* mean to be rude, but I'm not going to point that out. Hell, I'd be much worse if I were in her shoes.

"I'll go get Dr. Ansley for you. I'm sure you're eager to talk to him." Nurse Jackson smiles warmly before turning toward a hallway where the doctor is presumably located.

"Look at me." I take Bella's face in my hands, brushing her cheeks with my thumbs. "I want you to know that no matter what the doctor says, you're not alone. I'm here. I'll always be here."

Bella closes her eyes, which had begun to water, and slowly nods her head in acknowledgment.

"That's my girl." I bring her face to mine, softly placing a kiss on her forehead.

"Ms. Moretti, Mr. Hawthorne," Dr. Ansley's voice greets us from down the hall. We walk toward him, pausing right outside Aiden's room. "Good evening. I understand it's rather late but your father has been presenting signs of awareness and I wanted to let you know as soon as possible."

"No, you did the right thing calling. I want to know of any changes right away, whether big or small." Bella rushes to say.

Dr. Ansley nods before continuing. "This is great progress and lets us know he's moving in the right direction. He is currently in what we call a minimal state of awareness where his consciousness is minimal but definite. He is making conscious eye contact and presenting cognitive movement of his limbs."

Bella lets out a deep sigh of relief. "This is good news. This is very good news." A soft laugh falls from her lips.

"Yes. This is very good news. We are hopeful that he will be making continuous progress with his awareness, though there are some things I would like to discuss with you before we continue any supportive treatment."

"Of course, anything to help," Bella answers cheerily.

"Mr. Moretti's current mental state is very fragile. We aren't sure if he can tolerate any extremely emotional information or scenarios, so we want to keep everything as light as possible when discussing things in front of him. As of now, Mr. Moretti currently goes in and out of his states of consciousness so we want to be constantly aware of our conversations. It's also possible there might be a lapse in memory, as the prefrontal cortex suffered significant trauma in the fall. Don't be alarmed if he doesn't seem to recognize people or things pre-injury."

At Dr. Ansley's last words, Bella's smile falls and her lips turn downward.

Quickly wanting to bring her smile back, I finally interject myself into the conversation.

"This doesn't prevent him from eventually regaining his memory, right?" I ask the doctor while keeping my gaze on Bella. "If there's even a problem with his memory to begin with. He could just as well remember everyone and everything, right?"

"Correct. We won't know until he is fully conscious," Dr. Ansley responds. "How about we step inside so you can say hello."

Taking Bella's hand, we push Aiden's door open and step inside. Unsure of what we will see, we both take hesitant steps toward her father and my good friend.

"Hey Dad." Bella's voice is soft and sweet, at complete odds with what she must be feeling inside.

Aiden blinks hard at the sound of Bella's voice, spurring on hope that he does, in fact, remember her.

"Aiden, my man," I say jovially while patting him on the leg. "I think you've had plenty of time off work. It's time to get you back in the saddle." I grin ear to ear, hopeful that he hasn't lost his sense of humor.

For a brief moment, I swear I see a hint of recognition flash across his eyes, but it's gone just as quickly as it arrived.

"Keep doing what you're doing. Just remember to keep it light. We don't want to trigger any negative emotions that might revert any progress he's made."

Bella and I shoot each other a look, coming to a silent understanding of what this might mean for our relationship, at least in front of Aiden.

"Yes, of course," I say once I've pulled my gaze from Bella. "How long do you think this state of consciousness will last?"

"We can't really say at this time. We'll continue to monitor his progress and keep you posted on what we find." Dr. Ansley walks toward the door, placing his hand on the handle. "I'll be back in a couple of hours. Have the nurses page me if you have any pressing questions."

I turn back to see Bella crawling onto the hospital bed with Aiden and smile. "I'm going to step outside and call Ren. He wanted me to give him an update as soon as possible. Hopefully he hasn't gotten on his flight yet."

"Okay. I'll be right here." Bella snuggles into Aiden's side, the sight of her curled up like that making her seem so small and fragile.

I quickly step out before I'm unable to control the urge to gather her in my arms and hold her. That would definitely throw Aiden for a loop.

Shutting the door behind me, I take my phone out to dial Ren's number. But before I can press send, the phone begins vibrating and Mariana's number flashes across the screen.

"Hello, William?" Mariana's somber voice clues me in on the nature of her call.

"Mariana. I'm guessing you have some information for me, and by the sound of it, it isn't good."

"I'm sorry, William. I wish I didn't have to tell you this," Mariana says apologetically.

"I understand, it's your job. If it makes you feel any better, I would rather it come from a friend than a complete stranger."

"I should be the one trying to make you feel better. Not the other way around. Trust me..."

"Okay. Now you're worrying me. It isn't like you to drag out news like this. What is it? Do you have a lead?" I ask eagerly.

"I presume Dallas PD contacted you about the car they found in the river, right?"

"Yes. Based on evidence they found, they suspect the Moretti hit and run accident was intentional. Last I heard they were trying to identify the owner," I say, piecing the information together as best I can remember.

"Well they found the owner." Mariana lets out a loud breath before continuing. "The vehicle was purchased from a small used car lot and the buyer paid in cash. The driver's license the buyer used was fake, however, the photo that was used in it was not."

"Alright. Does the photo identify the driver?" I ask.

"Yes. We think the driver of the vehicle was your mother."

Nothing but shocked silence follows Mariana's last statement. Utterly horrific and devastating silence.

What in the holy fuck did she just say? She has to be kidding. This has to be a joke.

Speaking only after what feels like an eternity, I finally gather the courage to ask Mariana a question. "How certain are you that my mother was the one driving the vehicle?"

"Based on the evidence recovered from the scene and the testimony of the car salesman, we're pretty damn sure she was the driver."

"*Well, fuck.*"

Chapter Twenty-Two

WILLIAM

IF I WAS HESITANT about sharing the affair with Bella before, there is no way in fucking hell I'm telling her now. At least not right away. I need to figure out how in the world I'm going to soften the blow, if it's at all possible.

I could see it now... "Hey, beautiful. Let's order pizza tonight. Oh, by the way, my dad had an affair with your mom. Oh, and no big deal but the FBI suspects *my* mom was the driver who plowed into you three years ago."

Yeah. Not happening.

I need to get with Ren so we're on the same page regarding this new information. Don't get me wrong, we aren't going to keep this from Bella forever, the team and I just need to get some facts straight before we tell her.

Even if I don't want to see it, there's a correlation between the two tragedies that forever changed our lives and Bella's recent attack. Once everything has been tied together neatly, I'll come clean about everything. Rip it all off like a proverbial bandage.

"William, there you are," Daniel Mathers greets me from behind.

I've been standing at the steps of the courthouse for the past few minutes, patiently waiting for my lawyer to arrive. I'm back in Dallas and it's the day of my hearing with Heather. Needless to say, I'm eager to get this dog and pony show over with.

"Good morning, Daniel." I nod my head and give him a half-smile. "I'm ready for this hearing and not willing to waste one more minute being married to Heather than necessary. Hopefully, Heather Hawthorne will soon be Heather Moody. We can force her to take her maiden name back, can't we?" I ask while walking into the courthouse and toward the courtroom we'll be in today.

"I'm sorry but it's highly unlikely," Daniel says apologetically. "Were you able to find any connections between Heather and the judge who presided over your case?"

"No. But Heather is definitely acting unhinged. I wouldn't put bribery past her, though I couldn't find anything that would indicate it."

"Well, let's hope that whatever connections she might have had with the other judge don't extend to this one." Daniel raises a brow while motioning toward the courtroom.

"From your lips to God's ears," I mumble under my breath before stepping into the room that holds the answer.

"What fucking horseshit is this?!" I exclaim loudly, not giving a damn who hears me.

"William. Quiet down, we're still in the courthouse and I wouldn't put it past anyone to eavesdrop." Daniel places his hand on my shoulder trying to quiet me. "Especially after the hearing we just went through. I'm now certain more than ever that Heather has an inside connection with the judges presiding over your cases. You *need* to find out what it is. Our firm will do what we can to investigate, but you are the head of a security company. If anyone can locate the information, it's going to be you."

"I know. I know. I dropped the ball with everything we had going on with Aiden, I put the possible collusion on the back burner. I can assure you, I won't be making that mistake again," I huff out bitterly.

"Good. Today's hearing was another anomaly but I believe we could still get around this. Heather's attorney is basically implementing delay tactics. I have never seen a judge order marital counseling before. It's possible, I just have never seen it. It's such an archaic practice when it comes to the legal dissolution of a marriage." Daniel furrows his brows as he shakes his head. "The closest I've seen to it is a judge ordering a cool off period, but the evidence in your case file clearly indicates this has been a long time coming and you are way past the point of marital counseling. Appointing a mandatory guardian ad litem for your child? Yes, that is totally reasonable. Appointing a mandatory marital counselor? Preposterous, given the circumstances."

"Well good to know my case is the exception." I let out a bitter laugh. "I'll let you know how it goes with the counselor. Who knows, maybe Heather and I will work things out and I'll be able to stop giving you all of my money."

"Stop speaking such blasphemy. Sarcasm doesn't suit you, old friend." Daniel chuckles. "We'll let you know if we find anything on the judges." Daniel starts to walk away but turns back at the last moment. "William? Watch your surroundings at all times. This woman has connections in high places and you never know who's watching."

"Ten-four," I say with a mock salute before walking toward my car.

As I approach the parking lot, I notice Heather is waiting by my Range Rover—again. This seems to be a post-hearing tradition for her.

"My dear husband. When will you get it that we are destined to be together for all eternity?"

Well that didn't sound creepy as fuck.

"Heather, please step away from my car. I have nothing to say to you," I say as calmly as possible.

"Sure. I'll step aside as soon as you unlock the car and take me home. I'd love to see our daughter." Heather's smile widens comically at the mention of Harper. "By the way, how's Aiden doing?"

"Great, actually. No thanks to you." I narrow my eyes at her and glare. "Answer me one question, Heather. Why? Why did you set out to hurt Aiden?"

"Silly William. I didn't set out to hurt Aiden, he was just a casualty." Heather rolls her hand in the air, as if waving away a nuisance. "The real target was Bella. Is she still playing house with you?"

"What I have with Isabella is none of your business," I spit out between gritted teeth.

"Oh but I beg to differ. You are *my* husband, and I'll do whatever it takes to keep *my* husband. Including sabotaging Aiden's recovery. How do you think he will react when he finds out his precious daughter has been sleeping with an older man—a *married* older man?"

Lowering my voice to a whisper, I issue my first real threat. "Stay the fuck away from Bella's family. If you value your pathetic life even a little, you'll do as I say."

"Tsk, tsk, tsk," Heather admonishes, pulling her phone from her bra and waving it back and forth. "That sure sounds like a threat, William. A threat I've fully recorded."

I lower my head and let my eyes drop closed, trying to take in a centering breath. Instantly recognizing that I've fucked up.

How could I let this psychotic woman get the best of me?

I know how. I let anger blind me and I can't afford to let that happen again. That little recording has the power to damn my court case and threaten my role in Harper's life. I need to get it in my hands and destroy it.

"This changes things, doesn't it?" Heather giggles, fully aware that what she's just done has the potential to destroy me. "Here's what's going to happen, I need you to take me home. To *our* home. And then I need you to tell that homewrecker she needs to stay in California. Far far away from us. Then you're going to bring Harper home so she can be with her real mommy, not some second rate stand-in." Heather grins maniacally. "Doesn't that sound wonderful?"

"Just peachy," I force out, biting my tongue.

Isabella

What a whirlwind couple of weeks. Dad has been undergoing supportive therapy with Dr. Ansley and it really seems to be making a difference. It feels as if I'm getting a little bit of my father back each day.

The kids and I have fallen into a routine as of late. Every morning we visit Dad before making our way to Griffith Park. I use the trails, merry-go-round, and observatory as bribery, letting them know they can have their pick of activities if they behave while at the hospital. *So far so good.*

We've just gotten back from the observatory and I've finally gotten the kids settled down for their naps when my phone rings.

God, I hope it's William with good news about his hearing.

"Hey hot stuff, how'd it go?" I ask impatiently.

"Hello, Isabella," I hear a familiar woman's voice say.

"Bella, you're on the car speaker. I'm with Heather and we're on our way home right now," William's voice interrupts Heather's greeting.

"William?" I hesitantly ask, my voice cracking in confusion.

Why is Heather in William's car? Why is he taking her home? To his home?

"Heather is moving back in with me," William responds after a long pause, his words stabbing me straight in the heart.

I feel as if all the air has been sucked out of my lungs. I'm gasping, unable to catch my breath. How can a few measly words cause such excruciating physical pain?

"Bella, we want you to stay in California. Heather will be watching after Harper from now on, so we'll be sending for her soon."

Another stab to the heart. I'm stumbling, needing to grasp onto the wall to keep me from falling.

No. This can't be real. This has to be a nightmare.

"William?" His name comes out strangled, caught between a sob and a groan. I try to add more to the question but all that comes across the line is my ragged breathing.

"Yes, bitch. William and I are going home and I'll be packing up all of your shit—"

"Enough, Heather," William booms, cutting off Heather's words. "Bella, we'll be sending your things via courier and Ashley will be there later this week to pick up Harper. Are you okay with caring for her until then, or shall I arrange for an earlier pickup?"

My head is full of cotton as I try to make sense of what William is saying. *What is happening right now?*

My mind might be confused but my heart knows full well what's going on, it's being shattered into a million pieces with William stomping on its remnants for good measure. He's leaving me for Heather. I let myself love him and even opened up to the possibility of a future, only to be dumped over the phone.

How could this man make love to me one day and then throw me out like yesterday's garbage the next? How could he promise me he'd always be there and then abandon me at a time when I need him the most?

The phone drops and my entire body begins to shake, overwhelmed with the sudden barrage of thoughts and emotions running through me.

I'm a joke. Nothing but a fucking joke. They're probably laughing at me right this very second.

I drop to my knees, unable to support the weight of the world seemingly crashing down on me all at once.

He's leaving me. He's leaving me all alone. My rock, my everything. I don't understand. He promised he'd always be there.

Oh god, I'm going to be sick.

My stomach churns, letting out a noise before heaving out its contents onto the floor.

I'm sitting there—bent over and grabbing on to the wall—watching my tears mix with the literal bile that's crawled up my throat, when it hits me. Like a ton of bricks, reality hits me. *It was all a lie.* William never cared for me. It was all a ploy to bag the nanny, the convenient pussy.

I blink several times, my tears continuously falling despite my best efforts to stop them. Realizing William is still on the line and waiting for an answer, I pull myself together and pick up the phone. I *will not* let him hear me cry. I *will not* let him hear me fall apart.

He might have taken my heart and soul, but I *will not* give him my dignity too.

Clearing my throat, I finally speak. "No. That won't be a problem. I'll pack all of Harper's belongings and make a list of her current schedule. You can do with it what you'd like. If that's all, I have to get to the laundry before the kids wake up."

Not wanting to hear Heather's grating voice, I cut the line and pray the worst of this betrayal is behind me.

Chapter Twenty-Three

ISABELLA

I'VE OFFICIALLY SURVIVED the week from hell. Ashley arrived a couple of days after William's call of doom, claiming to know nothing more than the fact that she was there to pick up Harper. I haven't spoken to William since the day of the hearing and I can safely say I'm still very depressed.

I've been doing the bare minimum around the house. Unsure of what's going to happen next, I try to keep myself motivated and at least visit Dad every day. I have to constantly remind myself that the boys need me and I can't just drop everything because of William's dickass behavior. Well, that's the plan at least. The reality of the situation is that I'm a hot mess most of the time.

My phone bellows out Gin Wigmore's *"Girl Gang"*, alerting me to an incoming call from Cassie, so I answer.

"Woman! It's about time you picked up your phone. Open your damn door, already," Cassie rushes out in excitement.

"What? Why? Are you here?" I scrunch my brows together as I make my way to the front door.

"Yes, bi-atch. And I just cleared the million security guards you have surrounding the house, so let me in."

I open the door, squealing in delight at the vision that sits before me—Cassie holding a bottle of tequila in one hand and a pint of ice cream in the other. *I seriously couldn't have conjured a better surprise.* "Oh my god, Cassie! How did you get here?!"

Cassie steps across the threshold, thrusting her gifts into my hand before embracing me in a bear hug.

"An airplane," her smart ass replies. "A little birdie told me you were moping around here like some pathetic excuse of a woman. And *that* my friend, is unacceptable."

"Is it now? I'm not allowed to grieve the loss of a man—A man who I thought was the love of my life?"

We're walking toward the kitchen when Cassie stops in her tracks. Whirling around, she shoots me a glare before starting in on me. "First of all, that man was not the love of your life. The love of your life wouldn't just abandon you like that for some psycho bitch who is a *terrible* mother." Cassie waves a finger in the air while pursing her lips. "Second of all, no. You are not allowed to grieve that piece of shit garbage of a man."

"Okay. So what do you propose I do then?" I ask, a small smile lifting at the corner of my lips.

"You put your badass woman panties on and put yourself out there again. Literally. Go put on your sexiest panties and meet me out here in thirty. I'll watch the boys while you get ready for dinner. I made the four of us reservations at this new restaurant in Malibu right on the water." Cassie opens her arms wide, spanning an imaginary oceanfront view. "The fresh air will do you good and it's about damn time you do something outside of the house besides visiting the hospital."

I blow out a breath in surrender, releasing it slowly. "Okay. You're right," I mumble as I shove the ice cream into the freezer. "I'll be ready in thirty."

"Take your time. That hair is going to need all the help it can get. When's the last time you washed it?" Cassie shouts from the kitchen as I walk away.

"Ha. Ha. I get it. I'm a hot mess," I say, disappearing into my room.

"I loooove Malibu!" Cassie squeals. More cheerily than I could stand at the moment. "So many fun places to eat."

"I know you're trying to help, but could you tone down the happiness just a bit. It's making me want to strangle you, and we can't have that. Who will care for the boys if I'm locked away on murder charges?"

"Well, that escalated quickly," Cassie murmurs, shooting the boys a side glance as they giggle.

"I know. Sorry. Couldn't help it." I shrug while taking a sip of my drink—a double shot of tequila on the rocks.

I'm no longer able to drink whiskey without remembering William's mouth on me. *So tequila it is.*

A flash of dark hair catches my eye somewhere to the left, but it's gone just as quickly as it appeared. I put my drink down, swearing it's making me hallucinate.

"I met someone," Cassie blurts out. "I know you are going through a lot right now but I think you should listen to what I have to say."

"Oh my god, Cassie! That's amazing!" I cheer, apparently finding joy within me I didn't know existed. "Tell me everything."

"I'm not telling you to rub this new relationship in your face, Bella. I swear there's a point to this conversation." Cassie purses her lips, scrunching them to the side. After a pause, she continues. "A while ago, I met a man who I thought was the one. Things were progressing rather quickly and then all of a sudden he dropped me like a sack of potatoes, leaving me destroyed."

"How in the hell did I not know about this?" I shove at Cassie's shoulder in disbelief.

"You had a lot of stuff going on. I didn't want to add to your worries." Cassie shrugs her shoulders. "Anyway, the point is I didn't let myself wallow. I got right back on the horse and ended up meeting an amazing guy. We've been dating for a month now and I think it's serious enough for you to meet him. What do you say? Want to meet my beau and his bestie?"

I squint my eyes at Cassie in suspicion. "Are you trying to set me up and disguise it as meeting your new boyfriend?"

"Who me? I would never. I just thought you wouldn't want to feel like a third wheel is all."

"Uh huh. Sure you didn't," I say sarcastically. "As tempting as your offer might sound, I think I'll have to pass. I'm definitely not ready to put myself out there again. Now if you'll watch the boys for me, I have to go to the ladies' room."

Cassie nods. "Okay, but we're resuming this as soon as you get back."

I get up from my seat and make my way to the bathroom, needing to get away from Cassie's matchmaking antics as quickly as possible.

I'm just about to close the door to the single stall restroom when a hand appears, preventing me from shutting it all the way.

I know that hand.

Sure enough, William steps through the crack, shutting the door behind him.

"William." His name comes out as a whisper. I take two steps back in shock, thinking this can't be real. It's clearly a figment of my imagination.

"I'm so sorry, Isabella." William walks toward me. His eyes full of regret, trying to convey an apology I'm just not ready to accept.

Realizing this isn't some hallucination, I finally react. Lifting my hand, I slap William across the face, wishing I could transfer all of my pain with that one contact.

"Why? Why are you here, William?" I say through clenched teeth, my whole body beginning to shake with rage.

William steps closer, until we're a mere breath apart. "I'm here because I love you."

"Don't. Don't you dare tell me that." Feeling that familiar tingle in my nose, I try to tamp down my emotions. I *will not* let him see me cry.

"I'll tell you that as many times as I have to." William grabs me by the waist and pulls me into him. "Until you realize that you are it for me. I want no one else. There is no one else."

"What was Heather then?" I ask, my voice so little I barely recognize it.

"It wasn't real. Heather was blackmailing me. She said she had a recording of me threatening her, and that recording would have ruined my legal case as well as kept me from being present in Harper's life. I had to get my hands on it and destroy it, so I played along with her demands. I'm so sorry you got caught in the middle. I thought you would've understood that there could be no one else but you." William searches my face for understanding, but it's just not there.

"You thought I would've understood?" I scoff. "For someone so brilliant, you're such a dumbass sometimes. How the fuck was I supposed to understand? Through goddamn telepathy?" I try to take a step back but William's grip on my hips is unrelenting. "For fuck's sake, at the very least you could have told Ashley. She could have warned me."

"You know Ashley can't keep a straight face to save her life. She would have ruined the plan if I'd clued her in on what was going on."

"Well, did it work? Did you find the recording?" My lip quivers as an unbidden tear falls down my cheek. "Was my pain and suffering worth the charade?"

"There was no recording," William whispers, the decibel of his words doing nothing to soften their blow.

Closing my eyes, I suck in a breath and take a moment before asking him to explain. "Did you just say there's no recording?"

"After some maneuvering, the team was able to hack into her phone. Once they were in, they realized she never made a recording. Her phone doesn't even have an application that would allow her to create one." William's bitter chuckle snaps me out of my stupor. "Thankfully, Ashley was already watching Harper so I could send Heather packing immediately."

"Hold on. Are you telling me that you broke my heart—into a million pieces—for a recording that didn't even exist?" My head falls back and I stare at the ceiling in disbelief. *How could this man, this man I trusted with my life, hurt me so bad for something that wasn't even real?*

"I'm sorry." William's voice comes out choked and thick with emotion. "I thought the threat was real and I didn't think it through. In my head, I truly thought you knew that what we have is what's real. That nothing could ever shake us. Especially not some psychotic ex of mine." William brings my face to his, pressing our foreheads together. "You have to believe me. I thought we'd be okay. I never meant to hurt you, little moon. You're my woman. There is no one else. There will never be anyone else."

"Did you sleep with her?" I ask, unable to hide the mixture of skepticism and hope evident in my tone.

"Fuck no. Since you, there has been no one else." William presses us together, letting me feel his hard length twitch against me. "My dick only wants you. It comes alive for you and no one else."

Looking into his clear blue eyes, I let myself fall once more. "I believe you, but that doesn't mean I fully forgive you. What you did hurt me a great deal and it's going to take time for me to trust you again."

"I'll apologize for the rest of my life if I have to, Isabella Moretti. But understand this, you're mine whether you like it or not." William grinds himself into me while simultaneously lifting me by my ass, causing me to reflexively wrap my legs around him. "I've missed you, little moon," William murmurs before crashing his lips into mine.

I return his kiss with all the pent up emotion I have inside, our tongues dancing together in the purest form of expression. The kiss is raw and urgent, letting me know he needs me as much as I need him.

"Inside me, now," I urge William while I claw at his pants, needing all the layers between us gone.

"Yes, ma'am." William grins wide, placing me on the small vanity and pulling me to its edge.

I unbuckle his pants while he tugs at my leggings, both of us wanting each other exposed as quickly as possible. As soon as he's pulled my leggings off, he grabs me by the waist, driving his massive cock into me without warning.

I gasp at the sudden invasion, grabbing onto his ass and wanting him deeper. Needing him deeper. Losing myself in the moment, I revel in every spark, every tingle. My eyes roll back as my body is invaded by a multitude of wonderful sensations. The fullness of him inside me combined with the steady and unrelenting thrusts his throbbing cock delivers are almost too much for me to bear.

I never want to be without this man again.

"Fuck, I've missed you so much," William whispers against my hair as he slows his thrusts, savoring the sensation of his thick cock pressing in and out of me. "You feel so damn good, baby. But we're going to have to make this quick. Cassie and the boys are waiting for you."

I mumble incoherently, unable to form words with how good it feels to have him inside of me. I just want to keep going and never stop.

Smirking, William brings his thumb to my mouth. "Open wide and suck me."

Doing what he asks, I take his thumb into my mouth and swirl it with my tongue, making William groan. With a loud pop, he removes himself from my mouth, bringing the digit down to where our bodies meet.

His thumb connects with my clit and my body jolts from the contact. My entire body is alive with sensation and I instantly feel him everywhere all at once. It's a connection I've only ever felt with him, and in that moment I know, it will only ever be him.

"You're mine, little moon. All mine." William kisses my neck before biting and sucking it.

"Yours. All yours." I moan in ecstasy.

My whole body turns into liquid heat as he rolls the tiny bundle of nerves round and round while thrusting into me faster and faster. I'm close, so fucking close, I can feel myself clenching around him. Unable to hold back my release, I come hard, seeing nothing but black as my pussy spasms around William's glorious cock.

"That's right, baby. Come for me, and only me." William's pace becomes urgent. Each thrust a declaration of possession. "You're mine. This pussy is mine," he grits out, his jaw clenching.

Reaching below, I grab hold of the family jewels and softly squeeze. "I am yours and you are mine."

At my words, William throws his head back, roaring his release—filling me with his cum and marking me as his.

"Fuuuuuuck." He moans while pulling me into his chest. "God, I could never get enough of you."

"Well then it's a good thing the feeling is mutual." A genuine smile spreads across my lips.

William reaches for a paper towel, wetting it with warm water before bringing it to me and cleaning me off. "I'm sorry this was quick. I promise I'll make it up to you later. But for now, let's get you cleaned up and back to your friend."

Despite still having some reservations, I'm smiling like a loon as William and I walk back to my table. Dreading the reaction we're going to get, I prepare myself for Cassie to be angry with us, but the expression marking her face as we approach the table is of complete elation. Looking around, I see the boys are overjoyed as well.

Happy but confused, I quicken my pace, needing to find out what's got them in such a mood. As soon as we're within earshot, Cassie shoots straight up from her chair, answering my question.

"Ren called," Cassie blurts out, her grin practically splitting her face. "Aiden is talking!"

Chapter Twenty-Four

ISABELLA

THE FAMILY WAITING area is humming with anticipation as we fight over who gets to see my father first. The hospital only allows five visitors in a patient's room at any given time, so we're currently trying to figure out the logistics of our visitation schedule.

We decide on family first with Ren, the twins, and me taking first shift along with Cassie, seeing as how she's practically family; followed by William, Titus, and Hudson taking second. Ashley and Harper are back in Dallas, otherwise we would've had to have added a third shift.

Nerves wrack my body as we walk toward my father's room. A barrage of questions assault me all at once, two of which are playing on constant repeat.

Will he remember us? Will he remember the accident?

Finally at his door, Ren reaches for the handle, glancing back at us and giving us a reassuring smile. "Everything is going to be okay. Just smile, and remember, don't spring any highly emotional information on him. He's still recovering."

We all nod in agreement before Ren pushes the door open, letting us in.

My dad sits up in his bed, staring out the window. As soon as he hears us, he turns his head, his eyes landing on everyone all at once.

"My family," he murmurs to himself. A slow smile appearing on his lips.

Instantly, my eyes well up with tears. *He remembers.* "Daddy!" the twins shout as they rush the bed.

"Boys!" my father exclaims. "Come here and let me hug you."

"Where's Dr. Ansley?" I ask, wondering where the genius doctor is. I have no doubt his experimental therapy had a great part in my father's recovery and I feel the sudden urge to hug the man that brought us our father back.

"I spoke with him on the phone earlier today," Ren answers. "He had to fly back to New York for an emergency but will be back tomorrow morning. Assuming Aiden's tests go well, he can travel back home as early as tomorrow evening. We will need at-home care for a while, but I'm sure Aiden won't mind a hot nurse at his beck and call, will you, brother?"

My dad chuckles as I roll my eyes. If I weren't so damn happy, I would smack Ren for his chauvinistic humor.

"So then this is it? He's fully recovered?" I look back to Ren for an answer.

"As soon as he clears his tests. This is it."

The boys cheer, jumping up and down and hugging Dad all over again. "We made you so many cool drawings, Dad. You're going to love them."

"That's amazing boys. I can't wait to see them... I can't wait to get out of this bed. My body feels as if it's been lying here for months. It has, hasn't it?" Dad's expression grows somber as he looks between Ren and me for an answer.

"What's the last thing you remember?" Ren asks my father hesitantly.

My father's eyes close and after a long pause, he answers, "A job site. I remember a phone... smashing my phone."

"Yes! That's good, Daddy!" I exclaim, hoping he can finally answer the question that's been plaguing me for months. "Do you remember what made you so angry you smashed your phone? William said the loss of communication was the catalyst to your injury."

"Isabella," Ren chides. "We're not supposed to push him like this."

I turn to look at my father, needing answers but also not wanting to make him regress. "I'm sorry. I just couldn't, for the life of me, figure out what would cause you to destroy your phone. That isn't like you."

My father's expression grows dark. Turning to Cassie, he motions toward Matt and Max. "Cassie, would you mind taking the boys out for some fresh air? I'm sure they're tired of seeing their dad in a hospital bed."

"Nooooo," the boys wail. "We want to stay here with you!"

"I have to talk to your uncle and sister about grownup stuff right now, but I promise we'll be home soon and you can spend as much time with me as you want. So much time, you're going to get sick of seeing me." My father strokes their heads in affection.

The boys finally relent and follow Cassie out the door as I mouth a silent thank you.

"I remember," my father blurts out.

"Don't push yourself," Ren urges.

"Stop fussing over me, Ren. I'm fine." My father waves his hand in the air. "I got an anonymous text. It had very detailed information about trips Lucia had taken when she was alive, as well as photos of her and another man in very compromising positions."

My jaw drops as the nightmare from three years ago begins to haunt me all over again.

"Fuck," Ren mutters under his breath.

"And that's not the worst part. We knew and trusted the *other* man," my father adds.

My face pinches trying to recall the memory of my mother and the man. But try and try as I might, I can't see his face.

Without warning, my father speaks, revealing his identity. "It was William's father."

My heart drops and my throat clogs, heavy with emotion. *What the fuck did he just say? Surely, I must have heard him wrong.*

Shifting my gaze toward my uncle, I see that his face is frozen in horror and I'm pretty sure it's a mirror of my own expression.

Moments pass and the room remains eerily quiet. If it weren't for the beeping of machines, I would think we were all stuck in a state of suspended animation. Shocked into stasis by the sudden revelation my father has just shared.

Ren is the first to break the silence. "The photos could be fake. They were clearly sent to knock you off-balance, right?"

"Well besides the damning photos, the mystery text confirmed dates of travel and such. So, yeah. I'm pretty fucking sure."

"Fuuuuck." Ren shakes his head, though by the look in his eyes I'm not sure it's from disbelief. *Did he already know?*

I begin to question my memory but I really don't remember seeing the man's face. *Did William know?* No... he would have told me.

"Bella?" My father's worried voice pulls me from my thoughts. "You haven't said a word. Are you okay? I know you took your mother's death pretty hard."

I smile, choking back the angry sob trying to escape me. "Yes, Daddy. Now I think you should rest. That's a lot of information you just rehashed and I'm sure Dr. Ansley wouldn't want you stressing yourself out. That can't be good for your recovery."

"Sprout is right, Aiden. I think we've evoked enough excitement for one day. Besides, it's time we gave the rest of the team their turn for a visit."

"The guys are here?" my father asks, a smile reappearing on his face.

"Yes. I'll go get them on my way out," I chirp. "I'm heading back to the house so I can get the kids and I packed. We'll be ready to fly back home tomorrow."

Kissing my father on the cheek, I walk out of the room as fast as my legs can carry me. I need to tell William about this tidbit of information as soon as possible. I'd hate for him to be blindsided like I was.

William spots me as soon as I approach the waiting area. The whole team stands, waiting for news of my father's recovery. I plaster the sweetest smile on my face as I walk into a chorus of "How is he?"

"He's really good. You should go see for yourself." I motion toward my father's room, urging the team to go but shooting out my hand and grabbing William's arm before he moves past me.

Lowering my voice to barely a whisper, I pull him in closer. "Would you mind staying behind for a second. I have something to tell you."

William nods his head, his face full of worry. "What happened?" he asks as soon as Titus and Hudson have cleared the waiting area.

"My father remembers. He remembers what made him smash his phone," I blurt out in a hushed tone.

William's face pales as if he's seen a ghost.

"He got an anonymous text. It revealed my mother was having an affair with your father."

William's eyes begin to dart around the room, settling on a multitude of objects but never on me. I would have expected horror, confusion, or even disgust... but not this.

"You already knew that. Didn't you?" I ask, arching a brow as I stare at the man who had just declared his love for me a mere hour ago. "Didn't you, William?"

"Yes. But it's not what you think." William's face turns panicked. "I only kept it from you to protect you. You were going through so much and I didn't want to add to the stress."

"You and I have a major communication problem, William. First the thing with Heather, and now this. Is there anything else you've been keeping from me? Anything else you've been hiding for my own protection?"

William stares at me blankly, his arms hanging at his side, unable or unwilling to say anything.

"This is fucking unbelievable. You say that you love me. That there is nobody else, but this isn't love, William. You can't love someone you don't even trust." I shake my head incredulously. "I can't be here right now. Please tell Cassie to bring the boys back to the house. I'll meet them there later."

Without a second glance back, I walk away. Unsure of where I'm going, just knowing it needs to be far away from here.

Chapter Twenty-Five

WILLIAM

I CAN'T BELIEVE I just stood there like a fucking idiot. I didn't even try and stop her from walking away.

After talking to Cassie, I was able to convince her to let me take the boys back to the house. This gave me the perfect opportunity to wait up for Bella without looking like a crazy stalker, and also giving me a chance to hang out with her little brothers—it's been a while since I schooled them in some *Mario Kart*.

After a couple of rounds of video games and some pizza, I've finally managed to get the boys to bed. It's bordering on ten o'clock and there is still no sign of Bella.

As much as I would like to avoid a confrontation with her, we need to hash out the reasons why I omitted important information. She needs to understand that I love her and what I did was for her own good. *Her own good.* I repeat the words over and over in my mind, asking myself if it's really the reason why. But the front door opens before I'm able to answer my own question.

Bella steps inside, her hair looking wind-blown and her eyes bloodshot from tears and exhaustion. Her eyes meet mine and a frown instantly forms on her pretty lips.

"Where's Cassie?" Bella asks, her voice hoarse with emotion.

"I told her I would watch the boys until you came back." I motion toward the formal sitting area. "I need to explain. I was caught off guard at the hospital, but I swear, if you give me a moment to explain things to you it will all make sense."

Hesitantly, Bella takes a couple of steps forward into the adjoining room. I grab her hand, surprised she lets me, and bring her down onto the loveseat by my side.

"Everything I did was done out of love. Well, fear and love," I try to explain but my thoughts are all jumbled up and I'm finding it hard to get things straight. "I've never had a real relationship. You are the first woman I've ever wanted a forever with and I'd be lying if I said I wasn't absolutely terrified of losing you."

"Sure didn't seem that way when you broke up with me last week." Bella huffs out, clearly exasperated with my reasoning.

"You already know why I did that." I blow out a breath, feeling exasperated myself. "I fucked up. I'm human. I make mistakes just like any other man. But I can assure you that no other man will love you as much as I do. You and I, we were made for each other and I will always put you first in everything that I do. I will always do what I can to protect you." I shoot her a precarious smile. "You're my little moon. Keeping you happy and safe is my job."

The corner of her mouth lifts in a half-smile. "All that is beautiful, but I still don't understand how keeping that information was protecting me?"

"In all honesty, it wasn't just one thing. You say I don't trust you but that isn't it at all. I love you so much I can't bear the thought of you suffering any more than you already have in your short life. The thing with your father was weighing heavy on you and I couldn't bear to throw another bomb on top of what you were already dealing with... I also wasn't sure you'd want to stay with a person whose father helped ruin your parents' relationship."

"That's where you're supposed to trust me, William. I'm strong. I can handle whatever you have to tell me. I'll be okay. Besides, I would never blame you for the actions of another. That was between our parents. It had nothing to do with you." Bella looks into my eyes, concern and love shining through despite her own pain.

"I know that, but you can't blame me for wanting to keep you safe and away from any unnecessary suffering. I love you. You are so precious to me, and I never want you to feel anything other than joy."

"I love you too, William, but thinking like that is unrealistic. If you want something with me, something real, then we have to be a team. You have to be upfront with me about everything." Bella's gaze flicks back and forth between my eyes, searching for anything untold. "If there is something else you're keeping from me, now is the time to tell me. I don't think my heart could take another bombshell."

Letting out a breath, I let go of a half-truth. "There are other things that are under investigation. Nothing is confirmed which is why I haven't told you about them. I didn't want you to have to stress about something that could potentially be nothing."

"William, so help me God..." Bella narrows her eyes and moves to stand.

Reacting quickly, I grab her by the waist and pull her down onto me. "Bella, this is a two-way street. You also have to trust my judgment. If you want to be with me, you have to let me be a man and protect you. To some degree, at least. I understand that you're a strong independent woman, but you are still *my* woman."

Bella relents, softening her body into me as she pouts her pink lips. "I understand that. I just don't want to be blindsided when things happen."

"I get that," I say, wrapping my arms around Bella's waist. "I'm about to tell you something else and I need you to remember what you just said about not blaming me for the actions of others, okay?"

Bella nods, worry etched across her beautiful face.

"We recently discovered my mother was the one who ran into your car three years ago." I hang on to Bella, fully expecting her to bolt out of my lap, but she just sits there quietly—staring at me blankly.

Out of nowhere, Bella begins to laugh, and what began as a small giggle soon turns into full-blown fits of laughter.

"Bella? Are you okay?" I ask, concern riddling my voice.

"Oh, the irony. I've constantly avoided relationships, not allowing myself to love because of some fucked up notion that my mother's death was somehow my fault. Only to turn around and fall in love with a man whose mother was the real reason my mother died. I can't escape this. I will somehow always be linked to my mother's death."

Grabbing Bella's face between my hands, I force her to look at me. "Little moon, it's time you practiced what you preach. How can you blame yourself for the actions of others?" I ask as I stare into her tumultuous silver eyes. "It was my mother who decided to drive into your car, *not you*. It was our parents who decided to have an affair, *not you*." I wipe her tears away with the pad of my thumb before bringing her face to mine and kissing her forehead. "You and I, we were just pawns caught in the middle of their poor decisions. None of it was your fault, Bella. None of it."

"I get it. Really, I do. I just…" Bella cries out.

"Just let it go, Bella. Stop trying to atone for the sins of others and let it go. Let yourself live."

Bella falls into my chest, her silent tears soaking my shirt as she finally gives herself permission to let it all go.

We sit there in silence for a long while before either of us moves. Deciding to be the first, I lift Bella's face to mine and place a soft kiss on her lips, silently asking her if she's okay.

Bella's eyes flutter open, her eyes piercing me with their intensity. "I wanted to know everything." A sardonic laugh falls from her lips. "Be careful what you wish for, right?"

I smile a sad smile. "I promise, I won't keep any important information from you. But you have to understand that if I only have partial information, I'm still likely to keep it to myself." I stroke her hair, playing with the ends. "I never want to see you like this. Ever. It's my job to keep you happy, not to make you sad."

"Speaking of making me happy..." Bella shoots me a mischievous smile. "What are we going to do about our sleeping situation once we're back home? I'm sure Dad will want us to stay at the house and it will get tricky keeping our relationship from him."

"That reminds me, there's something else I have to tell you."

"Oh, god. I'm really regretting telling you I wanted to know everything." Bella lets out a self-deprecating laugh. "Okay. Seriously though, what now?"

"Heather was threatening to tell your father about us. That was another one of her sources of blackmail."

"I hate her!" Bella shouts.

"Shhh. You'll wake the boys." I press a finger to Bella's lips. "But, yes. I know. She's a piece of work."

"She's a piece of something, alright." Bella shakes her head in disgust. "So what's the plan then? Lay low for how long? We can't keep our secret forever, it's bound to get out."

"I think until your father is stable, and based on how well he handled himself today, I'd say that will be sooner rather than later. Also, the guys and I are working on a plan to take Heather down so it definitely won't be long

before we can resume our regularly scheduled activities."
I playfully waggle my brows.

"Good." Bella laughs and gently swats my shoulder.
"I've missed you like crazy and hate sleeping without you.
I'd hate to have to go and replace you."

"You wouldn't dare. I'd hunt you down and spank
your bottom raw." I bring my mouth to hers, swiping my
tongue across her plump lower lip, taking it into my
mouth and biting it hard.

Bella squeals. "You wouldn't..."

"Oh I would, and you don't even want to know what
I'd do to the poor schmuck who'd try to take my place."

"Is that so?" Bella moves to stand, wiggling her ass in
my face.

"Are you trying to tempt me, little moon?" I swat her
peach of an ass and let my hands linger, squeezing her
cheeks hard. "How about we go back to our room and
enjoy the little time we do have?"

Bella nods enthusiastically, eager to get started on our
fun.

Chapter Twenty-Six

ISABELLA

WE'RE BACK IN the Lone Star State and I find myself missing California every second of every day. Don't get me wrong, I'm happy my father is home and on his way to a full recovery; I just really miss the home I shared with William and our ability to be out in the open, without caring who saw us.

I stuff those feelings deep down and remind myself that this too shall pass. *This is temporary.*

We have an appointment with Dr. Ansley later this week and I'm hoping Dad will be fully discharged from his care, aka we won't have to tiptoe around him anymore.

"Morning," my father greets me as he enters the kitchen. "It smells so good in here."

"It's our weekend tradition. I make the boys pancakes and this week it happens to be blueberry, your favorite." I wink at Dad, wondering if he remembers.

"Of course. Thank you for making them. I never told you how much I appreciate your help around the house and with the boys. After your mother—" Getting a distant look in his eyes, Dad stops mid-sentence.

"You're welcome," I cut in, unsure if he had anything more to say.

Shaking his head as if to clear it from a fog, Dad continues where he left off. "After your mother died, I relied pretty heavily on you. That wasn't fair and I want to apologize. You deserved to be a kid if just for a couple of years more. I took that away from you."

That familiar burning behind my eyes begins to form, and for once I let it. "Thank you for telling me that, but I stopped being a child the day Lucia died."

Dad's bitter chuckle bounces off the marble surface, echoing through the room. "So you aren't calling her mother anymore?"

"She betrayed our family. I'd say she lost that right the day she decided to step out on your vows."

"Her vows to me and her role to you as your mother were two very different things, Bella." Losing the menacing glint, my father's eyes go soft as he reaches for my shoulder and squeezes. "Just because she was a shitty wife doesn't mean she was a shitty mother. She loved you and the boys very much. You were her world."

I scoff at his declaration on my mother's behalf. "If she loved us, she wouldn't have done something that ended up destroying her family."

"What are you talking about, Bella? How was her affair the catalyst to our destruction?"

Fuck. I've said too much.

"I'm just saying that infidelity breaks up a marriage, and the marriage is what holds a family together," I quickly say, hoping he's buying what I'm selling.

"No, Isabella. Love is what holds a family together and you have given that to us in spades. *You* are what's held our family together."

I turn away, unable to look my father in the eye. *If he only knew.* All these years of trying to be the perfect everything, when in reality I was just a fraud. An empty shell of a girl trying to find atonement for the sins of others instead of living my life and fighting for my dreams.

"I'm not going to college," I blurt out, unable to hold it in any longer.

"What did you say?" My father narrows his eyes and stares at me as if I've just told him I'm joining the circus.

"Going to college was never my dream. That was yours and Mom's. I want to write. I've already written a couple of books and I think I'm going to start shopping them around." I place the stack of fluffy pancakes on the table and try to act as if I hadn't just dropped a big bomb. *Way to keep the conversation light.*

"After all the money I've spent on private schooling, you're just going to drop out of college before you even start?" The look of bewilderment on my father's face transforms into anger. "No. You *are* going to college. What you do after that is up to you, but I've worked my ass off to give you this opportunity. I sent you to the best preparatory schools and made sure you always excelled in all of your classes so that when the day came, you would go to college. So you're going to fucking college."

"Between the car accident with Lucia and the work incident with you, I've learned that life is too damn short and I refuse to spend it doing something I don't love. I'm tired of just surviving, I want to thrive, and going to college for some stupid degree I'll never use isn't going to help me do that." I whip around the marble island and head for the pantry in search of the maple syrup. "And don't act like you contributed to my grades. While you were off on assignments, *I* was the one busting my ass to get good grades, *I* was the one who pushed myself to do better, always trying to compensate for the loss of a woman who wasn't even worth it."

My father's hand extends, slapping me across the face and making my head swivel to the side. "Don't speak of your mother like that. She may have been a cunt of a wife, but she was still your mother."

I hold my hand to my cheek, the sting of his slap still prickling on my skin. "You *slapped* me."

"I'm your father. I can discipline you as I see fit."

I stand there frozen in shock, unable to form words though I have plenty to say.

"Now, I hope our conversation has cleared up any confusion as to whether or not you're going to college. But in case it hasn't, let me spell it out for you. If you decide to veer from the path I've set for you, then you will be cut off financially. If you choose to pursue this ridiculous dream of yours, then you will do so on your own. I will not be a part of throwing your future down the drain." And with those words, my father walks out of the room, leaving me there in stunned silence.

I'm at the water park with the boys, still reeling from my conversation with our father earlier this morning. The whole scene keeps replaying in my mind, and I can't seem to shake the feeling that something just wasn't right. Besides the fact that I'm an adult and he can't tell me what to do, there's the fact that the man hit me. *He fucking hit me.* Something he hasn't done in the entirety of my eighteen years.

I make a mental note to ask Dr. Ansley about any behavioral changes the accident might have caused. I get that he was trying to be a concerned father, but he has never treated me like that before, always acting like more of a big brother than an actual father figure.

My phone vibrates and I see that it's William. Hoping this call will help change my mood, I slide the button to answer.

"Hey, hot stuff. Hope your Sunday is going better than mine."

"What happened? Whose ass do I have to kick?" William's concerned voice settles my nerves and soothes my aching heart.

"Oh it's nothing. Just a little father-daughter quarrel. No biggie. What's going on with you this morning?" I say lightly, hoping he'll drop the subject.

"What happened with Aiden? Is something going on with his recovery?"

Nope. He's not going to drop it.

Letting out a slow breath, I fess up, "I told him I didn't want to go to college and he freaked out on me. Said he was going to cut me off financially if I decided to pursue my dream of being an author, but not before smacking me across the face for bad-mouthing my adulterous mother."

"He fucking slapped you?" William seethes, his rage so palpable I can practically feel it coming through the phone.

"Yeah. I think something's up with him. He's never been one to physically discipline his children. Much less now that I'm an adult. I really need to talk to his doctor about that later this week. But for now, I'm just going to steer clear of him."

William lets out an audible sigh. "Baby, I don't like the fact that he put his hands on you. I'm tempted to go pluck you from his house and bring you here. If Aiden shows any other signs of aggression, I want you to take the boys and move in with me right away. I mean it, Bella."

"Thanks for the offer but that wouldn't go over well with the Wicked Witch of the West. Speaking of which, how are things going with Heather?" I ask, eager for some good news.

"Really good. We've gained access to her emails and are hoping to find something real soon. In the meantime, I think you should send your book out to agents and see if you get a bite. I bet you dinner and a blow job that you get an offer before the summer is over."

My dirty dirty man.

I smile to myself, shaking my head at his boyish behavior. "That sounds like a win-win to me, Mr. Hawthorne. I'll take the bet and reap its reward either way. But I'll have you know, in full disclosure and fairness, I've already submitted my books to a couple of literary agents as well as entered a contest for a publishing house. Hopefully one of those will take."

"So productive, my little moon." William's pride in me never ceases to amaze me. This man has always been my biggest supporter, even when I didn't know it, he was there, cheering me on and being my rock. "See. There's no way we aren't going to win this bet."

"William, you do know that normally there's only one winner when it comes to betting, right?"

"Well, you and me? We're anything but normal," William quips.

Letting that sink in, I know he's right. We lost the notion of normality a long time ago. Between the huge age difference and William's friendship with my uncle and father, our relationship is anything but normal.

A self-assured smile grabs ahold of my lips as I say, "I wouldn't have it any other way."

Chapter Twenty-Seven

WILLIAM

WE'RE SO CLOSE I can almost taste it. For the past couple of hours, the team and I have been scouring Heather's emails for any sign of nefarious activity. If I could just find something to bring her down, Bella and I wouldn't have to hide our relationship and Ashley could go back to her life in Florida. I feel terrible for having to impose on her, asking her to watch Harper again, but there really is no one else I'd trust my daughter with besides her or Bella.

Speaking of my sister, Ashley pokes her head into the study. "Hey guys, you've been in here for a while. Do you want me to whip y'all up something to eat? Chef doesn't get back until next month so you're stuck with my cooking." Lifting a finger into the air, she adds, "I might not be Michelin rated, but I can make a pretty mean sandwich."

"Thank you, Ashley. We'd really appreciate it," Titus answers.

I look back at Ashley and see that a blush has begun to appear on her face and neck. *That's odd. Titus is making my sister blush?* I make a mental note to talk to Ashley about that before speaking up. "You're already helping a ton with Harper. How about you order something from Marco's. My spare card is in the kitchen drawer. Get whatever you think we'll like."

"You've got it. That's my favorite kind of cooking." Ashley winks at us before slipping out of the room.

I look over at Titus and notice that his eyes are still lingering on the door where Ashley had been a moment ago, his gaze unwavering. *Something's definitely going on there.*

Hudson clears his throat, breaking the suspicious stare I was giving Titus. "I think I found something.

There's a set of encrypted emails and they all seem to be between the same two sources."

"Great," I say, praying that this is what we've been looking for. "Point us to them and we can all work on decoding. Hopefully we'll have our answer by this afternoon."

"First one to break through gets a bottle of their favorite liquor!" Ren bellows.

"It's on like *Donkey Kong*!" Titus chimes.

"Who even says that anymore?" I say, rolling my eyes and shaking my head back and forth. "But in case y'all were wondering, I'll be the first to find the source. Gentlemen, prepare yourselves, you're going to lose," I rib the team, stoking their competitive nature.

Three hours later and we still haven't found anything. Ashley came in about an hour ago with take-out from Marco's, practically forcing us all to take a break and eat. I have to admit, it's nice having her home.

I decide to take another break to check on Ashley and Harper. I've barely seen them all day and I like to make sure I spend enough time with them on the weekends.

Our parents were never home, my father was always working and my mother off at some event; and if by some miracle they were home, they would hide themselves away in their respective corners of the house. My father in his study and my mother in her room, constantly downing martinis to numb herself from reality.

They never had enough time for Ashley and me—we were a nuisance. A mere disturbance they could pawn off on the multitude of nannies.

I squeeze my eyes shut, trying to forget the memories. *I never want to be like them.* Once I found out I was going to be a father, I vowed to never be like them, making sure to always dedicate time to my child. So far so good. I do work a lot but I also have a special daddy-daughter date once a week and make time for her on the weekends.

Stepping into the playroom, I see Ashley and Harper playing with her lovey collection. I swear that girl has more stuffed animals than Ashley does shoes.

"Did you find the source?" Ashley asks as she waves a stuffed panda in front of Harper.

"No, the team is still working on it."

"You're going to lose out on that bottle of liquor if you don't find it first." Ashley purses her lips, trying to bite back her laughter.

"You know I don't need it. It's a good incentive for them though, you know how they like to win at everything."

"Yes. I know." Ashley smirks, her face flushing from a memory.

"What's up with that?" I ask, pointing at her face.

"What?"

"You're all pink. You turned all pink earlier when Titus talked to you too." I arch a brow and notice how her face manages to turn an even brighter shade of red at the mention of Titus. "There!" I shout as I point at her face. "You're doing it again."

"Calm down, I'm not doing anything. It's just hot in here." Ashley fans herself, trying to add credence to her lie.

"It's sixty-eight degrees in here, Ashley. It's the constant temperature in every one of my homes and you know that, so cut the act and stop flirting with my team. Besides, won't your boyfriend back home be upset if he knew you were getting all hot and bothered by someone other than him?"

"That piece of shit can go fuck himself for all I care," Ashley growls, practically foaming at the mouth.

"Language! Little ears." I motion toward Harper.

"I'm sorry." Ashley brings her hand to her mouth, her eyes as big as saucers. "I don't know what came over me."

"I'm assuming it's whatever that POS did to you. So what happened with the boyfriend? Do I need to go kick his a—, I mean, behind?" I look toward Harper and wonder if 'behind' is a bad word under this context.

"You're correct in assuming he did something. We're no longer together and no, you don't need to go kick his patootie." Ashley waves me away. "Now go back to what you were doing, I really don't want to talk about it. Besides, Harper and I were having a good time until you showed up. Wanting to talk about things that are best left in the past is definitely not our idea of fun, right Harper?"

Harper coos at Ashley while mashing a pacifier into her baby gorilla's mouth.

"See? Harper totally agrees with her auntie Ashley."

"Hint taken. I know when I'm not wanted." I chuckle as I head toward the door.

"It wasn't a hint. It was an outright statement," Ashley grumbles.

Before I can reach the door, it flings open and Ren stumbles through. "Found him!" Ren shouts over his shoulder before turning back to face me. "We've got something. You definitely want to get your ass into the study."

"Language!" I exclaim. "Poor Harper is going to have the mouth of a sailor thanks to y'all."

Ren cringes. "Sorry, man. Not used to little ones being around."

"Yeah, yeah. Just show me what you found," I mutter and follow him out of the playroom.

The entire team is huddled around me as I click open a thread, exposing the other party as one Shannon

Daugherty. *I've never heard of her before.* It looks like she's been in constant contact with Heather, with their conversations getting lengthier on the dates of my divorce proceedings.

"Look here." Ren points to a particular thread. "This Daugherty chick is basically assuring Heather she will win her hearing. Wasn't this the date your first case was dismissed by the judge?"

"*Fuck me.* It sure is," I say, sucking in a deep breath. *This is it. This is the link we've been looking for.* "Titus and Ren, I need you to search for anything you can find on Shannon Daugherty. Where she lives, who she's associated with, and what her damn schedule is like. Hudson, you and I keep searching through the threads and see if we can dig up any additional information that could help us possibly reverse the court's rulings thus far."

"Ten-four," the team responds all at once.

"Great job, men. I'm so fucking happy, I'm getting every damn one of you a bottle of your favorite liquor!"

Hoots and hollers are heard across the study before the men buckle down, digging for the rest of the information. The information that will finally let Bella and me just be.

Thank fuck. Despite my best efforts to reassure Bella everything will be okay, I've felt a notable distance growing between us.

Between Heather's threats, Bella's preconceived notions of not deserving love, and dreading her father's disapproval and relapse in recovery, it's safe to say this relationship has been an uphill battle.

Despite all that, I know the reward will be worth it. She is, without a doubt, the love of my life and I can't ever see myself without her.

"Found something!" Titus shouts. "It appears our Shannon Daugherty is constantly mentioned as the companion to one judge in particular, the Honorable Andrew Dawson. Isn't this the first judge who ruled on your case?"

"It sure as fuck is." I close my eyes and send up a silent thank you to the powers that be. *This bitch is going down.*

"I can't find any actual images of her, though." Titus narrows his eyes as he continues to scroll through information on his laptop. "I'm going to see if I can find her on one of the society pages in the local newspaper. She's bound to appear at some charity function, seeing as how she's the arm candy for a prominent Dallas judge."

"That's a great idea. Ren, how about you search for any social media presence?" I suggest, rubbing my palms together in anticipation.

"Already on it." Ren waggles his brows while shooting me a face splitting grin. "These ladies are going down."

"Between the damning emails assuring a courtroom victory, and the social ties this mystery woman possesses, they better go down." I sour my face in disgust. "Heather's balls never seem to amaze me. They seem to be bigger than an elephant's. Who in their right mind would go up against someone who owns a private security firm?"

"Someone with nothing to lose," Hudson adds, raising a brow.

"I suppose you're right." I nod once, agreeing but not fully understanding. I still think the bitch is crazy.

Ren cuts into my thoughts, "It looks like Shannon Daugherty didn't exist beyond three years ago. She appeared out of thin air and has managed to stay out of the media since. All of her social media accounts are active but her profile image is always of some generic outdoor scene and her posts are never of her, just random shots of Dallas. Nothing with her face on it."

"Keep looking. Try and see if you can find anything where she's been tagged or appears in the background. Look at accounts for people who run in the same circles and see if you spot a woman repeatedly by the judge's side," I urge, knowing there has to be a way to uncover this woman's true identity.

The whole team nods in agreement before looking back down at their laptops and resuming their search.

Hours later, I find myself rubbing my tired eyes and looking around the room. The men have been working since five a.m. and everyone looks exhausted. I'm about to call it a day when someone clears their throat.

"William?" Titus questions, sounding apprehensive. "I think I found Shannon Daugherty."

"Okay, why do you sound like you're about to deliver an apology with that?" I bring my brows together in confusion.

"Yeah. About that... do you happen to have any pictures of your mother lying around? I could be wrong, but the woman who keeps appearing by the judge's side bears a strong resemblance to the woman who used to live in your home and threw back martinis like they were alkaline water."

My entire body goes rigid and a cold sweat begins to form down my back. *That* was the last person I expected when discussing Heather's source... *my mother.*

Chapter Twenty-Eight

WILLIAM

"THAT'S DEFINITELY HER. There's no mistaking her eyes," I say after inspecting the photos on the screen.

"You mean those empty pools of black? Yeah, it figures. They look about as dark as her soul," Ren adds bitterly. There's no question as to how he feels about the woman who intentionally ran into Bella's car three years ago. Hate would be putting it mildly.

I blink multiple times, trying to clear my mind from the shock this new information has added to the ever-growing pile of shit I'm going to have to tell Bella.

It just had to be my mother.

I run a hand over my face, unable to repress the hysterical laughter bubbling out of me.

"I'm the perfect catch, aren't I?" I roll my neck, trying to release the tension this new piece of information has brought on. "Let's look at the facts, shall we? My father had an affair with my secret girlfriend's mother; a girlfriend I have to keep secret because of my psycho ex who happens to be in cahoots with my mother; my mother who tried to kill my secret girlfriend and her mother by running into them with her car. Oh, and did I mention that my mother has a new identity? An identity she's using to sabotage my relationships and make it impossible for me to divorce my psycho ex."

Another bout of hysterical laughter rips from my throat, giving the rest of the team pause. No doubt they think I'm in the middle of some sort of mental crisis.

"I'm fine. Really," I try to assure the men as I wipe away the tears of laughter. "Seriously. We have a lot of work to do. I need to find a link to the second judge and present it to my attorney as soon as possible. The faster I get this done, the faster I can move Bella in."

"You still have to worry about Aiden." Ren arches a brow. "And don't think we're done with our conversation about that. Remember... bodily harm." Ren pounds his fist into his palm.

"Yeah, yeah. I get it. Now get back to work. I need that information."

Titus cuts into our banter with a loud clap ringing through the air. "Shit, I've got it!" Titus calls out. "I can't believe it. Your mom outright promised Heather she'd win, twice. That woman is *not* cut out to be a felon. That's like criminal activity 101, don't put anything down in writing."

"What can I say, the woman is a piece of work. At least her ineptitude as a criminal is working in our favor." I close my eyes and rub at my temples, needing this all to be done. "Send me what you've gathered thus far and I'll start preparing it for my attorney. The next step would be to try to access my mother's email and see if we can catch the judge responding to her. I think what we have should be sufficient to reverse any of the prior rulings, but I want to make sure those dirty judges pay for the bullshit they've put Bella and me through."

"Hear, hear," the men speak in unison.

"William, what can I do for you at this fine hour?" Daniel answers the phone sarcastically.

"I know it's the ass-crack of dawn but my team found the information we were looking for and I wanted to get it to you as soon as possible. Heather has been in communication with someone who is dating one of the judges who presided over our case. This person, who happens to be my mother—a story for another time— confirmed in writing that she was guaranteed a win in both cases. When my team dug a little deeper they were able to locate communications between my mother and the other judge as well as her current beau, substantiating our claims of collusion."

"It looks like your team has been very busy. Very busy indeed." Daniel slurps something loudly before emitting a noise of satisfaction. "Now that I've had my first sip of coffee, we can continue."

"I'd apologize but it wouldn't be sincere." I chuckle, knowing it was brazen of me to call this early but not really caring. "So where do we go from here?"

"Send me everything you've been able to acquire and I will channel the pertinent pieces to the appropriate authorities. We won't be able to utilize it as legal evidence because of how it was obtained but it will enable us to get warrants on electronics and such. These will undoubtedly lead us to the same or similar information, though this time through a legal venue."

"How fast can we get this done?" I ask, already thinking of how I'm going to get Bella home.

"Pretty quickly. I have a great team that handles this sort of thing."

"What, psycho exes and criminal mothers?" I ask in jest.

"I'm glad to see your sense of humor is back. But no, I'm talking about taking fruit from the poisonous tree and turning it into manna from heaven." Daniel laughs at his own brand of joke, quickly stopping once he realizes I'm not laughing with him. "Don't worry, William. We will handle everything and you will be divorced sooner than you can say rule in perpetuity."

I shake my head as Daniel makes another attempt at a joke. "Why don't you stick to your day job. I don't think you were cut out to be a comedian."

"Oh pish posh. That was funny. I know, funny." Daniel laughs, mumbling something about perpetuity under his breath.

"Sure, you keep telling yourself that. I'm just glad you're a damn good lawyer. Keep me posted on any progress. I want to know everything, every step of the way," I say emphatically.

"Yes, of course. I'll get my staff on it right away. We should be able to get warrants on your mother and Heather very soon, providing you're not objecting to either."

"*Fuck no.* It's time these women paid for their actions and stopped destroying the lives of others."

"Very well then. I'll be in touch."

The line goes dead as I stare at my phone in contemplation. *Could this really be over?*

I'm about to tuck my phone away when the screen lights up showing an incoming call. It's Mariana.

"Hello?" I answer, curious as to why she's calling this early.

"Morning," Mariana greets with a matter-of-fact tone. "There's been developing information on my sister's car accident and we need to question Aiden. I wanted to give you a heads up that I'll be visiting him later today to talk to him about what we uncovered and figured you'd want to tell him what you know beforehand."

"Thanks for letting me know. I'll head over to his house as soon as I'm able to rally the team," I say, thankful for the notice.

"No problem. Take care."

Hanging up my phone for the second time that morning, I make my way to the coffeemaker. "I can't believe I've accomplished so much before my first cup of coffee," I say to myself as I pour an extra-large cup, making sure to fill it to the brim. *Lord knows I'm going to need every last drop if I'm going to be playing alarm clock to the team.*

"Aiden, you really need to hire a full-time nanny," Ren complains. "I can't fill in for Bella all the time."

"Bella can't hold out on me forever. She loves the boys and will be back to her regular self in no time." Aiden waves away Ren's concern.

The whole team has managed to crowd around Aiden's kitchen island, scarfing down the kolaches and coffee we brought over, knowing the information we were about to deliver was less than ideal.

"What's going on?" I ask without trying to sound overly interested.

"Bella has gone on strike ever since dear old dad over here shut down her dreams of becoming an author," Ren answers before turning back toward Aiden. "You need to bite the bullet, man. Apologize to her and hire a damn nanny. You were going to do that once she started college in the fall anyway. What's the big deal?"

"The big deal is she dropped out of college before she's even begun!" Aiden shouts, his vocal cords vibrating with each word. "If I hire a nanny, she will think that it's okay for her to forgo all of her responsibilities to pursue a fruitless dream."

"Fruitless?" I curl my lip and sneer. "Have you seen her work? She's brilliant. There's no doubt in my mind she could have a successful career as an author if she wished to be one."

"What is this, gang-up-on-Aiden day?" Aiden argues in defense.

"No. It's keep-it-real-with-Aiden day. Bella told us you were released from Dr. Ansley's care and that means no more sugar-coating things," Hudson adds.

"Well, shit. If you've been sugar-coating things before, I can't wait to hear what you have to say now," Aiden quips.

Hudson runs a hand through his hair, nervously shifting his gaze between everyone. "The reason we're here is to talk to you about your wife. Well, more like something involving your wife."

"You mean my adulterous spouse? By all means, please tell me what could be worse than finding out the woman you've idolized was sleeping with one of your friend's father," Aiden grits out.

"It's not worse, per se," Titus states, turning his palms up and shrugging his shoulders. "It's just news that could be considered shocking."

"Well, what is it then? We don't have all day," Aiden prompts.

"We found out who the driver was the night of the car accident," I rush to reply, needing to be the one to tell Aiden this information. Thankfully, the team seems to understand and they all back off giving me the floor. "Aiden, before I tell you, you need to understand that the authorities believe it was an intentional hit. The person who ran into your wife and daughter did so with the intent to harm, and most likely kill."

"You mean to tell me someone set out to hurt my wife and daughter? How the fuck could I not know about this?" Aiden's face contorts in outrage. "When did you find out about this? Is the person still out there?"

A female voice responds in my place.

"Oh, she's very much out there. Isn't she, William?" Heather trains her wild gaze on me, cocking the revolver nestled between her outstretched hands.

At once, we all turn our eyes toward the madwoman who's begun to pace back and forth in Aiden's kitchen.

"Heather, what are you doing here?" Aiden asks, his brows furrowing in deep confusion.

"You mean they haven't clued you in?" Heather laughs, waving her gun in the air in a circular motion. "Well, sit down, darlin'. I'm about to fill you in."

Chapter Twenty-Nine

ISABELLA

I'M COMING BACK from a run when I see William's SUV parked in front of my father's house. *That's odd. I didn't know he was planning on a visit.* I'm about to enter the house when a familiar car catches my eye. Heather's pink SLC Roadster sits empty across the street, which could only mean she's already somewhere on the property.

I'll be damned if I'm going to let that woman threaten me. If anyone is going to tell my father about William and me, it will be me.

I march up the entryway stairs and into the open living space but can't hear any commotion. Suddenly, a loud pop reverberates throughout the entire home. *Was that a gunshot?* The loud pop sounds off once more and now I'm certain someone is shooting off a gun in the house.

I lower myself to the ground and quickly dial the police from my smartwatch, praying it's close enough to the actual phone to catch a signal. *I knew I should have gone with the cellular version.*

"911, state your emergency," a voice greets from my wrist.

"Hello, yes. We have an intruder at five fifty-five Romansky Way. They have a gun," I answer as quietly as possible.

"We've already received a request for service from that location. It appears a silent alarm was triggered and help has been dispatched. Expect someone to arrive soon."

As soon as the woman finishes speaking, I'm able to hear shouting in the kitchen. "Ma'am, ma'am, if you could please stay quiet, I'm not sure how to lower the volume on my watch and I don't want the intruder to hear me."

I crawl a little closer to the commotion once the operator agrees to remain silent. I definitely don't want to insert myself into the middle of a shootout, so I quietly step into the kitchen hallway, and immediately my jaw drops at what I see.

Heather is restrained in a chair and her hands are being cuffed by Hudson while William picks up a revolver with a large freezer bag.

"Where the fuck is your security team, Aiden?" Titus asks my father.

"I gave them the day off. I'm a fucking SEAL. I don't need a damn security detail," my father rebuffs.

"You gave them the day off?! You might not need the security but Bella and the twins do. For fuck's sake, what would've happened if they were in the room when Heather came in wielding her gun?" William roars, the veins in his neck pulsating wildly.

"I'm here. I'm okay." I step into the kitchen, letting everyone know I'm uninjured. "And the twins are over at the neighbors for a play date."

"You got lucky." William glares at my father while making his way to me. As soon as he reaches me, he pulls me into an embrace and presses a kiss to my forehead. "I'm so fucking glad you're okay." He breathes into my skin.

ACTS OF ATONEMENT

"What the hell is going on?" My dad looks between William and me, no doubt confused with the sudden affection.

"You didn't know, did you?" Heather cackles from her seat. "Daddy's perfect little angel isn't so perfect."

"Shut your mouth, Heather," I growl out before turning to face my father. I'm about to tell him about our relationship when William beats me to it.

"I'm in love with your daughter, Aiden," William says matter-of-factly.

And just like that, all the air leaves my lungs. To hear him declare his love for me so openly, *to my father*, brings me an immense sense of peace.

I hadn't realized how much our sneaking around was affecting me until this very moment. Having to constantly worry about keeping things from my father, or letting something slip out in public was weighing me down and this moment of liberation has left me feeling so light and free.

"How fucking sweet." Heather breaks into my moment of joy, wrecking it with her sarcasm. "Well fuck you and your happily ever after. Marissa—Oh wait, she goes by Shannon now." Heather rolls her eyes and shakes her head before continuing. "*Shannon* promised me this would be easy and that everything would be okay. She and I were supposed to be on some remote island sipping daiquiris by now, not having a care in the world. But nooooo. William wouldn't take me back because of *this* little bitch." Heather points her head toward me as I sit there stunned by all the verbal diarrhea that's coming out of her mouth.

"Watch yourself, Heather. You will not talk about Bella like that," William warns her through clenched teeth.

"You can't control me." Heather scoffs. "I will not let you hold me back, William Hawthorne. You screwed me over once with that damn prenup and I will not let you do it again." Heather seethes as everyone watches her verbally spar with William.

"Is that what this is about? The prenup?"

"Yes! If you would have let me walk away with some money, this wouldn't even be happening right now. Once I realized I wasn't going to get anything from you, I had to come back. Otherwise I'd be left with nothing. That's when your genius of a mother approached me, talking about some hair-brained scheme to clean you out once you and I were back together. Apparently her stash of money had run out and she was in need of replenishing her funds too."

"Fucking money. It all boils down to money and greed. Coveting that which isn't yours to possess." William shakes his head in disgust.

"Of course it's about money. Haven't you been paying attention? Well, the part where your mother killed your father... *that* was more out of blind jealousy. But I mean, someone was threatening to take away her cash cow, so could you really blame her?"

"Yes!" everyone shouts in unison.

"Whatever. Just be glad I didn't try to kill you and Bella, like your mother did with your father and Lucia. Though trashing Bella's car felt pretty damn good."

"That was you?" I gasp in surprise at the same time as William shouts, "Of course it was my mother!"

"Yup." Heather pops her P, seemingly unaffected by being handcuffed to a chair.

"Yes to what? You were the one who vandalized Bella's car, or my mother was the one who murdered my father?" William asks.

"Yes to both of those. I shot Bella's tires out with that gun right there." Heather points her head toward the gun inside the plastic bag. "It was a gift from your treacherous mother. Said she couldn't look at it any longer, something about it being the gun she used on your father."

William shares a knowing look between Ren, Titus, and Hudson. I'm guessing they already suspected as much.

"I never should have trusted that woman. But she assured me over and over again that she could make it so I could win my hearing and get back into William's good graces." Heather laughs maniacally. "We hadn't counted on William fucking the nanny though. That definitely threw a wrench in our plans." Heather turns her head to look at me. "You dug your heels in real good, didn't you honey?"

I narrow my eyes at Heather, unable to keep quiet any longer. "Don't blame me if you never appreciated what was right in front of you. You were the one who walked away from a life with William and Harper. Throughout this entire breakdown of yours, you haven't even mentioned her once!"

"You could have them both for all I care. I just needed the money. Instead, I get a call from the mastermind herself telling me that the jig is up. That there are warrants out for our arrest and she's going into hiding. Do you think the brain decided to take her underling with her? Noooo. That's too much to ask for. After all, I only did every little thing she asked of me, including keeping her damn secrets. Did y'all know she was the hit and run driver that killed Lucia? If only she could have killed Isabella too." Heather hocks a loogie, aiming it toward me but missing by a long shot. *Thank god for small miracles.*

A second later there's a loud bang at the front of the house. We all crane our necks in an attempt to see what caused the noise, but we're unable to see anything because of the way the kitchen is closed off.

Luckily, we don't have to wait long for an answer. A team of heavily armed police officers and FBI agents descend into the kitchen.

"Looks like your time is up, Heather," I add a little too cheerily for the occasion. "You're going down after that beautiful confession you just delivered."

"I have no idea what you're talking about. I haven't said a word this entire time, and you can't prove otherwise."

The entire room goes silent. *Surely she can't get away with everything she just admitted to being a part of, can she?*

"Ma'am? Ma'am? Are you still there?" A woman's voice breaks through the silence. Everyone turns to look at each other trying to figure out where the voice is coming from when it speaks again. "Ma'am? Ma'am, this is the 911 dispatcher."

"Yes! I'm still here," I say, bringing my wrist closer to my mouth. "I'm so sorry. I forgot you were there."

"Oh, don't worry. I just wanted to let you know that it is our protocol to record all incoming calls. This entire conversation has been recorded and can be pulled up for future review if you'd so wish."

"*Well, shit,*" Heather mumbles under her breath as the entire room breaks out into a combination of snickers or outright laughter.

Chapter Thirty

WILLIAM

THE AUTHORITIES HAVE cleared out and Heather has been taken into custody. *One down, one to go.* I may be a cold-hearted bastard, but a son can only take so much from his mother, and I think my mother has far exceeded my limit for forgiveness.

Looking around the room, everyone appears to be as shell-shocked by this morning's events as me—especially Bella. I'm just now getting a chance to really look at her, and the sight of her in her tiny shorts is making my body react in ways it shouldn't while in the presence of her father. She must have been coming in from a morning run when Heather decided to stop by with her antics.

Bella is wearing a black sports bra with matching running shorts. Her hair is up in a high ponytail with loose strands clinging to her skin, damp with perspiration. I love her like this. Fresh with no makeup on and with her skin showing the slightest flush—*though I prefer to be the reason behind her flush.* My eyes continue to rove over Bella's barely dressed figure and it takes everything in me to keep my hands to myself out of respect for Aiden.

Unfortunately, my perusal of Bella's body doesn't go unnoticed. Feeling a set of eyes boring into me, I reluctantly look up and meet their owner.

"Done eye fucking my daughter?" Aiden asks me, his voice rasping with restrained anger.

"We were going to tell you, Aiden. But with your injury, we needed to make sure that it wouldn't set back any of your progress." I try to remain as calm as possible, hoping this conversation doesn't turn physical. It's not that I couldn't hold my own, but the man just suffered a brain injury for fuck's sake, he doesn't need to be getting into any brawls at the moment.

"Daddy." Bella speaks from behind me, her voice sounding so small. "It wasn't like we planned this."

"Silence, Bella. This is between William and me," Aiden admonishes while simultaneously cluing in the rest of the room that this is a private conversation. The guys take the hint and start to file out, giving us some privacy. "How long? How long has this been going on right under my nose? She just turned eighteen, William. Did you sleep with her before then? Do we need the police to come back?"

"Daddy!" Bella exclaims, visibly upset by Aiden's reaction.

I bring Bella forward, tucking her into the crook of my arm and place a kiss on her temple. "It's okay, baby," I whisper into her hair before looking back toward Aiden. "No you do not need to call the police. We started our relationship well after she turned eighteen."

"Well after, *my ass.* She's still a little girl, William. She doesn't even drink, for goodness' sake." Aiden shakes his head back and forth.

"If you truly paid attention to your daughter, you would know she stopped being a little girl a long time ago, and you would also know that she has very fine taste in whiskey." I smirk, giving Bella a side glance.

"Thanks for ratting me out," she mutters under her breath, shoving her elbow into my ribs.

I look toward Aiden who is standing in silence, no doubt second-guessing what he thinks he knows versus what is reality.

"This isn't a fling, Aiden. I love her and I think she loves me too." I look over toward Bella who is nodding her head emphatically. "Bella is mine. She's my forever and there will be no other—regardless of whether you approve or not."

"Over my rotting corpse." Aiden growls. "You with your insane family genes. Do you think I want that around my daughter? *Fuck no.* I saw your face when I revealed Lucia was having an affair with your father. *You already knew.* You knew it and you never told me about it." Aiden's gaze narrows into small slits. "What kind of brother, honorary or not, thinks it's okay to keep such important information to themselves? You were just sitting on that information, all while taking advantage of my sweet daughter."

"Daddy, it wasn't like that. It was for your own good," Bella pleads, her eyes big and round.

Aiden turns his gaze on Bella, his brows furrowing before speaking. "You knew about this too, didn't you?"

"Yes. But I only kept it from you to avoid causing you any unnecessary pain. She was gone. What good would telling you do?"

"How long, Isabella? How long have you known your mother was stepping out on me?"

"Since the day of the car accident," Bella whispers, her voice barely audible. "I walked in on her and..." She trails off, the room going silent at her admission.

Did she know it was my father? She couldn't have, she seemed just as shocked as everyone else.

"Not only do you go and sleep with your father's business partner and friend, but you also go and keep important shit like this from me too? Oh, and you're dropping out of college before even attending your first class. Let's not forget *that*." Aiden sucks in his lips while shaking his head. "You are *not* the perfect daughter I thought you were."

At his words, Bella sucks in a sharp breath.

"*Enough!*" I roar. "You will not talk to her like that. She *is* perfect. She is unbelievably smart, extremely patient, and one of the most supportive people I have ever met. You will not belittle her for keeping something from you when her actions were driven by love. She loves you, Aiden. You are her father and the only parent she has left. While you've been busy with your head up your ass, she's been raising herself and the boys, all while balancing the guilt of her mother's death and holding on to a toxic secret, bearing the pain of it herself in order to protect you from it."

Aiden's face twists in pain. "I'm your father, Bella. You should have told me."

"You haven't exactly been present." Bella chews on her bottom lip while focusing on the ground as if it's the most interesting thing she's seen all day. "You've been gone a long time. Since Mom died. Physically, you're present, but emotionally you've checked out."

"I'm your father, Isabella! You should have told me!" Aiden shouts, repeating his words from earlier.

"When?! When was I supposed to tell you?!" Bella shouts back. "Whenever I would try to talk to you about anything remotely emotional, you would shut me down—either changing the subject or just straight up walking out of the room." Bella wipes at the tears streaming down her face. "So tell me father, when the fuck was I supposed to tell you?"

Aiden takes a step back upon hearing Bella's words, as if they've physically struck him. "You will not disrespect me in my own home. If you want to go behind my back, keeping secrets and doing things I don't approve of, by all means, go ahead. But you will not be doing it while living under my roof. As of this moment, you are no longer a part of this family. You are nothing." Aiden lifts his hand and points toward the door. "Get the fuck out!"

Isabella

I stand there trying to process my father's words. *I'm alone. I'm utterly and completely alone.* My worst fear has come true and I've lost what remains of my family.

I wipe the tears rolling down my face and will them to stop, but they don't.

I knew this day would come, where both of my parents would abandon me. *I don't deserve their love. I don't deserve* any *love.* Time and time again, life has proven this to be true, so why should this time be any different.

My mother turned her back on me the moment she decided to step out on our family, and now my father is abandoning me out of some jacked-up sense of betrayal.

Surrendering to what is, I place one foot in front of the other and begin to make my way out of my father's home.

Maybe Cassie will let me crash at her place for a while.

Vaguely, I hear people talking behind me but it's all a jumbled mess as I try and figure out where I belong, if anywhere.

You are nothing. You. Are. Nothing.

My father's words keep replaying in my head over and over again, as another slicing pain rips through my soul.

I need to run. Run until I'm numb and can't feel this deep ache in my chest. I stop and close my eyes for a second, needing to catch my breath. The pain is so excruciating it feels as if I were being cut from the inside, making it impossible to breathe.

Letting the emptiness swallow me whole, I crumple to the ground, unable to walk any farther.

Just when I begin to wish I could disappear into the ground, a strong set of hands scoop me up. I crane my head up to see a set of pale blue eyes staring back at me.

William. I blink hard, trying to clear my vision and regain my sense of surroundings.

"Baby." William's soothing voice cuts through my mental fog. "I stayed behind to talk to your father, and I come out to find you like this. Did you fall? Are you okay?"

I shake my head no, unable to formulate any words. The hurt running through me, shattering my soul and rendering me speechless. I just want to hide from the pain. Dig a deep hole and bury myself.

William presses a kiss to my temple and carries me to his car. When he places me in the passenger seat, I realize he must be taking me home with him.

"No. Take me to my car," I manage to say.

"We can pick it up later. You're in no condition to drive," William states, his tone letting me know there's no room for argument.

But then again, I'm not one to listen.

"No, William. You need to take me to my car. I need to get to Cassie's."

"Isabella." William lets out a frustrated breath. "Stop being so damn stubborn and just acquiesce for once. You're coming home with me. That's where you belong."

"I don't belong anywhere. *I. Am. Nothing,*" I grit out, my words coming out choked as the lump in my throat grows.

"Do *not* say that. You are everything. Do you hear me? Everything!" William grabs me by the shoulders and shakes me until my tear ridden eyes are looking directly into his. "You belong with me. You are my everything and I will show you your worth every single day for the rest of our lives if you'll just let me." William's eyes are pleading, seeking permission into my soul. "Let me in, Isabella. Let me show you how amazing you are."

I stare blankly at William, not knowing what to say. I love this man. I really do, and that's why I can't go live with him. "No, William. I'm broken. You deserve someone who is whole. Someone who could give themselves fully to you and to Harper. That's not me, no matter how much I want it to be."

"But don't you see, Bella? That *is* you. Without you, I'm not whole. You take my broken pieces and put them back together with your love. When you've shown up for Harper every single time, you've made me whole. When you've been patient with me, unwavering in your love, you've made me whole. When you've shared your smile on some of my darkest days, you've made me whole. You, Bella, are what makes me complete. Let me do that for you, always. Come live with me, and I promise you I'll do whatever it takes to make sure you never feel empty again."

Wiping away my tears, I nod my head in agreement—realizing that William is just as broken as I am and that maybe, just maybe, we could help each other heal, erasing the jagged wounds of our past.

Chapter Thirty-One

ISABELLA

THREE MONTHS LATER...

I'm rocking Harper to sleep when William walks in
holding a large envelope in his hand. It must be good
news because his face can barely contain his joy. Lifting

one finger, I signal that Harper is asleep and move us toward her crib.

After some stealthy maneuvering, I'm able to get her down for her nap and tiptoe quietly out of her room. Once outside, I look up at William and see that he still possesses the same wide grin.

"What has you so excited? Are those your divorce papers?" I ask, curious to find out what's got him so giddy.

"No, but it's just as good. As your literary agent, I took the liberty of sending a couple of letters out." William's mouth splits into a mischievous grin as his teeth bite into his plump lower lip.

At his confession, my jaw drops and my eyes practically bulge out of their sockets. To say that I was surprised would be an understatement.

"I had no idea you were my *agent*." I look up at him beneath my lashes and smirk. "Or that you were sending out letters on my behalf. Despite the fact that you seriously overstepped, I have to admit, I truly am grateful." I raise both brows and let loose an excited smile.

"I *did not* overstep. I have a college buddy who works at a publishing house. I pitched him your books and he wanted to take a look at them. No big deal. I figured I could send them on your behalf, and if it wasn't a good fit then you'd be none the wiser, so no harm no foul."

"William, you can't protect me from rejection." I purse my lips and shake my head. "I get what you were trying to do, but I don't want someone to like my books just because of a social connection."

"Matthew is a smart businessman. Trust me, he wouldn't just sign someone as a favor." William pulls me into him, waving the large envelope in his right hand. "This is his response. Don't you want to know what it says?" William asks, practically bouncing on the balls of his feet.

"Ummm... yes?" I respond, my answer coming out as more of a question.

William hands me the envelope and I hesitantly pull the letter out. My heart quickens and my hands begin to shake as I read the words over and over again.

"They want my books," I whisper, looking up at William.

"Yes. You got an offer for the entire *Little Moon* series." William's previous grin transforms into a self-satisfied smirk.

A multitude of thoughts assault me as I stand there staring at the paper that holds a piece of my future.

Is this really happening? How did I get so lucky?

"William, thank you." Unable to contain my gratitude, I wrap my arms around his neck. "Thank you. Thank you. Thank you," I whisper into his chest. "You have no idea what this means to me."

"I think I do, little moon. These past couple of months have shown me what it's like to feel complete. As if everything is where it should be. I wake up every morning feeling so at peace I have to ask myself if this isn't all some sort of dream." William strokes my hair as he looks into my eyes. "I want to make sure you feel that way too. I want you to have everything your heart desires, including the career of your dreams."

I close my eyes and breathe him in. This man, the man of my dreams, has given me more than I've ever thought possible.

The past few months have healed so much hurt, and slowly but surely, William has managed to fill the jagged hollows of my heart. He and Harper are my home, and though I still miss my father and brothers, I now know there is nowhere else I'd rather be. Nowhere else I belong.

"I should frame this letter and mail a copy of it to your father." William arches a brow as he takes the letter from my hand.

"Don't," I hurry to say. "He doesn't want anything to do with me and I'm positive that also includes anything that might prove him wrong."

"I think that's exactly why we need to send him a copy. Show him how ridiculous he's acting and that he needs to be supportive of his amazingly talented daughter." William lifts me in an embrace, holding me up by my ass, causing me to wrap my legs around him. "We'd have to ship it to Seattle since he's decided he's only accepting contracts as far away from home as possible."

I purse my lips and shift them to the right. "He's being ridiculous alright. I can't believe he sent the twins to boarding school. I can't visit without hopping on a plane and I bet he didn't even add me to the visitor list." My lips turn down as a deep ache settles in my chest. "I wonder how they're doing."

"Everything will work out the way it's supposed to. I promise. I don't care if I have to move heaven and earth for it to be so." William places soft kisses down my neck as he walks us down the hall.

"I know, I've said this before, but thank you. You've given me so much in such a short period of time..." My voice trails off, unsure anything I could say would be enough to show my gratitude.

"I love you, Isabella. I want you happy. This is part of making you happy and there's no need to constantly thank me. Although, if you really wanted to show me how grateful you are, you could just let me have my way with you whenever and wherever I wanted." William waggles his brows playfully, though the bulge in his pants lets me know there's some truth to his request.

"Why Mr. Hawthorne, are you propositioning your nanny?" I tease, as a devious smile spreads across my face. "How very inappropriate of you. Besides, you're so much older than me. Does your cock even work at such an advanced age?" I tease, trying to contain my laughter.

William squeezes my ass and grins. "Keep it up and I'll leave that gorgeous ass of yours raw. Show you just how good my cock works." William slips a hand down the back of my shorts, sliding his middle finger between my cheeks. "Has anyone ever been here before?" William asks as he softly strokes my puckered hole in small circles, making me squirm.

"No," I manage to say, the one word coming out all breathy and barely audible.

William lowers me onto our bed. Apparently he'd been walking us to our bedroom this entire time and I hadn't noticed, too wrapped up in what his hands and mouth were doing to even care.

"Good. Because it's mine." William's stomach vibrates against me as he lets out a soft chuckle. "Don't worry, it won't be tonight."

I let out a breath I didn't know I was holding in. "Thank god, because the thought of your massive cock inside that tiny hole..." I trail off as my eyes go wide.

"We'll go slow. I promise." William leans over, pulling a package out of his nightstand. "For now, we'll start with this." He waves a shiny metal object shaped like a teardrop in my face.

I reach out and touch it, the cold metal sending shivers up my spine. I'm not sure if it's from fear or the

ELEANOR ALDRICK

excitement of trying something new. I was never with anyone long enough to experiment, so this is all uncharted territory.

"Relax, baby." William positions himself between my knees before spreading them apart. "This will only feel good if you trust me and let yourself relax."

I nod my head and give William a timid smile. "I want this. I want to try this with you."

William lifts my leg, placing a soft kiss to the inside of my ankle. "Thank you for giving me this." He slides his hand down my leg and over my pussy, giving it a quick slap before opening the bottle of lube he'd brought over with the plug.

Pouring some into his hand, he coats the metal and lowers himself onto me. "You're so fucking beautiful. So perfect," William whispers into my skin as he trails my stomach with wet kisses.

His lips find my hardened nub, latching on and causing me to arch my back from the sudden jolt of pleasure coursing through me. I grab ahold of his hair, pushing him deeper into me, never tiring of how good his tongue feels on my clit.

I'm reveling in the feeling of his mouth on me when I feel a cold prodding at my rear. I jerk involuntarily, shocked by the different sensation. William steadies me by placing his open palm on my pelvic bone, and pressing me back down onto the bed.

331

"Easy, *little moon*," William coos as he rubs the tip of the plug back and forth over my hole before gently pressing it in, slowly working it in and out until the widest part makes it past the tight ring of muscle.

I gasp at the sudden feeling of fullness. *It's different but not bad.*

A wicked grin flashes across William's face. "My little moon likes ass play. How much more perfect can you get?"

I slap at William's chest, my face turning pink with embarrassment. "I'm pretty sure I'd like almost anything as long as it was with you."

William's face softens and his previously predatory glare transforms into one I've never seen before. In that one moment, William and I exchange a thousand silent words, recognizing our other half in each other. He is the missing part of me, and I'm his.

"I love you," we simultaneously declare before breaking into soft laughter.

"Jinx, poke, you owe me a coke," I rhyme.

"Oh, I'll give you a poke, alright," William teases as he rolls me over onto my stomach.

The massive head of his cock teases my clit, once, twice, three times, before slowly and deliciously entering my channel. William works his thick cock in and out of me until his entire length is plunged deep inside me.

My breath catches in my throat as I try to decipher what it is I'm feeling. Unable to contain the plethora of sensations running through me, a half moan, half groan escapes me.

The fullness is unlike anything I've ever experienced, with nerve endings I never knew existed firing up, lighting my body like the Fourth of July.

It feels so fucking good. Everything with him feels so good.

William begins to rock himself into me. Immediately, my body responds without prompting—pushing and pulling in synchronicity with his—as if our bodies were speaking their own language.

In a matter of seconds, I feel that familiar tingle enveloping me, where everything becomes fuzzy and I lose all control—falling into the abyss of intoxicating pleasure.

William snakes his hand around, his middle finger finding my clit and detonating me into orgasm. Wave after wave of pleasure crashes into me, my body shuddering uncontrollably under William's hold as he reaches the climax of his own crescendo, slamming into me one last time before roaring his release.

Completely spent, William collapses on top of me, nuzzling the crook of my neck and depositing a lingering kiss. "Forever mine, Bella. You are forever mine."

A contented smile forms on my lips. "Forever yours, William. I'm forever yours."

Epilogue

THREE MONTHS LATER...

    "It's so peaceful here," I whisper, a sense of calm washing over me as I look out toward the water and into the rising sun. The beach is deserted on our private stretch of sand with only William and I here to bear witness to its beauty. Taking full advantage of the seclusion, William set up a picnic blanket, complete with pillows and candles surrounding our own private nook of Cape Cod.

"You've picked the perfect place to celebrate being newly divorced. Who knew it would have taken you so long to get unshackled from a felon?" I poke William in the ribs, winking at him before taking a sip of my coffee. I normally don't wake up this early while on vacation but William coaxed me out of bed with a full carafe and promises of unparalleled beauty.

"I'm just glad everything is resolved and everyone and everything is as it should be." William wraps an arm around me as we continue to stare into the ocean where the sun has now lit up the sky into a visual cacophony of purples, pinks and oranges.

I try to focus on the beauty in front of me but the memory of my father and brothers causes a dull pain to dampen my mood. As if sensing my sadness, William turns to me and lifts his hand to cup my cheek. "Retraction. Almost everything."

"Almost," I repeat, a warm smile touching my lips.

"Don't worry. I haven't given up on my promise to you. Aiden will see the error of his ways. Sooner rather than later. You'll see."

"Mhmm. I know you deliver on your promises." I turn my head to kiss the strong hand laying on my shoulder, softly rubbing my lips back and forth across the grooves of his fingers. "You were right. This sunrise most definitely qualifies as unparalleled beauty."

William reaches out with his other hand, turning my face to his. "That's not the beauty I was referring to."

My cheeks heat up as his eyes look into mine, so full of love the emotion flows right into me, warming the coldest and darkest parts of my broken self.

It's been six months since I officially moved in with William and everything has been perfect. The combination of his love and patience has helped heal my wounds a great deal and I've come a long way, but I'd be lying if I didn't admit there were times of doubt. Not about my love for William—that's the one constant I know will never change—but about whether or not I'm worthy.

"What's going on in that gorgeous head of yours?" William's brows knit together as his thumb gently strokes my cheek.

"That I love it when you look at me like that. Like I'm enough." I squeeze my eyes shut, not wanting him to see all of the uncertainty I carry within.

"My sweet Isabella. If you could only see what I see. You are more than enough. You are everything, and if you let me, I will spend the rest of my life showing you how worthy you are." William shifts, dropping his arm from my side and I instantly feel the heat of his body leave mine.

"Open your eyes, baby." William caresses my cheek with the back of his hand.

Slowly, I pull my eyes open, and the sight before me causes my heart to skip a beat. William is on one knee and in his right hand is a small box, the perfect shade of robin's egg blue. My eyes tingle and my stomach flutters, feeling as if it houses a million butterflies.

Tears begin to stream down my face as I fling myself onto William. "Yes. *Oh my fucking god*, yes!" I say between kisses. "How? How are you so perfect?"

"I didn't even ask the question yet." William chuckles as he kisses me back. "I had a whole speech prepared."

"You can tell me later after you fuck me senseless. This calls for celebratory sex!"

A throat clears from behind me. "Well, this is sure going to make a great story for the grandkids." Ren points toward the phone in his hand. "And we've got it all on video."

A snicker comes from behind Ren before I realize Matt and Max are here too. Looking back toward the rental we booked, I see the whole team is here along with Ashley, Harper, and Cassie.

"Oh my god. When did y'all get here?" I wipe at my tears, thankful it's too early for makeup, otherwise, I'd have major raccoon eyes.

"We flew in on the jet last night." Cassie gushes while popping open a bottle of champagne and shooting me a salacious smile. "How about you come inside and we settle for celebratory mimosas instead of the sex, at least until we've all cleared out?"

I feel my cheeks redden for the second time this morning and it isn't even seven a.m. "Yes. Of course. You guys realize I had no idea you were here, right?"

"You said *fucking!*" Matt sing-songs before he and Max burst into a fit of giggles.

And there it goes again, my face turning a crimson shade of red for a third time.

"Boys, come here!" I shout, opening my arms wide for an embrace. "I've missed you so much. How did you get here?"

"I picked them up from New Hampshire last night. I'm their emergency pickup, and I think this definitely qualifies as an emergency. It's not every day we see a grown man propose to a teenager." Ren gives William the side-eye while snickering under his breath.

"*Fuck you.* You're just jealous I found my forever and you're still out there playing the field with nothing to show for it." William shoves Ren playfully.

Just then I notice Ren and Cassie exchange a look. I'm about to prod Cassie about it when Ashley cuts in, "So much for watching our language. I swear, these kids are going to grow up fluent in profanity." The room breaks into a mixture of belly laughs and giggles, knowing this is probably a very accurate prediction.

Ren walks up to me, wrapping me in his arms as the laughter subsides. "Congratulations, Sprout, you know I was teasing about the age, right?"

"Yes." I tilt my head and look up, the corner of my mouth lifting ever so slightly. "Everyone here knows I've lived two lifetimes in my short nineteen years of life. I might still be young on paper but deep in my soul, my ass is old. I'm ready for the next stage of my life. I want to belong to a family unit. Officially."

"You already do," a familiar voice rumbles from the doorway. Silence descends on the room as we watch my father make his way toward me.

"Daddy. How did you get in?" My brows scrunch together trying to figure out what's going on.

"I let him in," Cassie admits, shifting from foot to foot.

"Don't be mad at her. I didn't really give her a choice." My father looks back at Cassie apologetically before returning his gaze to me. "I received a call from the school letting me know Ren had picked up the boys. Then I discovered the company jet had traveled to Massachusetts carrying an unusually large list of passengers. Putting two and two together, I figured something big was going down." My father picks up my left hand, inspecting the new addition. "And it looks like it has."

"Aiden." William nods toward my father as he wraps a protective arm around my shoulder. "Thank you for joining us on such a happy occasion. I do hope you're here to offer your congratulations. I'm afraid anything else would be unacceptable. I don't want this day to be tainted with anything but joy for Isabella."

"I understand. And don't worry, I give this union, albeit an unconventional one, my blessing." My father extends his hand toward William, who reaches out and takes it, pulling him in for a bro hug. "Thank you for letting me crash your party, but if it's okay with you." My father looks between William and me before continuing. "I'd like a moment alone with my daughter. There's a lot I need to tell her."

William turns to me, kissing the top of my head. "I'll be in the next room if you need anything."

Everyone clears out and it's just my father and me, both unsure of who speaks first. Deciding to be the one to take the plunge, I part my lips and begin to speak. "I'm sorry for never letting you see the real me. For letting you believe I was still your little girl, unchanged and unaffected by the actions of those around me." My voice shakes as I lay it all out there, fearing my father might reject me for what I'm about to tell him but not caring because I am enough. Just as I am. *I am enough.*

"I walked in on Lucia and her lover the night of my art exhibit. The room was dark, so I had no idea who the man was, only that I'd caught them in a compromising position... I argued with Mom on the drive home, telling her she needed to come clean. Tell you what she had done. She offered excuses, of course, all of which were inadequate. Before I knew it, we were spinning out of control and by the time the car had stopped, it was too late."

My father reaches out to wipe the tears from my face, his unexpected affection giving me the courage I need to continue. "All this time, I've lived with the guilt of my mother's death. If I hadn't fought with her on that ride home, maybe she'd still be here. Maybe the two of you would have worked it out. Maybe the twins would still have their mother instead of being raised by a pseudo-mother like me or at boarding schools." I stop and wipe my nose with the sleeve of my shirt, unable to look my father in the eye. "From the time of her death and up until recently, I engaged in self-destructive behavior. I truly believed I needed to atone for what I'd caused, never allowing myself the joy of love, and only seeking numbing release in alcohol and men."

My father's eyes go wide and his jaw clenches. I think he's about to walk out, but instead, he nods his head and silently urges me to continue. *So I do.* "William helped me to heal, showing me that the sins I carried for so long were not my own. That there was no need to atone for the actions of others and that the accident, however tragic it might be, was not my fault. I may not be the perfect daughter you thought I was, but despite my flaws and inappropriate behavior, I am enough. I am worthy of your love. I am worthy of a family. And I will never let anyone take that away from me."

Hard sobs wrack my body as my father pulls me into him, stroking the back of my head as I cry into his shirt. "You are worthy, Isabella, and I'm so fucking sorry I never made that clear." He kisses the top of my head before continuing. "None of that was your fault. You were fifteen for fuck's sake, I should have known better than to assume you could handle a loss of that magnitude on your own. But instead of helping you cope, I loaded you up with responsibilities that were beyond your years. I'm so sorry."

"It's okay. You were grieving too." I look up into his eyes, so full of pain and regret.

"It doesn't matter. You were my fifteen-year-old daughter, still under my care. I should have been there for you, not forced you to grow up before your time."

"Like William always says, everything happens the way it's supposed to. If I hadn't been thrust into the situations life gave me, I wouldn't have been ready for the wonderful man that is William."

"So what you're saying is that it's my fault you two are getting hitched?" Dad raises a brow, a playful smile forming on his lips.

I lovingly shove at him and smirk. "I guess you could look at it that way."

"Did I hear my name?" William asks as he walks into the room, donning a shit-eating grin. I have no doubt he was eavesdropping the entire time.

"I was telling Bella you should thank me for bringing you two together. Who knew a nannying gig would turn into a marriage proposal?" My father's eyes glitter with something between mischief and happiness. "I'm glad Bella found a man who will love her the way she deserves. And hey, at least this isn't a shotgun wedding."

Now it's *my* turn to look like the cat who ate the canary.

Deciding there's no time like the present, I place my hand on my stomach and shoot them an excited smile. "Why can't it be both?"

The End... *for now.*

by ELEANOR ALDRICK

Acts of Salvation
September 2020

Acts of Redemption
December 2020

Acts of Grace

Acts of Mercy

Be sure to sign up for my newsletter where I'll be sharing the prologue to Cassie and Ren's story. You won't want to miss out!

Connect with Eleanor

Let's stay connected. I'd love to hear what you thought of the book, what's on your TBR list, or simply how your day is going.

www.EleanorAldrick.com

Instagram
@EleanorAldrick

Goodreads
www.Goodreads.com/EleanorAldrick

Twitter
www.Twitter.com/EleanorAldrick

Facebook
www.Facebook.com/EleanorAldrick

Acknowledgements

They say raising a child takes a village, and this can also be said of writing a book. My tribe, I love you to pieces and I am truly blessed to walk through this journey with you.

My husband, the real MVP, who always encouraged me and never complained about my late night, early morning, or all-nighter writing sprints. I love you to the moon and back.

My family, Bella and Linda. Thank you for being supportive and always keeping it real. I love you both more than words could say.

My girl tribe, Taralyn, Natalie, Ivette, Susan, and Kellie. the ones who listened to me incessantly go back and forth between cover model options and formatting. I love you and I'm so glad you aren't sick of me yet.

My writing besties, Domino and Annie. Though I met you at the tail end of this journey, your friendship and feedback have been priceless. I hope that we may continue this journey together and I look forward to what the future holds.

My street team, the Sinfully Seductive Squad. Thank you for all that you do. Y'all are social media wizards!

And of course, you. Thank you. Thank you for taking the time to read my book. It honestly means the world to me. I hope that we can continue this journey together.

XOXO,
Eleanor Aldrich

Made in the USA
Monee, IL
03 March 2023

29085445R00215